Benn Flore

Three Religions, one Killer

Original tittle:
'Drie hoofden op een kussen'
Published by Uitgeverij Lemmens
English ISBN: 978-94-91599-17-0

florad publishing
Benn in Books

Benn Flore

Three Religions, one Killer

florad publishing

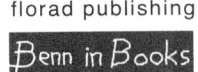

© 2011 Florad Reclame Marketing
Cover image: ingimage.com
Cover design: Florad
ISBN: 978-94-91599-17-0
NUR: 332

Publisher Florad Reclame Marketing - Netherlands

Geneva 1938

Jonathan Kerzner was in Geneva, his tall thin frame stretched out on his hotel chair as he thought about his blond 14 year old son in America. David consistently had the best school reports and grades. For his age was he not only academically gifted, but also rock solid and well-built. That must have been a result of the swimming; he had already competed in his 10th youth championships in Boston, and in two years' time was set to go to the All-America Championships. Jonathan saw him in his mind, swimming in the pool at the foot of the hill where his stately white house stood. It was the largest mansion in the city and had an ocean view. It stood in the middle of open countryside, surrounded by undulating grass as perfect as a golf course.

It wasn't often that 42 year old Jonathan thought about his children while in Europe. But now he did, and with good reason. His son David had displayed a keen understanding of the situation. 'There was no way he was going to come with me to Amsterdam, and it's not just because he doesn't want to say good-bye to his sport', mused Jonathan. According to Jonathan's gifted son, Amsterdam in 1938 wasn't safe for his mother and little Esther. That was fair enough. There was good reason to feel that way. The Olympic Games had been an unsettlingly political affair, and you heard terrible things about how difficult things were for Jewish families in Germany. In fact, many were now fleeing the country. But that was Germany—and Holland was nothing like Germany.

Amsterdam, the centre of the diamond trade, is in Holland. And Jonathan, with his background in business, could not easily ignore that.

He stared at the reflections of the window pane in his Swiss hotel room, where a floor-lamp sparkled near the knuckles of his hand. His decision seemed to be carved in stone. He had wanted to live with his family in the area surrounding Amsterdam for some time. He had pictured in his mind a classic villa on the outskirts of the city.

The problems in Europe wouldn't take them unawares. And so what if they did? He had money, lots of money, and therefore he could surely handle any situation.

His ideal future played out in his mind as he relaxed in the large luxurious hotel room on the shores of Lake Geneva. He contentedly waited with his business partner Abdel Amini Sabagh for the man who was bringing their money, hopefully now on his way from Germany laden with two suitcases filled with gold, jewels and especially diamonds. From his armchair Jonathan glanced through the tan-colored room that smelled of wood and of the dark brown leather with which the walls were upholstered.

He looked at the back of his partner, who was standing by the window.

Abdel Amini peered over the checked tiles on the balcony to see outside where, through the rain and darkness of the dreary night, there really wasn't much to see. On other days you could see clear across to the mountain on the other side of the lake, and further beyond that, the snow-capped peak of Mont Blanc. But the visibility tonight wasn't more than about thirty meters or so. It felt as if the chilly dampness was even penetrating inside.

The grey weather of today made the little man from the British protectorate between the Mediterranean Sea and the Jordan River wistful. Jonathan sensed his mood. The two business partners were spending more and more time together and were thus getting to know each other well. The diminutive Abdel Amini, who was easily ten years older than Jonathan, was as always immaculately dressed, today in an expensive but very showy white suit. He was recounting again, as he too often did, the old story which Jonathan now knew so well that he could have told it to you backwards. You couldn't say he had a particularly high opinion of the older Abdel Amini. But then, who could you say that of these days? So once again, in the early hours of the morning Jonathan heard the story once more, not really listening but flicking through the financial pages of the newspaper with his free hand. Abdel Amini stood before the window, talking to the blackness of the dark lake.

A strange guy, this little, balding man from the old land of the Philistines. He was maybe a hundred times as rich as Jonathan, but not half as clever. Jonathan knew that Abdel Amini had lived in America for many years in the past, and would return there after his job was completed.

But for himself, Jonathan first had to fight a new battle in Amsterdam, centre of the diamond industry; because money was something you never had enough of!

Adbel Amini continued speaking while wiping the condensation from the pane of glass with his fat fingers so he could have a better view of the wooden moorings. It wouldn't be long, surely, before he would spot the German with his two guards on board. But the rain lashed down on the water's surface, and it was pitch black above Lake Geneva, as you would expect at four in the morning.

Abdel Amini told, as he had done countless times before, how he had become rich almost overnight through buying and selling weapons.

'It was all by chance really,' so he had begun for the thousandth time reminiscing about his childhood not far from Jerusalem. 'If as a child I hadn't seen my bigger and stronger, although defenseless, friend Nabib beaten almost to death by a priest using a huge cross as a weapon, then maybe I wouldn't have seen the need for weapons.' Jonathan saw Abdel Amini shiver as he relived his old history again.

'Palestinians must arm themselves—and not only against fanatical Christians. That has always been the same.' And that was true; even the film industry now made films about the so-called heroic crusades against the Arabs. Someone had to provide the weapons. And it wasn't just about the money. The need for defense arose again for some as the Zionists from 1900 wove a web over the district, trying to make Theodor Herzels a Jewish state. There were families in that meager land that were treated as savages and they needed protection. I know that you will probably see it otherwise, but I didn't choose this career, arms trafficking came to me. I would a thousand times over have rather just worked the land.' Abdel Amini sighed deeply. 'I would happily hand all my riches over if my next child, may he be a son, could lead a different sort of life', said Abdel Amini, sorry for himself.

'Well that's easy enough to say when you don't yet have a son,' Jonathan answered annoyed.

'Well you do,' was the unexpected, snappish answer from his partner. 'Perhaps you should think about that!'

Heinrich had arrived; the older German man was flanked by two large, broad-shouldered young men wearing boots and dark black leather jackets. He walked purposefully over the slippery mooring quay carrying two square trunks richly filled with stolen treasures. His over-sized wet moustache made him look both ridiculous and pleasant at the same time, and it seemed as if Heinrich was aware of that fact himself.

'He's an old police constable who evidently doesn't have a high regard for his employer,' thought Abdel Amini, now that the three drenched men had reached the hotel room. 'He does his work reluctantly. Are we are all slaves to our destiny?'

The man who brought their money looked unsteady on his feet. He was a corpulent yet likeable man. For the next three days he stayed at this luxurious hotel as well, at the cost of his employer. He chattered on about his Dutch girlfriend and about what, according to him, was about to become of Germany.

'Dark times are coming,' warned the mustached Heinrich more than once over lunch and dinner. 'And much worse than any of us ever experienced before. For myself I've decided not to go to Amsterdam. If I'm permitted, I'm after a terrific house to live in a long, long way away in America. Let me give you this advice; take your suitcases and join me in that Promised Land. There's enough stolen gold in there to last 100 lifetimes. Pay attention to my words; Germany and the rest of Europe are heading in a dangerous direction. That is to say, for men like you.'

Abdel Amini nodded. 'I'm going via England to New York. That's been the plan for a long time and, as soon as the little one is born, I'll get Tannous to join me.'

'And you Jonathan?'

'Not me old man. My family is coming to Amsterdam. After all, The Netherlands are neutral. We'll start off in a hotel—it's already booked. If the situation remains stable, we'll buy a villa in The Gooi, not far from Amsterdam. If it doesn't we can always travel further. The gold in my case won't be invested in weapons this time. From now on my interests are going to be directed to a new market, and if you want to trade in diamonds it's essential to be in Amsterdam or Antwerp.'

As the three separated for the night, Heinrich couldn't rest easy about the future of the ambitious businessman. He slipped a letter into Jonathan's inside jacket pocket for his Dutch girlfriend who was twenty-five years his junior.

'If you won't forget about this plan of yours, then take Margaret my letter, as I'm not sure that the Dutch Nationalists aren't reading my mail. Margaret is resisting the growing group of Dutchmen that are eager to support the Germans. The Dutch Nationalist Socialist Movement has in many ways much in common with the Nazis. Maybe she will be able to help you if you come into danger.'

'Nonsense,' was Jonathan's last word on the matter. 'I'll not have need of it.'

Three rainy days can turn three completely different adults into three firm friends. The intentions towards the two well-filled suitcases would be altered dramatically though a friendship which would, in fact, play an unexpected role in world history.

On the second day, something important happened. Abdel Amini received a telegram; far away in Jaffa his first son was born.

That evening, the three men sat at a richly decked table. The two who weren't bound by the laws of Islam had been made languid and listless by the pheasant and the glasses of Chateau Neuf du Pape that they'd been enjoying.

The telegram really touched Abdel Amini and all of a sudden he leaned over the table while he addressed the two reclining men. 'I have a proposal and Heinrich is to witness it', he began. 'We have here two cases and two grown men who, on the one hand have provided others with weapons in this hellish Europe but, on the other hand, want to present their sons with a good future. We can't change what has passed, but maybe we can change their future. Let us, for at least this one time, do something for our children with this money; your David and my new-born Jassar.'

He took a gulp of water. His glance met that of Jonathan, who was sitting uncomfortably across from him looking like he wanted to object to something. But he stayed quiet, and Abdel Amini continued. 'Let's make a solemn promise that we'll open the cases just one time only; and that's to put some instructions in there for our children so they can make a better life for themselves, that their lives will take a different course than ours.' Again he leaned over the table and Heinrich applauded theatrically.

Jonathan didn't move. He thought it was a stupid idea which would actually short-change the boys. Thus he wavered during a long painful silence, while Abdel Amini played with his serviette and Heinrich didn't know what to do with himself but take another bite of pheasant. Jonathan knew he'd never be able to talk him round.

Slowly and thoughtfully, he finally raised his glass reluctantly with a forced smile in the direction of his emotional partner; Jonathan couldn't do otherwise. He knew that for the coming ten or maybe even twenty years he would have to do business with this stout man in the white suit. And he knew that behind that friendly face lurked a ruthless businessman. To contradict him now would mean an abrupt end to their business relationship. It was a calculated decision.

That very night the cases were given their new intended role. The three men packed the two letters, in dark heavy envelopes, with the gold and jewels. Abdel Amini and Jonathan promised, with Heinrich as their witness, that they would not talk about the contents of the letter with their children until they were grown up. 'Grown up! When is that then, in your eyes?' Jonathan wished to know. That wasn't too far in the distance for his David.

'Grown up is the moment when our sons are old and wise enough to make judicious, discerning decisions,' answered Abdel Amini.

Those instructions in the two identical letters would define the course of Jonathan's son David's life, who was, for now, thinking only of his studies and of winning gold medals in swimming at the highest levels of competition. Dreams could become realities in America.

Boston 1938

David had finished his homework for the day and was strolling past the black Ford that always stood on the gravel in the drive. Of all the cars that his father possessed, David admired this middle-class model, recommended by Ford for the simple man, the most. The rest were too pompous and not sporty enough. The Art Deco style of the car with the large grill really appealed to him. Moreover, it was the only cabriolet that the family had. He just couldn't wait until he could drive.

David followed the lane to the bottom of the hill to the old town centre to meet up with Ted Bates on Acorn Street. In his day, Ted had been Boston Sportsman of the Year. Now he had an electrics shop. Inside on the walls hung newspaper clippings and photos of the young Ted Bates with a big curled moustache, wearing a woolen gym suit that showed off his bulbous muscles. Now he was an old man; anyone over forty was old!

The locals bought their bulbs into Ted's shop when theirs had burned out. His little shop window was full of incomprehensible pieces of equipment and a few large radios. In the middle a Murphy A42V was on display, a dark-brown square cupboard, the same color as the radios. On top was a cover which was always open, it was necessary to see what the machine was all about; a little convex window of grey glass with rounded corners. David estimated the screen to be about ten by ten centimeters. 'That's a television', Ted Bates told him. 'That comes from England. Next year I want to replace it with a DuMont 183. That's American. It has a larger screen, more reliable than the 180. This is the future. It's sold really well in America, most of all in New York. Within five years, ten thousand people there bought one, although not all of them are DuMonts.'

That seemed incredibly far-fetched to David. Ted was probably one of the few in Boston who would have a DuMont. Not many Americans could spare the seven hundred dollars needed to buy one, for that price you could also buy a car. For the ordinary man everything was expensive. Bread cost nine cents now. Families really didn't have the time or the money for such novelties.

In David's eyes, Ted was an enthusiastic workaholic whose hobby had driven him mad. A workaholic but also a fantastic swimming coach. Early evenings and mornings at five, David picked him up to go to the pool. He closed up shop an hour earlier than the others so they could have this time.

Every day David traveled down the hill to the shop where Ted was usually waiting in the doorway. The shop bell rang as he closed the door behind him. Together they wandered around the old houses along Louisburg Square. He knew that the twenty-two householders here managed their own possessions and surroundings without the municipal authority's input, and that Louisa May Alcott had based her classic novels on this romantic setting. Ted always had something interesting to say.

'Next year NBC and RCA want to do a live broadcast from the World Exhibition in New York,' Ted Bates said enthusiastically.

'Why would they do that when there are only a few who will be able to see it?'

'Well maybe I'll show it from my shop window. That would be a fantastic publicity stunt! Believe me, sooner or later, this machine is going to change the world.'

David could see how that statement was possible. At that moment he had a thrilling feeling that he was going to live through something momentous that would begin with that intriguing wooden cupboard in Ted Bates' shop.

Purmerend 1940-1941

David felt he was old and wise enough to resist his father's plan. Nevertheless, a year later he was on his way by ferry to Amsterdam with his mother and four-year-old Esther. He was very wound up. He was not happy about the situation in Europe and Dad, in his eyes, was taking too risky a chance. He thought it really important that Mother and little Esther should not travel alone.

The journey took nearly a month by ocean steamer. The journey through Spain made it feel almost like a holiday for his mother. For David it was the dullest four weeks he'd ever spent. It's true that there was a swimming pool on the deck, but it wasn't more than seven meters long and was usually full of old men with fat pot-bellies who just hung on to the sides. Around the pool were recliners with bathrobes hanging over the armrests. Women in swimming costumes lay by the pool the whole day and moved only to smear themselves with something that made them glisten in the sun, or to sip on a drink through a straw. David watched the women over the course of the four weeks go from lobster-red to deep brown. He also had a little more color himself by the time they reached Amsterdam.

Boston was an old city, but Amsterdam had its own tempting charm. David thought it seemed to be full of doll's houses. The bricks were the same colors as in the paintings by Old Dutch masters that he had seen in textbooks. To David, the canals and bridges of the old quarter downtown appeared to have been unaltered in three hundred years. That gave him a pleasant, settled feeling; he didn't enjoy the hustle and bustle and sounds of the city. The Netherlands were completely different though. This country had a history, even a castle, but that didn't seem anything special to anyone here. For an American like David it was unique. Everything here seemed to be on a small scale and the unity and friendliness of people surprised him; it was as if everyone knew each other.

For a short time life went smoothly. David had taken up swimming again and swam in open water. As soon as possible he wanted to dovetail himself into a swimming club, and for this reason was trying to learn Dutch. He spent a lot of time on the racing bike his father had insisted that he bring on the journey. That's how he came to know not only Amsterdam but also the surrounding areas.

In 1940, the Dutch were dealt a blow which initially the Kerzner family didn't see as having serious consequences for them. Over a period of three days, the German armies marched into the Low Lands. Queen Wilhelmina and her family fled the country. The Dutch burst the Grebbenberg dikes to try and halt the German army's progress, but to no avail.

Jonathan and David could still move about freely. In their hotel they heard about the establishment of a Jewish Council and about the first raids. From the beginning of 1941, Jews were forced to wear the Star of David; as unknown foreigners, the Kerzner family managed to avoid having to do that.

Soon Reich Commissioner Seyss-Inquart issued a regulation which stated that anyone who was wholly or partly of Jewish descent, and who was a resident in the occupied Dutch territory, had to make themselves known. Jonathan decided he would not go along with this and that it was now, in fact, time to leave the Netherlands. Doing this, though, did not turn out as he expected.

Shortly after the first raids in February of that year, Jonathan got caught up in the middle of a disturbance involving the National Socialist Party. All those who wore the Star of David were picked up. Moved by fear, the next day he went as fast as he could from the comfortable hotel on the Amstel River to Margaret. She lived in a humble neighborhood in downtown Amsterdam, her home was on the ground floor of a tall house on a narrow street.

Margaret was a confident woman with wavy brown hair and dark eyes, and she agreed to help Jonathan just as Heinrich had predicted. She gave him an address where he could go into hiding with his family in a damp, smelly basement.

From that day forward, David found his father a changed man. Not only was he tall and thin, but he was now also deathly pale with a glazed look in his eyes that revealed nothing.

The address Margaret suggested was a cramped musty basement

partly under street level. It was also in the old downtown area, in its narrow streets, winding lanes and dark houses four stories high. The young slightly built Huigje Colijn, who lived next door with her older spouse Sjoerd, said that the room was being used to store books. For this reason the cellar also stank of wet paper. Church books, literature from religious dissenters, and many science books were thrown into the unaccommodating wet space. What Huigje didn't know was that her husband had rearranged the books to provide a provisional living space.

Colijn, a small man with shifty eyes, always wore the same dark suit with shiny, worn spots on the elbows. Sjoerd and Huigje went regularly to church in Durgerdam and it was here they had heard about how many frightened Jews were appealing for help. That was how Sjoerd came up with the idea of harboring rich Jews in this very basement.

David named the perilous shelter the 'book cave'. The thin room that ran from the street to the miniscule garden at the rear was about nine meters long and five meters wide. Originally it was one large storage area, now only accessible from the rear. The door which had been on the street side was permanently sealed. To get to the back of the building you had to go through the house of Sjoerd Colijn.

Sjoerd Colijn had creatively sectioned off the area into little rooms by stacking up all the books to form walls. The rest of the books were stacked to line the walls running along the sides of the basement. The living area at the garden end of the room was about four by five meters and, on the street side, Colijn constructed two tiny bedrooms. The surroundings were bizarre and dreary. The books seemed to absorb what little light there was; and that was just the sprinkling of light that fell through the hatch leading to the garden.

In this basement David had plenty of time to think back to the period when he'd had relative freedom. He'd been able to discover much of Amsterdam and its surroundings. It had been pleasurable to see the canals, bridges and splendid facades of the old buildings on a daily basis. He'd been able to escape every day on the racing bike his father had insisted he bring with him. He had ridden to the east where it was dry heath land, by Laren. Above Amsterdam, on the other hand, lay the wet, verdant polders.

On one of the trips north of Amsterdam, through the village of Dur-gerdam, David had happened to meet Brenda. About a year before, when the German soldiers were about ten days away from invading Amsterdam, David had been enjoying cycling with the wind behind him through the polders. He was following a long strip of the North Holland Canal, on his right was a ditch, and the pastures stretched out beyond. In some places the view of the meadows were obscured by dikes.

He had suddenly heard a cry for help from beyond one of the dikes. David pulled sharply on his brakes.

Brenda, with shining blond hair wearing bright blue overalls, appeared on the top of the dike at that same moment. She was running in his direction, nervously looking behind her. What she was running away from and was so afraid of wasn't yet clear.

Brenda hurried towards him stumbling, with her arms stretched out to him. David in the meantime had dismounted and was running to meet her. Following Brenda was a young man with dark curls. He also looked behind him as he reached the top of the dyke. He did not seem to be very frightening. He stopped at the top of the dike, gesturing for David to be careful of what was following behind him.

David heard several sharp bangs in the distance that didn't emanate from the boy on the dike. Suddenly the boy seemed to receive a blow, and he collapsed forward, hobbling in Brenda's direction with a look of astonishment on his face. Out of breath, he put his arm around David's shoulders to hold himself up.

Back in the book cave, as soon as he got the opportunity, David mentioned the story to Margaret.

'A little less than a year ago, did a blond woman and a dark man from North Holland pay you a visit?' he frantically wanted to know from her. His father had insisted he always carry Margaret's address. 'This is the address of a girlfriend of a well-trusted friend of mine,' his father had entrusted to him. 'I don't think it will ever be necessary for any of us to have need of it, but you never know. If we do come into unexpected difficulties she can help us.'

David had known that he had to help the duo escape out of the hands of their pursuers by getting them across the canal. First he dragged the man by the shoulders to the water, and from there swam with him to the other side. The blond woman swam behind them, pulling his bike. On the other side they took shelter behind the bank. Their pursuers, who were dressed in uniform, and could have been either Dutch or German, stood a long time on the other side of the canal evidently discussing what they should do. Eventually it appeared as if they had decided to give up the chase. However, David feared that perhaps they had simply gone back to their vehicles to find a bridge to cross over the canal.

David described to Margaret how they'd managed to reach Brenda's farm. There he had quickly realized that she was a strong willed young woman. Against the advice of all the know-it-alls in the village she had married the adventurous swarthy gypsy boy who was at that moment lying in bed, his leg in incredible pain. Margaret then explained that even before the war had broken out, there was a lot of prejudice in the Netherlands towards gypsies. Despite this, Ricardo had remained a cheerful person and had known Brenda and her father for a good year by then.

David was now very inquisitive to know how the tale unfolded, from the moment when he had given Brenda Margaret's address. Had the pursuers come to the farm? Had she actually met Brenda? Was Brenda able to escape in time and had Margaret been able to help her? And…had the personable Ricardo survived?

David bombarded Margaret with these questions because he had the impression that Brenda wouldn't let the grass grow under her feet, and felt she probably would have fled the very next day. She realized surely that she would have to keep one step ahead of their Dutch or German pursuers, who would undoubtedly come looking for them at the farm.

Brenda had indeed brought the matter into Margaret's hands. Within a short time she made for the address in Amsterdam that David had given her. She was with Ricardo, who was much more seriously injured than she had realized. Margaret then directed them to Sjoerd Colijn; this situation might have been what had given him the idea of using his cellar.

What Margaret didn't know was that Sjoerd Colijn had refused shelter to Brenda and injured Ricardo. The carefree Ricardo died out on the street in Brenda's arms while they were looking for another address along one of Amsterdam's canals. Neither Margaret, nor David could have known that at that moment, Brenda had sworn revenge on Colijn.

Now sixteen year old David lived with his docile mother, little Esther and his stubborn father at the same address that had been given to Brenda. They had gotten used to the penetrating stench of wet books and couldn't even smell it anymore. The walls of stacked books of all shapes and sizes were no longer strange. David's mother cherished the small glimmer of light that pressed through the uncared-for, overgrown garden. There was actually only a little light in the garden itself; it was too small and the surrounding block of houses too high. In one corner of the garden stood two gnarled apple trees that his mother could have made good use of, just like the pair of raspberry shrubs and tomato plants.

The faint light that fell into the improvised living room fell through a window which was no longer glazed. At night they slid a shutter over the blistering paint on the frame to keep out the cold. This was the only exit to the outside world, so it was as well that is was obscured by all the greenery.

On the street side of the basement, the windows had been boarded over long ago so now no one would ever expect that there was a dwelling behind them. Church goers from Durgerdam knew that the books from the old library had been stored somewhere around here. Sjoerd Colijn was a faithful member of the congregation and had taken care of the religious and science books, as well as the many books on nature, electronics and economics.

The family that had gone into hiding in this dreary, acrid pit realized they had to keep their head above water. The accommodation didn't seem to bother Mother; she remained mentally and emotionally strong just like David. He killed time reading the copious supply of books. Sometimes he allowed himself to stretch his legs among the thickets in the garden.

Partly to kill time and partly to try and drag his father back to the land of the living, David tried to engage him in conversation. 'Ted Bates believes in a future with a new exciting invention, Father.'

'Don't be so stupid boy. What sort of future can you possibly look forward to in this world anymore?' Jonathan shifted uncomfortably in his chair. He could not share David's enthusiasm about what lay ahead.

David peevishly tried to explain to him. 'Let me put it to you this way; it's like you'll be able to see the people that you telephone. You'll be able to see with a turn of a button in Amsterdam whether it's raining in Boston,' his son predicted.

'The books you're pouring over every day are clearly not doing you any good', sneered Jonathan the same way he had done on previous occasions. Nevertheless, David remained encouraged by the idea. Jonathan thought that David's ideas were the mindless dreams of a child not ready for this world, where everything revolved around money. As a result he got to hear of David's ideas less frequently. And it also made Jonathan less inclined to tell David about another matter. He revealed nothing to David about the case which was later to become his, which was at the moment being stored safely by Sjoerd Colijn in the house. In Jonathan's eyes, David was not yet ready for it.

'The radio is going to be surpassed by the television', David predicted one day. 'But that won't be for at least another fifty years, because development costs such a lot of money.'

'Since when have you had an interest in money?'

'I'm not interested in money, Father. I'm just wondering what the future will bring. I'm wondering if people would still fight this kind of war if everyone in distant countries could see each other in their kitchens.' Jonathan wouldn't be drawn to that and wouldn't talk further about money.

'You must have an opinion about that, Father'.

David tried month after month to win his father over. As the months passed, Jonathan became thinner and paler than he already was. Increasingly he withdrew further into himself, just sitting in the only wooden chair in the room richly decked with books. The conversations became shorter and shorter until it was as if Jonathan didn't even exist.

David tried not only philosophizing about the distant future but also about the situation that they found themselves caught in right now in 1941. 'We need to find a way out.' Jonathan was with him on that one for once. Jonathan himself now searched for a way out—together with Sjoerd Colijn.

Only Sjoerd Colijn seemed to get through to him. He seemed to come to life for a short time, actually get some color in his cheeks, when he got to know his neighbor better through the things they discussed.

Durgerdam 1941

Within a year, because of Jonathan, David saw all his ambitions evaporate, and he saw his father become a shadow of this former self. David was now almost 18,no longer a child, but a young man who wonders whether he can depend on his father anymore. He was now taking more of an interest in the family's fortunes and how their life would be after the war. That life would come; of this David had been persuaded. 'Hope floats,' he had read in the books in the book cave. He had found some beautiful passages in the part of the bible that Christians called the 'New Testament'.

'This accommodation is only temporary,' Jonathan promised David towards the end of 1941. 'Sjoerd Colijn has not only agreed to run the business for me as long as is necessary, but will also work out a way for us to leave the country. Colijn is a Christian and, think of them what you will, they have the same standard as us, and their 'Old Testament' has the same patriarchs and prophets as the Jews.'

David understood the situation perfectly without his father having to say a word. His father was a sitting duck. Sjoerd Colijn, with his ancient black suit, white shirt and black tie that was too short for him, could make or break him. That Jonathan knew well but would never admit it, especially not to his son who seemed to have an idealistic view of life rather than grasp the harsh realities of the business world.

The outside world seemed closed to the Jewish family whose only mutual language was English. David, therefore, seemed to take over his father's role. Only Margaret and the young, slim wife of Sjoerd Colijn with her little son Harm ever crawled through the casing in the back garden to visit them. They whispered earnestly in broken English to mother about 'women's businesses.' These conversations often left Huigje with tears in her eyes. 'Hey, leave us alone', was the only comment that David was able to hear…until one night he heard screaming and shouting in the adjacent house. Little Harm was also crying.

Instinctively he crawled out to the garden where he tried to get a grasp on the situation, hiding in the shrubs by the window where the sounds seemed to be coming from. The scene displayed before him was one that would stick in his memory for a long time.

In the neighbor's house, Huigje was being assaulted by her husband whilst a large man that David didn't recognize stood watching. Little Harm was tucked up in a corner near the cupboard.

The window was slightly ajar. All his hesitation had disappeared, and without a moment's thought, the agile David climbed through. Immediately he stood behind the heavy man who became unbalanced and awkwardly fell against the cupboard without David laying a finger on him.

David looked at the astonished face of Sjoerd Colijn. That didn't last long. Now that she was saved, Huigje set on Colijn with a fury. Not knowing really what she was doing, she drummed into his face with all her might—kicking him uncontrollably with renewed strength in her legs. She kicked him between his legs and he fell against her. She had the presence of mind to get out from under him. In the few seconds that followed, the heavier man grabbed hold of David but, seeing that Huigje was free, his anger suddenly blazed against her. He left David alone and started threatening her. David launched himself onto the man's back. The man shook him off and punched him. David summoned up all the courage and strength he could muster and hooked his fist round to the man's jaw. The man's eyes rolled back into his head and he was knocked out. Colijn now saw the opportunity to set about the stunned David, but Huigje quickly grabbed the candlestick on the bedside table and cracked it about his head.

Battered and bruised, David came home and didn't even attempt to hide anything from Mother; he could tell her anything. Father seemed to sleep and notice nothing.

To his surprise, his mother merely nodded as if she was expecting it. She said he'd done well to intervene. 'In every marriage things go wrong sometimes, but this was too far.' David had been a tough boy, and Huigje had every right to defend herself.

Later David asked how he and Huigje, both much younger than the other two, had been able to conquer them; to knock one out and leave the other semi-conscious, doubled over the bed. For that Mother had a simple explanation: 'David, you're much stronger than you realize because of your sports training. You've never chosen martial arts so you've never been able to measure yourself against another man. It's worked out for the best that you can stand up for yourself.'

After that event, Huigje came daily to the book cave. A bond soon formed between David and the young woman with the long, straight hair. David developed feelings he couldn't yet understand. Suddenly there were glances that weren't there before, and the attention Huigje used to give to Mother was now diverted to him.

It was evening and almost entirely dark in the small book room that David shared with his little sister. For the first time, Huigje crept into his room. Without saying a word she crawled to the edge of his bed. 'I must talk with you' Huigje declared as she shoved the covers back and found David's hands. 'There are many things I have to tell you.'

For the first time that evening David felt warm, and knew why he looked forward to seeing Huigje crawl through the window. His hands closed over the delicate fingers of the woman who, although couldn't be much older than him, was a parent. Mother looked over from the living room with the light of the candle, but withdrew at once as if she expected to find them together. 'I've also discussed this with your mother. But not everything: There is more.'

David got the feeling that she had planned this conversation, and although he was warm he felt unsettled and nervous. Did he really want to know everything? 'Why do you want to talk to me?' he asked uncertainly, 'and not just with Mother?'

'I've come to realize that it's you I have feelings for. It's the first time I have felt something for a man. And part of what I feel is also trust. Something that I've never had before…and that is the core of my story.' A nervous tension overwhelmed David but he forced himself to stretch out to listen to the rest of her story.

Huigje had grown up in the village of Durgerdam; the little village in the polder, with the little church behind the broad ditch, where David had often cycled. 'You must understand that not many people lived in the village. There was no one, almost no one, of my age. I so much wanted to talk to someone of my age. In the end, I only visited with Elsbeth and Jennifer. They were two elderly spinsters. They ran a little shop and a kitchen garden. I enjoyed helping them in the garden, weeding, or picking gooseberries. Afterwards I'd always go in for tea and a biscuit. And there was another friend of mine, his name was Hendrik. He'd been a friend of mine since I was about six years old. I think he was then around fifty or sixty years old, so he was more like a granddad to me. Now I'm an adult with a child myself I have a better understanding of the situation back then. If I'm honest, I think that Hendrik was the only one in the village who could see what my destiny was to be. Maybe there were others who saw it to, but only Hendrik let on. People in the village have always treated him as crazy, as disturbed. He wasn't crazy. He'd just withdrawn himself to his mill and didn't seek anyone's company. Perhaps for that reason he dared to say what he thought.'

Huigje sighed deeply, but her tone remained steady. In spite of the tears that welled in her eyes she continued firmly with the tale. 'That night with you and me and Sjoerd and my Father has made me another person', she said defensively.

'Your father!!!' David spurted out.

'Yes…my father. But stay quiet because I've got to tell you much more.'

'Your father,' repeated David.

'Quiet now, I'm telling you.' Huigje held his hands tightly. 'I still have much more to tell you so we don't have the time to intensify the drama.' Huigje kept hold of his hands. 'Look it's like this; my father is a big part of the story. I don't know if you can understand what it is like to grow up in the middle of a church community. My father is an elder in the congregation, and Sjoerd is someone who always sat at the front. He's fifteen years older than me. Always an important man; don't let how small or slight he is fool you. In fact, this part of my story is very simple. You mustn't be shocked at what I have to say now.'

In a daze David nodded.

'I was fifteen when I got my child, Harm, from Sjoerd. Not voluntarily of course. Not voluntarily.' Huigje's stomach turned as she said it. 'I was raped.'

'Raped.'

'Yes. Raped. You can't be that shocked after what you saw the other night.'

'Raped,' David mumbled again.

'David I'm not here for you just to repeat everything I say and to get even more upset. I've continually been assaulted, until we fought back last week. From now on, that won't happen anymore. Believe me; Sjoerd is dead scared of me now. He doesn't lay a finger on me anymore.' David took a breath, but Huigje wouldn't give him an opportunity to interrupt the conversation. 'You know David, I'm already healing from this long ordeal. There'll be enough times to cry about that later. First, I have to tell my whole tale. There are many more important things to tell.'

Huigje changed position and continued the story. 'I don't know how it goes by you, but it's the custom in Holland that you marry the person if they get you pregnant. Sjoerd was much older, but a prominent churchgoer. Anyhow, from the moment it became known, I was given the blame. My father insisted that I marry Sjoerd; Mother's opinion didn't count. Every woman who gets pregnant in the Netherlands must marry. Sjoerd's prominence and responsibilities in the church sealed the deal. No one suspected that he had taken me with violence. Only the Harms Sisters asked me something once, and Hendrik the miller. He was the only one who fully understood what happened. He was the only one who got angry, but that didn't change the situation. No one in Durgerdam dared say anything. So what happened?' Huigje took a deep breath and looked with large, childlike eyes into his to see how he would react. Huigje evaluated him cautiously and considered how she would proceed.

David asked her, 'why are you telling me this? Is there still more?'

'There is still much more. You are in danger.' Huigje put her fingers to David's mouth. She wasn't speaking loudly before but now she whispered almost inaudibly 'I've already said this isn't the time to snivel. I must tell you the rest, and you may not interrupt. I'm glad to talk to you. With you alone I feel at ease.'

David felt himself glow. He could hardly believe that Huigje felt the same way about him as he felt about her. She was lovely. 'But you are married.'

'Married? David, listen carefully. What I tell you now is more important than the fact that for the first time in my life I truly love somebody. I didn't know that would ever be possible for me. You are in grave danger. I must tell you why. That's the whole point of this conversation.' David was speechless. 'Hendrik is gone. Or dead.'

It was dead quiet in the book cave.

For the next few minutes Huigje told how Hendrik the miller had smeared the church doors of Durgerdam with white chalk messages about Huigje. 'As a small child I always played with him at the mill. You must know, Hendrik wasn't clever but loved children and especially me. He must have known what I'd endured. On the church doors he chalked "Keep off her!" Everyone must have had the idea he meant me. Hendrik also chalked messages about stolen church money on the doors. It was almost incomprehensible Dutch. Incoherent. But it made everyone wonder. "Where is the money?" was written there with a large question mark. That could only mean the church funds. The church had a fund for good causes which was controlled by Sjoerd and my father. In this quiet, neat community everyone concluded that these random messages could have only come from Hendrik, so all fingers pointed at him. He denied nothing, being as honest as he was. For two years no one thought any more about the matter—until the Germans came. Then Hendrik was arrested by nurses and men in uniform.'

'Arrested? On what grounds?'

'I can only guess about that. Perhaps Hendrik really did know something about some stolen money, and because of his strange writings and isolated existence they could use this as an excuse to descend on him. Your guess is as good as mine. If you're crazy, you get picked up and taken away to who knows where. An asylum, I suppose. Until now no one in the village has heard any more about him. You're not allowed to be crazy in this day and age.'

'But you said yourself that Hendrik wasn't crazy!'

'That's true. I think that my father and Sjoerd had something to do with the whole thing; that they had made some sort of arrangement with the Germans and that's why they came after him.'

David was bewildered.

'That's why I've come to you. Your father wouldn't understand me, or wouldn't want to understand me. I've also come to you because I think so much of you. How is that possible? I am glad that I feel happy for the first time in my life, though also scared. Sjoerd will also betray you. I feel it. He knows something changed that evening, that I've become independent and that I'd rather be with you. Sjoerd realizes that I think of you every minute of every day. I can't hide it.'

'That's ridiculous.'

'That I should be so happy to have found you?'

'No. That Sjoerd would betray us.'

Suddenly there followed a long tearful kiss from Huigje on David's lips. David's first kiss. A kiss in a dark book cave, in bed beside his little sister Esther.

'Betrayal?' David mumbled softly as Huigje's lips released his. He saw how she stroked her long hair back from her young face so that her large beautiful eyes seemed to sparkle in the dark night.

Huigje looked at his face and, despite the miserable lighting, could see that David was anxious, but she knew he was wise enough to pay attention to what she would say: 'He is extremely jealous, but it's not just that. He also craves money. He wants all the money that your father has. I have frequently heard them talking. Your father wants Sjoerd to invest all his money in airplanes, which are rapidly becoming essential to fight the war. Sjoerd's intention is to get his hands on that money—money and your father's mysterious case.'

Soon after the American newspapers communicated that the Netherlands had come under German occupation, Abdel Amini received a telegram. Abdel Amini had little to do in America. The war, which was being fought so far away, only made a little impression on them, so the average American didn't talk about it much. But someone who was experienced in international relations and arms-trading knew the situation was serious. London was being battered by German bombs. The opinion of America would turn, however, after the Japanese attack on Pearl Harbor. After the signing of the Atlantic Treaty by Roosevelt and Churchill on a warship in August 1942, they realized the seriousness of the situation.

Up until that time Abdel Amini had lived in relative peace. Along with Tannous, his three daughters and the baby Jassar, he had established himself in Washington. From there he did little more than invest in shares in industries connected to the war and scarce goods such as oil, and watch the share price on the exchange. The family Sabagh became a part of America. Everyone, including the servants that Abdul had brought over, spoke fluent English. The tall reddish-brown house that they had bought was immense. It stood in a suburb in the open countryside. The six servants all had their own quarters and there were still rooms spare. Washington wasn't an ideal spot for Tannous and the children; there weren't any schools in the direct area

He was warmed by the contents of the telegram which he had just been sent, however. The telegram from Holland spoke of a house with stately white pillars and high windows. The white house with its enormous driveway lay in beautifully mown pastures with a view of the old city and the ocean. Along the coast of America you could find even more mansions, but these were much too large for one family. This was probably the most picturesque of the bunch, surrounded as it was by huge trees which were stunning when they colored red in the autumn.

And, of course, the children would have the opportunity to study at Harvard. Tannous would love it there, and Nabib too. Abdel Amini smiled inside for the restless Jonathan and his simple older friend Nabib, who was now his gardener. 'Jonathan only ever wanted to know a little about Nabib's history', he thought. Abdel had always enjoyed teasing his friend by repeating the story again and again. Maybe he did it to keep the images sharp in his mind also. When he saw Nabib, now old and stiff, busy in the garden it seemed as if his friend of twelve years of age was there. Abdel Amini knew what sort of person he had been in his former days, before he had been beaten by a fanatical priest in Bethlehem as a child. The long brown robes that he wore must have been his habit. Much later, Abdel Amini had come to understand what the cross symbolized, and that Christians themselves would have seen it as insultingly blasphemous to use it as a weapon. Every faith has its own fanatical minorities. Didn't even his own? As on many previous occasions, Abdel Amini asked Allah if he had intended it to be this way; Nabib had almost bled to death in Bethlehem. For four months he had lain in a coma with desperate parents by his side, eventually to recover but not without considerable brain damage. Nabib had remained from that moment as a child, a dear child for whom the wide world held no attraction. Nabib lived in the paradise of a garden where he knew every petal and every bird. Sometimes it seemed to Abdel that Nabib was the one who really lived life to the fullest. Paradoxically it was sure that Nabib was better off than the restless Jonathan, who was always wishing for more. Of course, Abdel's Jewish friend wouldn't agree. He seemed to have a fanatical attitude to money but, if you knew him, you would realize that this was just because he wanted the best for his family. To the outside world he appeared to be cold and selfish. So Abdel was astonished that he offered him the house which he had so often bragged about.

The telegram, which Abdel Amini held in his hands in the hall of his home in Washington, did not come from Jonathan himself but from a Mr. Colijn who claimed he was handling the matter on Jonathan's behalf. That sounded plausible. Now that America was involved in the war you heard a lot more about the difficulties of living in Europe. And hadn't the sympathetic German, Heinrich, who they had met in Geneva, warned them of that? Abdel Amini wondered how Jonathan's son, of whom he had been so proud, was faring.

In Boston, Ted Bates put oil on the wooden counter of his Electronics shop. Ted was often alone in the shop and could let his mind wander free. Before the war had broken out in Europe, he had frequently received letters from David and his mother. They described Amsterdam as a pleasant city in which to live. 'So different from Boston,' Ted read. 'The houses downtown stand so close to each other that you can see right inside your neighbor's. They've mostly got three or four floors. I thought first of all that it would be one family living there but that's not the case. On every floor there lives a family, sometimes with five or six children, in two small rooms. The top floor's windows are so close to the windows opposite that you sometimes see the women up there hanging the washing out and chatting to each other. Everything in the city is miniature, in contrast to the farms in the surrounding areas. There's usually a large farmhouse where the farmer lives. The cows sleep on straw in the barns. The cows they use for milking here are a black and white spotted variety. And Ted, this is true, the farmers wear wooden shoes that they just slip off when they come indoors.'

From time to time Ted now saw pictures from the Netherlands and other parts of Europe. He pictured in his mind the young athletic David training in that green landscape with the water courses and dikes, just as he'd described in his letters.

Ted missed the talented ambitious boy and couldn't bring himself to train any of the less capable swimmers in town. The splendid house of the Kerzner family was languishing. It seemed as if moss grew in all its crevices and was no longer brilliant white. There was even talk of a rich Arab buying it. Even the exciting technology of television no longer inspired him. He cynically laughed inwardly at himself as he already felt like an old man with little to expect from his life. Ted had read that the Germans had a plan to broadcast propaganda from the Eifel Tower in Paris. The American authorities had decided that the commercial production of televisions had to stop until the war was over. 'There's not much more to live for,' Ted concluded.

Amsterdam 1942

Two summers had been spent in the book cave already, and now winter was around the corner. It wasn't clear how the war would develop. Germany fought on many fronts and, according to Jonathan, it was only a question of time before the allies would start winning their first battles.

Since Huigje had warned David about betrayal, David and his father started to talk more often again. The boy was nineteen now. The conversations didn't bring them closer to each other; Jonathan wasn't interested in the mundane things his son brought to his attention. Sure, he had to be afraid of Sjoerd Colijn. For a long time he had been promising a flight out, and Jonathan had already paid him a lot of money. It seemed to be taking a long time for Sjoerd Colijn to come forward with an escape plan. David thought it suspicious, but Jonathan continued to hope. It was difficult to find a way out. The Germans kept a tight hold on the Netherlands; Sjoerd Colijn had repeatedly made this clear to him. Nevertheless, Jonathan had the feeling he would remain true to his word. Betrayal; Jonathan didn't think so. But, time would reveal all. A year had already passed since Huigje had issued her warning and nothing had transpired since then. Jonathan and Colijn were business partners after all, so betrayal seemed quite far-fetched.

David had never got to learn how his father had amassed his fortune before the war had broken out. In America they'd lived in a huge home, and in Amsterdam they'd firstly been living in rooms in a prestigious hotel. 'We have to go to Amsterdam, as that is the centre of the diamond trade', Jonathan had said before their departure. Was that where his father had made his fortune?

The winter had become heavy, and there were rumors that Germany had been brought to a standstill in North Africa. In the Netherlands, there was nothing to see of the American, Canadian or British forces. The fact that that country on the other side of the North Sea had successfully resisted occupation by Germany gave the Dutch hope. 'The Allies are giving themselves time to get their weapons arsenal up to a level to be able to defeat the Germans. They've probably got their factories at full steam,' instructed Jonathan.

David noted that his father had remarkable knowledge about such things. As long as he didn't talk about the personal situation of the family, the conversations between father and son became more animated. Generally they tried to anticipate the course of the war based on the, sometimes contradictory, information from Sjoerd, Huigje and Margaret. The conversations did David's father good. The answers he gave were lively, and Jonathan liked having something to say about international affairs.

Sjoerd never came to the book cave. What David and Jonathan gleaned from him about the war came from Jonathan's meetings with him in his new partner's outhouse. As a result, David became better informed than Huigje and Margaret; although there were some things which Sjoerd would never learn about. And that was logical, everyone had their own mysteries. Margaret had her relationship with Heinrich, whom David had heard his father mention. Heinrich had now been stationed in Amsterdam. And Jonathan understood that this was something that it would be better for Sjoerd not to know.

On the evenings that Huigje and Margaret visited the book cave, they could somehow forget their situation and simply be sociable. They slid onto the benches around a square dining table which was in the middle of their small living room. The armchair where Jonathan sat was the only other chair.

Mother brought a calm atmosphere to the house; she had been blessed with a sort of naivety and a desire for a simple life. Her surroundings seemed to have no effect on her. It made little difference to her whether she was in Boston and had staff to do errands for her, or whether she had to do everything herself in the book cave, living off what she could get from Margaret or stolen things from the black market. She hummed children's rhymes and remained cheerful, even when Jonathan crawled back from his business meetings with Sjoerd. She arranged wild plants and unusual shaped branches that others would consider as ugly, tastefully into little displays in a tin can in the middle of the table.

Mother also introduced a daily routine. Although their lives played out entirely within the walls of their prison, Mother didn't act that way. In the morning, after their meager breakfast, Esther had to get a move on to be on time for school. 'Come on child', her mother would say then. 'Hurry up. School won't wait for you.'

David had the job of giving her lessons, Mathematics and English

Language. Also he taught what little Dutch and German he had picked up from Margaret. The lessons changed in the afternoons when the parents had their turn. Father only came out of his chair for this and his meetings with Colijn. Mother did needlework with her and Father limited his lessons to reading, as far as Esther was concerned, incomprehensible parts of the Torah.

No matter what the weather, the lessons were punctuated at fixed times with outdoor play, one day with David, the other with Mother. 'This way you'll get some fresh air when you breathe in deeply,' they said. 'It'll keep you healthy.' Hidden by the shrubs and high fence, there was a space of no more than two square meters for her to do some exercises and play some games. As in school time, also in playtime, Mother would watch by the narrow slit and softly clap her hands.

Mother also read. There was certainly no shortage of books!

If there wasn't a visit from Margaret, Huigje, or more frequently now, little Harm, David killed time by studying for himself. He made good use of the many books which Sjoerd had used for the partitions. He designed a complete program of economic and technical studies. He always discussed what he learned from the technical books with Harm, who now visited especially for that reason.

Huigje visited daily now and tended to stay for hours. Sometimes it was as if her life took place more often in the book cave than in her own house.

Besides Sjoerd Colijn and Huigje, Margaret was their only other link with the outside world. That outside world seemed to be suffering more and more under the German occupation. During the first year, Margaret had been able to bring them food with some regularity. It became noticeably less, though, as daily necessities were now scarce. And it wasn't only food that was hard to come by. Textiles and shoes had been rationed since 1940, soap and matches following closely after that. Rations were published in the newspapers that were still being printed. Sometimes Margaret bought one, in which she read that the potato ration was going from 1.5 kilos to 1 kilo, or you could choose to have 250 grams of certain vegetables or 250 grams of oats. The natives got less and less for themselves, so there was little to share with the refugees who were hiding in and around Amsterdam. The resistance succeeded in stealing vouchers, but this was of no real benefit as there wasn't anything to claim with them.

Money just didn't have the same value anymore; Jonathan questioned whether he was still as rich as he thought he was. Food was now bought with paper money with five zeros. Inflation was so high because the Germans continued to print money. 'If there's too much of something it reduces its value,' David had read during his study hours.

It was possible for David to discuss such things now and then with his father, and he couldn't help but mention again the miraculous nut-brown wooden machine with the small glass screen that, for all he knew, probably still stood in Ted Bates' shop window. 'Television will change the world,' David had prophesied at a young age.

'Nonsense. Money is what makes the world go round and so it will always be. The television you're talking about is simply a new product. It's similar to the film industry. You wouldn't say that Charlie Chaplin changed the world, would you?'

'According to Ted Bates television will go further—where you can watch what's going on in one country from another. No, further than that…from one continent to another. In America you could see how people are living in Africa.'

'How can they do that?'

'With radio waves.'

'From Africa to America?'

'For example, yes.'

'That's impossible, boy. Radio waves travel straight and the world is round. That way, radio waves would go straight up into the air.'

'They put a mirror there.'

'An immature boy's dream! You still have a lot to learn, boy. It's pure fantasy. And you can't make fantasies and sell those to the world.'

The conversations killed time and because of Jonathan's conversations with Sjoerd, the occupants of the basement were more or less up-to-date with what took place outside. One day David's father admitted, 'I'm astounded. Mr. Colijn wants to know more of this television of yours. He doesn't know anything about such apparatus.'

'America is about ten years ahead of Europe.'

'He thinks God will prevent them.'

'Maybe in Holland, not in America.'

'For some strange reason he thinks your idea may be profitable; a little cupboard with which you can see different countries.'

'According to Ted Bates, sooner or later everyone will have such a thing. That means someone will have to sell them.'

'Hmm.' Jonathan rubbed his chin while he seemed to be thinking about something. 'Colijn said something similar. "The whole world?" he mumbled as I told him of your idea. Maybe he took you more seriously than I did. He looked at me sideways and, I'm not sure if he was making fun of me, said "that's a lot of buyers." Afterwards Colijn told me about how many were skeptical about whether cars would ever catch on, until Ford made the Model T. And people have been skeptical about the increase of the German Reich, but they have been forced to eat their words. In fact, that has become an enormous customer base.'

'Is that German Reich of Mr. Colijn still growing then?' David asked out loud.

'If you believe the German publishers you would think so.'

In addition, Margaret and Huigje had much to say of what took place outside the book cave. Because of the German Reich of Hitler, things were constantly changing. A new phenomenon was the Arbeitseinsatz; Dutch men were taken to work in German workplaces, because the German workers had been sent to various fronts.

Margaret also informed them of a German order which meant that Jewish people from other municipalities had been compelled to move to the Jewish district in Amsterdam. That news forced Jonathan and his family to stay shut up in that suffocating room for about half a year. They heard that German Jewish refugees had to come forward for 'voluntary' relocation. Beginning in 1942, the first Jewish inhabitants from Amsterdam were brought to the special labor camps also under the name of 'Arbeitseinsatz'.

Apart from the times when these bulletins left the Kerzner family with a chill, they could often relax and have an enjoyable time when Margaret came to call. She had an excellent sense of humor. With great pleasure she told them some of the funny tales that were doing the rounds about the German occupiers. David had to laugh at them, but he couldn't figure out how she could be so caustic about the Germans whilst being involved with one of them: Heinrich, whom his father seemed to know.

'How is it possible that you have a German boyfriend?' he let slip one time.

'I'll tell you about that one day,' Mother answered rapidly before Margaret could open her mouth.

On one of these relaxing evenings with Margaret they heard a simple piece of news with caused an unexpected reaction. 'Heinrich heard something strange today', said Margaret. David, Jonathan and Mother expected to hear of some new ridiculous command. 'Sjoerd Colijn has offered some of Heinrich's superiors some small diamonds.' There was no tone of suspicion in her voice.

Jonathan never really paid much attention to their conversations but this time he suddenly sat bolt-upright as if he'd been stung by a wasp. 'Which diamonds?' David heard his father ask, as though Margaret would know.

'Why's that relevant?' David asked. 'The Dutch have need of money, so they need to sell, and Germans are willing to buy. And this is diamond city.'

Margaret also couldn't understand Jonathan's reaction. 'That he would trade diamonds isn't so remarkable. I just wondered how Sjoerd Colijn would have come by them. And it's odd that on the one hand he's helping you, but on the other hand he's dealing with the Germans.'

For the rest of the evening Jonathan was restless and moody. As soon as he had the opportunity, he would have a word with Sjoerd Colijn.

'And something else', said Margaret rapidly changing the subject, 'Sjoerd Colijn is looking for a secretary.'

David realized he couldn't do otherwise than plan their escape from the country himself. Even Jonathan was willing to discuss this with David, realizing that David would have to take this matter into his own hands. Sjoerd Colijn and Huigje's father were planning to go to America on business for two or three months. 'Maybe that would be a good time to take flight,' suggested David. 'If we can find a way in that short time.'

'On the one hand it is better that Sjoerd Colijn is gone and doesn't know what we're up to, but on the other hand maybe he could help us.'

'First we need to know where we can go,' said David, keeping quiet about the farm which he had in mind; the farm where he had come to know Brenda. Maybe that would be a good halfway house from where they could leave the country.

'Travel is not going to be possible.'

'I don't know about that. The Dutch still travel don't they?'

'Only within the Netherlands, I believe.'

'Then maybe we could just try and get to the border and reassess the situation there.'

It was indeed not much longer before Sjoerd Colijn traveled to America. 'I don't know how he managed to arrange that,' said Jonathan but then answered his own query with: 'Colijn must have good contacts with the Germans. That'll really help. The trip to America also has something to do with my businesses.' Jonathan wanted his son to know. 'The journey has other purposes: Trading diamond goods, property and mainly the sale of a large number of paintings and other works of art. That's where we've invested together because inflation has made money worth less and less. While Colijn is gone, his secretary is to prepare a large seventeenth century painting of one the Dutch Grand Masters for transport to Geneva.' Jonathan spoke frankly. 'That's not just to advance the fortunes of me and Colijn, but also that of some rich Germans.'

'Well that explains how it's possible for Colijn to travel so easily,' thought David quickly.

Before the time came for Colijn to depart he set about recruiting a secretary who would be able to begin working for him immediately. He also continued to discuss anything to do with money or business with Jonathan.

David continued to worry about the escape; this would only be possible if he made contact with reliable people outside of the book cave. Father could not know anything about it. Father still met regularly with Sjoerd Colijn in the house next door. 'I'm going over now to talk business,' he would say briefly as he crawled through the breach to the outside. Through the wet garden, protected by the high shrubs, he sloped off to the adjacent building only to return, more often than not, downhearted. David and Margaret seized upon the moment without Jonathan to think about various flight plans. The arrival of a secretary for Sjoerd Colijn gave David inspiration. 'It's no more than just an idea', David softly whispered in the little bedroom that he and Margaret used for this sort of conversation, the sort they didn't want Mother to get agitated about.

'Well, that's got me curious,' answered Margaret.

'My idea is to try and get someone we can trust in that little job as secretary. You don't know what possibilities that could open up for us.'

'That's a superb idea,' Margaret spontaneously reacted.

'No one, and I mean no one, must know what our plan is,' whispered David.

'No one,' Margaret agreed. 'Then we can develop all sorts of ideas without being afraid that someone might let it slip.'

'The little children mustn't know about it, and neither Father nor Mother. I'm afraid we must conceal it from Huigje also. It's not that I don't trust her; we'd just bring her into danger, and why make life unnecessarily difficult for her?'

'I'm absolutely with you on that one. I'll not even say anything to Heinrich. It's the same with him. I trust Heinrich absolutely, you understand that. But why make things more dangerous and complicated than they already are?' Margaret sighed.

David was silent for a short while, then looked Margaret in the eyes and continued, 'I've been thinking about this. I think that I may know someone for this job. But I can't ask her myself. That's something you'll have to do. But that won't be simple because, as far as I know, she doesn't live in Amsterdam but possibly in a farm in the neighborhood of Purmerend.'

'If you mean the young woman who you sent running to me before the war, then there's no problem with that. Provided you're absolutely sure your candidate is one hundred percent trustworthy.'

David rekindled Margaret's memory of Brenda; the North Holland country woman who radiated beauty, with blond locks and blue eyes. 'She's quite different from Huigje,' David followed with rosy cheeks.

'Oh really. How?' Did Margaret really want to know, or was she teasing him?

David indicated the shape of breasts with his hands while his cheeks blushed and even deeper shade of crimson.

'I think I understand what you mean,' Margaret sniggered. 'She seems like a perfectly suitable secretary for Sjoerd. Leave it to me.'

One week later, all was communicated to Brenda and not long after that she was presented at twilight one evening to the occupants of the basement. Brenda looked completely different in her straight suit to how David remembered her in her baggy blue overalls. Her blond hair didn't cascade over her strong shoulders, but had been pinned back neatly into a sophisticated chignon. The things that made the biggest difference were the glasses which she now wore. The large-framed spectacles really gave her the impression of a secretary, as if she belonged behind a typewriter. Her suit made her figure appear slimmer than it had looked at the farm. And Brenda used the brightest red lipstick. 'And it seems as if she's done something to her eyes,' David thought to himself. The difference between this Brenda and the one at the farm was so great you would have never have realized it was the same person. Especially as her demeanor was now so altered; she shook everyone's hand and was so cool and stand-offish with everyone in the book cave, and towards David too. She acted as if it were the first time she'd ever met him.

It was blatantly clear to David how Margaret and Brenda had been able to secure the job. She looked like a film star. David also understood why Margaret had been so certain that Sjoerd would never recognize her at the interview. 'The Brenda that Sjoerd would employ as secretary looks completely different than the farm-girl who was asking for refuge, standing in the pouring rain, with her victimized boyfriend,' Margaret had tried to reassure David when they forged their plan. She was right. He had to really look hard at this woman in the tight little skirt to see the farm-maid he knew. David glanced at her knees, which were just visible below the hemline, and couldn't help but anticipate how much more he'd be able to see when she climbed through the window to outside.

David had explained to Margaret how she could find Brenda's farm and now Margaret told David about her first visit to the North Holland polders. Brenda had taken to their plan immediately. Father Baltus protested, but this changed nothing. Brenda told Margaret of the death of Ricardo and how she had her own motivations for taking part in the plan.

David had been concerned about Brenda's suitability. 'She's a farm-girl, not a secretary,' David had warned. He thought Margaret wasn't seeing things realistically.

'Women have their methods,' Margaret had answered mysteriously. She had got that right because Sjoerd Colijn had yielded to Brenda's provocative beauty as soon as she'd stepped through the door, and it went just as Margaret predicted. He hadn't recognized Brenda, a fact which no longer astonished David.

David also talked with his mother in the living room about Brenda, and about Margaret. He was curious about her relationship to the German, and was even more curious about how Father also knew him. Not that Father had told him that he knew the German, but David had figured it out along the way.

As soon as Esther had gone to sleep, Mother had come to sit with him at the table and by candlelight had whispered, 'I think you're old enough now for me to talk to you about these things. You will by now have wondered why such a young woman as Margaret, not even 40 yet, can get together with a much older man, and a German at that.'

'I have sometimes wondered that,' David admitted.

Using the necessary euphemisms and talking in a roundabout way, it became clear that Margaret had been, as Mother called it, a 'lady of the night.' 'Before the war she would have come to know all sorts of men, men from all nationalities. She came to be fond of Heinrich. Thanks to him, Margaret managed to get out of that way of life.' And, according to Mother, she didn't have a single regret about that.

'She still works in the city centre,' said Mother with blushed cheeks; she meant in the red light district. 'In a cafe. There she meets daily with different sorts of men and women. Margaret knows exactly how to charm men such as Colijn. She knew exactly how to present Brenda.'

Mother told him something else. 'But you mustn't say this to Father. Sjoerd Colijn is not such a nice man as your father thinks. He…' Mother spoke even more softly. 'He can't keep his hands off Margaret.'

David happily chatted about Brenda though. She had a pretty fresh face which had now been greatly improved with her full flame-red lips. In place of the suit, she also sometimes wore a low-cut dress with a little cardigan that she left undone at the top. The gleaming, soft skin revealed for what talents Sjoerd had hired her; not her average typing skills.

'Brenda knows how to emphasize her strong points,' summarized Margaret.

Hereafter David dreamed of Brenda like he'd never done before.

America 1942

Abdel Amini Sabagh had always been interested in world politics. Not only because of his business with Jonathan of selling weapons; in Abdel's eyes politics were what made the world go round. He didn't talk about it often but he knew a great deal about the developments in Europe. He knew well that Hitler had come to power using the economic crisis in his country, as well as sentiment. The development of National Socialism, along with the appointment of Hitler as chancellor in January 1933, was the most important political factor in Germany. In that same year, in Dachau in Munich, the first concentration camp had been arranged. 1933 was also the year that Hitler dissolved all opposition parties, and Germany followed Japan in leaving the League of Nations. Meanwhile America was celebrating the end of prohibition. Life for most Americans, although in poor circumstances, simply continued.

The Belgian astronomer and priest, Georges LeMaitre, published 'Discussion on the Evolution of the Universe' in 1933. These were the first written theories about the 'Big Bang'. The cosmos we know had arisen, according to LeMaitre, from a cosmic egg, out of which all things had burst out. The beginning of all things lay, according to Abdel Amini, with Allah, whom Abdel considered to be the same God as that of the Christians and the Jews. And he would leave the account of what happened at the beginning to the God of Abraham and his prophet Mohammed. This wasn't a concern of the man on the street.

Of course the success of the black athlete Jesse Owens at the Olympic Games in Berlin was a humiliation for Nazi Germany, and thereby the talk of the town. Jesse Owens with his four gold medals had undermined Hitler's expectations for the Aryan super-race.

These were the days in American history where you saw the first electric iron with a thermostat. All sorts of clever machines were coming onto the market. Around the time war broke out, the Dutch company Phillips had produced a shaver with round heads. American law students had demonstrated a method of making numerous copies of documents: they called the process dry-copying or Xerox.

Globalization had become evident with the release of the film of the book 'Gone with the Wind'. The film was a success not only in America but over the whole world. Many devotees of the film had seen it more than ten times at the cinema.

Abdel Amini took a more professional interest in following the construction of the first jet engine powered airplane. The plane could reach top speeds of five hundred kilometers per hour. The American engineer Igor Sikorsky, born in Russia, devised the first helicopter, the VS300.

It would still be a number of years before Abdel would realize the significance of the research of Nils Bohr, and his arrival from Copenhagen to spend some months at Princeton. Much later Abdel Amini heard that he had come to discuss some abstract problems with Albert Einstein; also, interestingly, the discoveries of Otto Frisch and Lise Meitner, who had both fled from Germany. It was to these whom Bohr had revealed his idea that the absorption of a neutron would lead to an atom dividing into two approximately equal parts. This would lead to the release of a high amount of energy from an atom of, say perhaps, Uranium. This process quickly became known as 'splitting the atom'.

As the war progressed, Amini's attention moved slightly. The T-shirt was born. Sailors wore such shirts as underwear, but they had now become part of the uniform, and Abdel Amini had the contract to provide the shirts. Also he was the first person to sell 'freeze-dried' orange juice to the Americans. The process of 'freeze-drying' was used in the US for the preservation of food. And when the demand for soft drinks started, Abdel Amini was the number one supplier. Most importantly, however, the trading in weapons remained part of his business ventures. He did well in speculating on suppliers, just like he did in oil shares and aircraft suppliers.

In the winter of 1942, just shortly before America was drawn into the war because of Pearl Harbor, Abdel Amini received a visit from Sjoerd Colijn. The small man from the Netherlands was accompanied by a large chap who presented himself as Herbert de Yong, the father of Huigje and Council member. In the eyes of Abdel Amini, the mountain of flesh seemed to be more in the role of bodyguard. Sjoerd Colijn told Abdel Amini how he was married to the most charming daughter of Herbert and other mundane details of day to day life in Amsterdam before he got down to business. Sjoerd Colijn said he was there to represent Kerzner, which could be seen from the legal documents he brought with him. There was a written authorization from Jonathan which had been signed by him; Abdel Amini recognized he sharp and fast handwriting of his former partner.

It soon was apparent to the experienced Palestinian that his Jewish friend didn't have much more to sell. On the contrary, much of his property, if not all, was not in the hands of Sjoerd Colijn. 'It's just a formality so we are able to lead the Germans off the track,' explained Colijn.

Abdel Amini had himself placed a lot of his own fortunes in the name of his gardener and friend Nabib but, of course, not completely everything as it seemed Jonathan had done with Colijn and the strangely silent Herbert de Yong who disturbed him. 'Why am I worrying about this?' thought Abdel Amini. 'If the stubborn and cocksure Jonathan wants it this way, who am I to question his judgment?'

Sjoerd Colijn offered Abdel Amini all kinds of properties in America. 'Jonathan wants to sell as he can't do anything with these properties in America at the moment. He's staying with his family in a comfortable apartment but he can't set foot outside. So he'd rather have the money so he can invest it as soon as the war's over.' Abdel Amini bought most of the property for peanuts, amongst which was the huge property in Boston which he'd already been offered. 'You'd be doing your friend a favor,' reassured Sjoerd with Herbert nodding in assent. Abdel Amini found it strange that Jonathan was still unable to leave that small land.

'The Netherlands—twenty percent of it lies under sea level. Such a people must be very inventive,' Abdel Amini mused.

'Oh for sure, we're very inventive,' muttered Herbert de Jong on one of the few times that he opened his mouth.

Sjoerd Colijn and Herbert de Jong stayed for another three and a half weeks while they finalized the formalities with Abdel Amini. 'Now we have money,' Sjoerd whispered to his companion as soon as they were out of the neighborhood, 'Now we can do all that we want.'

'Until the war is over,' grumbled Herbert. He wasn't confident that all would turn out well. 'When this war's over then your Jewish pal will discover all that you've done. Then you'll hang.'

Sjoerd Colijn looked over at his friend and guard and, without a moment's hesitation, said evasively, 'We're not at that stage yet. This war's going to last some time more.'

After the three and a half weeks, the two men traveled back to the Netherlands. There they would undertake the transportation of the painting that Brenda had prepared. At the same time they'd be transporting objects of art for corrupt German officials. Colijn would smuggle some of his own assets through the occupied lands. 'By our return, the Old Masters' masterpieces should be waiting in large crates in a warehouse by the railway station in Den Haag, ready to be taken to Switzerland.'

Sjoerd Colijn had thought the scheme through thoroughly and had limited his own risk. The preparations began the moment he started on his way to America. If the corrupt German officers should suspect something was amiss, he would be out of harm's way. 'Your name will come up,' muttered Herbert in a dark voice.

'I doubt that,' answered Sjoerd with a little laugh. 'If anything goes amiss, the Germans will first come for my secretary Brenda. And then the trail leads to the Jew Jonathan, because all the business is traveling to Switzerland in his name. At the end of the day, all they know about me is that I'm a supervisory traveler, in a luxury first-class compartment, with my secretary Brenda. I know nothing more than that.'

'Together with Brenda,' Herbert repeated evocatively. 'That Brenda's a pretty girl.'

'She'll be more willing than your daughter,' assumed Sjoerd without a glimmer of shame.

David couldn't understand what was going on inside him. During that year, a particular link with Huigje had developed. After dinner they withdrew to the improvised room between the stacked books. There the two dreamed of how life was going to turn out. Not everything could be said frankly. Frequently they took turns whispering in each other's ears to ensure that they wouldn't be overheard in the living room. Usually, Esther slept on the edge of the bed while the two crawled to be close to each other. And that was not only to whisper more quietly to each other.

Sjoerd Colijn and Huigje lived increasingly more apart from each other. He did know that Huigje was now effectively a part of the Jewish family and that he would find her in the basement most days and evenings. 'He must suspect that there's something going on between us. I don't sleep with him anymore. Since you came to my aid he hasn't disturbed me anymore. Sometimes he grumbles that I don't do anything with him, but mostly I am nothing to him.'

'He does keep pestering Margaret, though' David knew.

'I know it. Margaret can't come in the house without him trying it on with her. He's figured out that she can't do anything about it because she comes to see you, and therefore can't just leave. It's terrible. If I were Margaret I couldn't live with myself, but she just brushes it off, as if it's not serious. She just laughs it off, it seems.'

David didn't know if Huigje knew of Margaret's history, but he left it that way.

David found the time that he was with Huigje very pleasant but it disconcerted him also. He found it harder to view her as his married neighbor; she was also his girlfriend. He dreamed of the woman who was so slight that, when she pressed herself against his strong body, he could easily put his arm all the way around her. Huigje sometimes whispered for him to stop if his hands drifted away from her waist, but then as other times she just pushed herself closer against him.

'I have to tell you something,' David said one evening. 'I think of you all the time when you're not with me.' Huigje looked at him silently. Was she annoyed or timid?

David thought about her far more often than he dared confess. The images he pictured when he was on his own in the evening he wouldn't say, or not completely. They unsettled him. He was conflicted thinking about the kind, lovely Huigje and the stunningly attractive Brenda. 'I feel…' he started sometimes, but then lost his nerve and shut up and stared at the ceiling.

'Listen. I am still married,' Huigje would then warn. Or she would say nothing and behave as hesitatingly and uncertainly as David himself.

Of course, sometimes Huigje would feel the need to have physical contact with David while they spoke. She would stroke his broad, naked shoulders under his sweater with her slender hands. 'That's not possible,' David thought and subtly pushed back her fine, caressing fingers. Not so fast.

Everyday Huigje was drawn to the book cave. For some reason she was compelled to see him. Sjoerd Colijn hadn't grasped that, or maybe he had. Certainly for David's mother everything was clear. Of course she never reacted against it; in fact, she would smile when Huigje would try to say casually after dinner that she wanted to discuss something important with David. The young couple was undoubtedly attracted to each other and that wasn't so astonishing really. Huigje wasn't much older than David, and she didn't have much else in her life than them in her isolated existence.

Both were meanwhile wise and adult enough to realize they couldn't keep on making excuses to see each other. They had to face the problems staring them in the face. Inevitably then they eventually came to speak of love. First in the abstract: concerning the love of others, of love such as in Shakespeare. And concerning the reproductive impulses of animals: how cats have many partners yet swans mate for life. Eventually it developed into talking carefully about their love for each other with words that became more serious and thorough.

David knew the Ten Commandments on the tablets of Moses. And Huigje well knew what the church had to say on the matter. 'What God had yoked together let no man put apart.' But had God had anything to do with this forced marriage? And wasn't it written that a husband could send his wife away? What if Sjoerd were to do that? And how would God judge the situation if the woman was to decide for herself to go?

'I don't know exactly how it is with Dutch law,' said Huigje cautiously to David. 'But I believe you must prove before the court that your husband has committed adultery. That's my only grounds for a legal separation.'

'I really wouldn't know how it goes with our law either. Our Rabbi in Boston would know. As a matter of fact, it's not looked upon favorably for us to marry outside of our faith. Not for orthodox Jews. Solomon had many wives but he was brought down by a foreign woman. But that was about three thousand years ago I know. I don't know what a Rabbi would think about it these days.'

'And what he'll think about it in ten years' time,' said Huigje hopefully. 'Times change. And perhaps in the Netherlands a time will come where women may leave their husbands if they're being badly treated.'

David let her words sink in. What should he say? He though a bit longer and said, 'I don't know. I've lived here long enough to know there's an awful lot of people here belonging to either the Catholic Church or the Reformed church. It'll never be permitted that church weddings are allowed to be dissolved. No, I don't believe that time will ever come. Except for, as you already said, on the grounds of adultery. You'd need to hire a private detective to get proof of that. That happens in America all the time.'

Huigje sighed. 'You're probably right. Maybe it's better that way, because if everyone were allowed to separate the floodgates would open. And then who could women like me and children like Harm look to for care?' She looked at David as she said this but he didn't notice. He was deep in thought, like he was trying to solve some complicated mathematical problem, and from that deep concentration his conclusion came: 'You're right. Your proposal to make it easier for husbands and wives to separate can't be good for the children.'

Huigje thought of Harm and became silent.

As David lay alone in bed after their long conversation, two thoughts wouldn't leave him alone. On the one hand there was still the thought of taking flight from the Amsterdam address where they'd been in hiding. On the other hand, that would mean he could no longer see Huigje.

The more David spoke with Huigje the more he fantasized about running away with her. In his mind he saw a girlfriend in a cabin on the Holland-America line, such as he'd had on the way from Boston to Netherlands. She then sat in a tight bathing costume at the edge of the pool. But there were more images which haunted David's mind. He had no control over them; it was if they had a life of their own. While thinking of that scene with Huigje, in shuffled Brenda in another swimsuit. He pictured the rounded form of her firm, naked shoulders and her blond hair cascading over them. And naturally she was emanating that carefree radiance that made you forget it was war-time.

Huigje would come and lay next to David on the bed frequently. The sheer substance of her dress, her slim body, was pleasant to feel. It was pleasing to lie in bed thinking of those times, but then Brenda would come creeping into his thoughts. That caught him unawares. She lodged in his thoughts and brought about a different feeling. He wanted to say things to Brenda, thoughts never raised in him about Huigje.

If her boss wasn't around, Brenda would regularly hop into the book cave. On one of these visits, David had come to know for the first time about what had happened after Ricardo had knocked on Sjoerd Colijn's door. David had carefully questioned Colijn about them previously, but he had shrugged his shoulders and said that the young man hadn't thought much of the basement and had gone to find another address. Sometimes David felt guilty that Sjoerd had allowed his family to lodge here. Why had he allowed them? Because his father had plenty of money? He had no idea what he had paid for their stay. But Brenda wouldn't go any further and seldom spoke about Ricardo. From time to time David caught a faraway look in her eyes, but then she straightened her back and looked as if she took her life firmly by the reins again.

When she came to visit, David could hardly keep his eyes off her, although he did his best not to look as she hitched up her skirt to clamber through the window. And he had to force himself to look in completely the opposite direction when she sat across from him at the wooden table. Supporting herself with her arms, it appeared as if her breasts sprung even further forward. David didn't allow himself to look. Or maybe just a little. It seemed as if Brenda noticed. Was he mistaken, or did she look at them and then at him? He was sure she laughed a little at him then.

David couldn't sleep very easily that night, and in his thoughts he saw himself with Brenda at the farm. Those voluptuous lips; there he wanted to press his own.

With Huigje he talked and thought about marriage. With Brenda? Marriage? Children? No…These thoughts never crossed his mind. With Brenda, David thought about something else…something which in turn made him forget everything else.

After mealtime Mother steered the conversation at the table around home life and the future. Jonathan stood up at these moments, paced up and down the little room and then nestled his long legs one over the other as he relaxed in the wooden armchair again. He listened to the conversation but rarely took part.

Saturday was for her family the rest day, the Sabbath; for Huigje and Sjoerd that was Sunday. On this day they would go to church, Huigje in her long black skirt, high buttoned blouse and her hair tied up under a hood. Sjoerd was in his Sunday black suit that didn't look much different from his weekday suit, except this had shiny spots where he put his hands in his pockets. The weekday trousers were too tight and too short. The Sunday trousers were of the same substance but were too long. To the outside world they seemed like a neat Amsterdam family, as Father had heard it said of them. Harm walked along with them, frequently hand in hand with his mother, even though he was now around ten years old.

Saturday evenings sat in between the two rest days. With luck, Margaret would bring something special from one of the local farms in the evening. Sometimes they'd have apples or pears that Mother had managed to save. Very rarely you got the tasty aroma of a warm apple tart or a thick waffle from the cake stall which masked the musty smell of paper in the house; but since flour had become scarcer this didn't happen often.

Jonathan had to give up smoking almost completely since cigarettes were so difficult to come by. Of course every now and then he got a packet thanks to Sjoerd and his good connections with different Germans. He saved these rare treats for a Saturday night and his cigarette smoke mixed in with the other fragrances. The cigarettes stank but they did bring a warm environment to the house.

On these evenings they didn't get up straight away after eating to do the washing up, but waited at the table for Margaret and Huigje to move the shutter by the window and crawl in. They shuffled along the benches to make room for them and chatted together.

Margaret could, in coded terms for Esther's sake, give tasty details about her earlier life on Amsterdam's ramparts. All kinds of strange individuals with the craziest desires came to the prostitutes' district.

Later, when the noise from the street died down, out came the candles and they spoke more softly so that nobody outside could hear them. They had to hold in their laughter, and sometimes tears, as life wasn't getting any easier.

Conversations about love and relationships between men and women were the preference of the women. David sat there and listened intently. The attention of Jonathan seemed to be devoted to his cigarette. There often lay an open book on his lap so no one had the impression that he was remotely aware of what they were talking about.

Margaret talked about how she and Heinrich would like to have a child. 'We don't know when we'll be able to marry, but we're not getting any younger,' she said. 'We wouldn't want to settle in my neighborhood, and I don't know if a neighborhood with so-called "proper" people would accept me.' She told them about her next door neighbor who was regularly beaten by her husband. 'I wouldn't tolerate such a man.'

It seemed as if Huigje had been waiting for an opportunity like this. 'David and I had a conversation about such a case. In such a situation as that, you should be allowed to leave your husband.' She didn't dare to say that this was something which affected her personally. 'But David wondered if that would be best for the children.'

'If a marriage isn't good, then it isn't good for the children,' Mother observed, level-headed as always. 'Just look at little Harm.'

Harm had often been the topic of conversation between Mother and Huigje. 'Harm is sick,' said Huigje many times. Mother had seen that for herself. She found it difficult to comprehend what must be going on in that little mind of his. He was a delicate little thing, and not as smart and forward in his abilities as David had been at that age. Harm looked like a lad she knew from back home called Levia, friend of David's who ate nonstop. A lovely little chap. He didn't say much, but you saw his eyes light up if you set a piece of cake in front of him. The little fellow would take a saucer with him to the corner of the room, sit down and hold it close to his mouth to catch the crumbs as he took tiny nibbles from the home-baked treat.

'Harm's so quiet. He never speaks at home. I've taken him to the doctor's about that. He said he's not right in the head.' She didn't want to say the word. 'Backward' was the word the doctor had used to describe him.

'Nonsense,' said Mother simply. 'He is sensitive. And he's had it hard. You can see that in him.' Huigje could endorse that, but didn't tell everything that the young boy had gone through. She didn't tell the doctor, who therefore couldn't have any other explanation for his strange behavior than being 'backward.' And she also didn't tell David because she knew there'd be nothing left of Sjoerd Colijn if David were to find out all that happened in that house. No wonder Harm's silence seemed unnatural to the outside world.

Without revealing details of their home life, Huigje did discuss her concerns about Harm's reserved nature with David. 'Harm is so vulnerable. It makes me worry. If he doesn't talk, how can he progress at school? Because he'd not said anything to his teacher, she thought that he couldn't talk, or that he was backward. The doctor said that too. And what could his future hold? He has no little friends. If I go with him to try and get him talking with another little boy, Harm just stares at the ground and says nothing. Or he lets go of my hand and walks away.'

'Harm is certainly not backward,' David protested. 'In fact, just the opposite. I think he's a genius!'

'What was that?'

David said to Huigje how he would read daily with Harm and Esther some of the books from the book cave. Esther preferred the fairy stories with happy endings; tales of princesses and princes. Harm, on the other hand, was totally absorbed with anything technical. It had been some time before David realized that Harm had a particular aptitude. On one evening he had knocked together a little lamp that would come on if you twisted it. 'The necklace that he wears he made himself. The pendant isn't a work of art but it's quite an ingenious piece of technical engineering. It's half of a shape which wonderfully clicks into the other half which he's given to Esther. Esther wears that like a princess. That's their token of friendship.'

Nevertheless, neither David nor Huigje really knew the half of how exceptional the talents of Harm were. Harm was certainly captivated, perhaps even obsessed, by the technical books from the book cave.

He'd read much more than that there also. David himself had a greater than average knowledge in a wide variety of subjects thanks to the vast library. He read everything from theology to economy. But he found Harm's technical knowledge extraordinary; everything he read, no matter how difficult, he understood immediately. For David to understand something required reading, studying, thinking and reflecting, but there was a limit. At some point everyone reaches a level where no amount of thinking and puzzling will bring solutions.

David read books concerning world economy, books by Keynes, other economists and also a book by Marx, banished by the church and had been left to rot for a long time in the book cave. The books fascinated him, but he never got the feeling he understood it all. Not like Harm. 'Harm truly understands anything technical,' David wanted Huigje to know, and he thought it would comfort her. 'I really don't know where you and that doctor got the idea that he's backward. And he's not quiet either. When Harm comes across a chapter with some sort of complicated formulae in it, then he talks incessantly about all the things he could invent using it. Anything to do with electricity, because that's where the future lies, according to him.'

Huigje listened captivated and hopeful as David spoke about her son. Initially she found it very difficult to believe him. Her little boy seemed to lead a double life: One at home and one with David.

The technical interest she recognized a little, especially after looking curiously at the books Harm read. The technical stuff certainly didn't hold any charm for her. Other books interested her more, and it was as if a new world opened to her. The books on people and art especially appealed to her. They awakened interests in her that she had never known before. Obsessed, she looked at reproductions of the female nude. 'If you've been forced to marry at age 15 to a man of over 30, then you've got other things on your mind than reading books,' she told David.

Her little Harm was not interested in her books, all he wanted to learn about was technical things. He still had some strange behavioral patterns. At home he still didn't speak a word; that he could speak so freely in the book cave still astonished her. 'What else does he go on about then?' she asked David. David told her that the last time it was about an apparatus through which you could see the whole world; televisions, such as David had come to know about from Ted Bates. 'The fantasies of a child,' thought Huigje.

'That's what I thought at first too. Did you know there's already an abundance of such an apparatus where you can see hundreds of kilometers away from you?'

'Yeah, in the cinema.'

'This goes further than that. Imagine me in a swimming competition in America and at the same moment you would be watching me in Amsterdam.'

'Amazing.'

'I'd win of course, and then the interviewer would come and ask me where I got the strength from. And I'll give this answer: I think of my Huigje in the Netherlands. She gives me my strength and my luck. You'll see it all, on a little screen. According to Harm it's not going to be so long before that's possible.'

Huigje laughed a little. 'And that's what you talk about? What does a child know about it?'

'Oh we talk about much more than that. Also about all the devices that will be in homes ten years from now. About radios and computers that will do work for you. I must say that Harm really lets his imagination go. According to him, in the future, no one will go to America via boat but will go in huge airplanes. And we'll even fly to the moon.'

'I'm really happy that he'll talk to you, but he must reel off such nonsense.'

'If you heard Harm talk, within a short while, you'd believe him too. We have a plan actually which proves it isn't nonsense.'

'Two scatter-brains instead of one.'

'That may be true…but the plan is that when the war's over we're going to start a business that produces these things and sells them. Harm makes them. I sell them.'

'How do you start something like that? Surely you need money to start with?'

'Well that's a different matter. We don't have anything, but there must be money in the family. In America we lived in an awesome house, and I won't begin to tell you about the hotel we lived in for nearly two years in Amsterdam. But Father won't talk to me about money. You'd think at least he'd tell me how he earned so much money so I could go and do the same.'

Her whole life Brenda Baltus had been able to live the way she wanted to. You could see that about her. She moved easily, almost athletically. She had a radiant face and clear, bright eyes. Brenda had a serious face which showed self-assuredness, but not to the point of arrogance. As Brenda's mother had died of TB when Brenda was still very young, her father had brought her up on his own. 'Please yourself what you will do,' said Baltus when Brenda had finished elementary school. 'You can work on the farm; you can stay on at school. Choose yourself.' Baltus was lucky in that that his daughter was not only a particularly lovely girl, but she was also extremely judicious. Brenda dictated the course her life would take, but she did nothing rashly.

No doubt Baltus had had his doubts when the carefree Ricardo came to their home. It had worked out rather well though, until the Germans hunted him down.

Then Brenda came home to him one night in January 1943, after the day's work at the farm, after mealtime, to say she'd got a little job in Amsterdam as a secretary. Farmer Baltus wisely swallowed down his objections. 'Secretary?'

'Yes. For a man called Sjoerd Colijn; the man who refused lodging to Ricardo at the beginning of the war.' She stopped abruptly without further explanation. Baltus well understood that there was more to this. The closed, indifferent face across from him made him realize that he clearly shouldn't ask any more questions.

Brenda had found a small bed-sit in Amsterdam, but every Friday at 4:30, when she finished work for the week, she made the effort to travel the twenty-five kilometer journey home. On Saturdays she worked at the farm. 'That's what I stipulated,' was her explanation, and Jan Baltus knew that Brenda generally got her own way. That she wouldn't work on a Sunday was logical working for a Reformed boss.

'Why in heaven's name would you want to work as a secretary?' Baltus asked her one of the weekends. Except for the cattle market, Baltus seldom left the farm and found it difficult to understand what towns-people occupied them with. Brenda always went at her own pace and was open and honest. Baltus felt he knew his daughter far better than other parents knew their progeny, yet he didn't understand this move.

'A secretary holds everything together. Makes appointments, looks after the finances, does the administration.'

'That's something you've never had an interest in before.'

'I have to tell you that I'm developing an interest in it now.' Brenda meant it.

Brenda and her father often spoke about serious matters in the evenings, after work, at the kitchen table. Their food was cooked on an ancient cast iron cooker which was stoked with wood from the orchard. The kitchen smelled of burning wood and farm animals. She heard the cows shuffle about in the barn. These were the smells and sounds that she missed when she was in Amsterdam. At the end of winter the dark red glow of the setting sun shimmered just before the night sunk into real darkness. Brenda brought her chair in closer to the table and began to explain why she had started to work for Sjoerd Colijn. Not that her father had asked anything, but the story just seemed to want to come out automatically. 'I think it's because the figures that I keep have a tale to tell. I know exactly what I'm doing, and I'm starting to fill in the gaps as to what Sjoerd Colijn is up to.'

'And that's the reason you're working for him?'

'In a way.' Brenda reached over the table to enclose her father's hands in her own.

'You want to ask me something,' Baltus knew already.

'True Father. You mustn't worry about this.'

'If you say that of course I'm going to worry now! But that won't stop you, I know. You're like me. Ask me.'

Brenda let go of her father's hands and they both leaned over the table towards each other so they could talk more softly. 'You make and repair all the tools here yourself, don't you?'

'That's correct.'

'Well, I want you to make a gun for me.'

Shocked, Baltus stared at his daughter. Brenda, in her short life, had been involved in all sorts of things that others would have shied away from. Baltus was well aware of that. But a gun? Brenda never undertook anything without thinking it though properly. What was her plan for this?

Without waiting for his reaction, Brenda told him about the paintings that were going to Switzerland by train. She had to arrange the transport herself for Colijn. 'I've arranged all the smallest details. I've booked the first-class carriage for Colijn and myself; I have to go too. Colijn then thinks he'll have me to himself. I haven't got a choice, you understand.'

Jan Baltus understood exactly what Colijn wanted from his daughter. If he wanted strong cattle on the farm, he would mate the strongest bull with the most beautiful cow. Emma had also been a terrific woman, truly loved by himself but not as wise as Brenda. The thought that his daughter should sit on a train with the man who had broken his son-in-law filled him with disgust. He would rather wring the guy's neck with his own bare hands. But it was something else to support his daring daughter in her plans for murder? There was sadness in Brenda's eyes as he looked at her. Everything had changed. Where had those times gone when she used to laugh all the time and almost float into the house after playing about with the cows?

'Revenge is not a good motive,' he said softly.

'I'm not doing it for revenge,' answered his daughter thoughtfully. Baltus knew that nothing he could say would change anything. He could protect her better by helping her. He had resolved to do that before she even revealed her motives. 'Revenge no longer concerns me. A secretary sees all sorts of papers. I know all about his finances and I've discovered that, with the help of Herbert de Jong, he is slowly but surely taking all of the money from the people who have gone into hiding there. They'll soon not have a single cent. Meanwhile, Jonathan Kerzner thinks that he can keep his entire property safe by means of Colijn and has already put everything into his name. The only thing he still has is a large trunk, and that's because the gold and other precious things that sit in there can't be placed in a bank. It also can't fraudulently be put into Sjoerd's name, not even with the false signatures and corrupt Germans that Colijn usually uses. This is literally the only thing that Jonathan still has, and Sjoerd has his eye on it. Revenge hasn't crossed my mind for a long time, Father,' she repeated, now even more gently. 'I have to rescue this family out of the claws of Colijn. They have a daughter and a son. The son is David; the boy who saved me and Ricardo before, and who gave me Margaret's address. That's how I got to find out about Sjoerd's hideout. Now they're there and have handed themselves over to him.'

Baltus saw the soaking wet boy with the earnest look in his eyes from before and sighed. 'You are, of course, right.' He said laboriously, 'we must do what we can for that family, and I'll help you wherever possible.'

'There is more,' Brenda interrupted her father. 'Sjoerd has a wife of about my age, whom he raped when she was about fifteen and got her pregnant. Fortunately he doesn't bother her any longer but they have a son, Harm. And I know for a fact that they can't stay with Colijn either.'

Jan Baltus stared for a while at his gnarled hands which were stretched out on the table in front of him. Then he lifted his head and looked at Brenda resolutely in her eyes. 'We two will do something, my girl. I'll help you. We'll make a gun. You practice. We'll discuss all plans in details and I'll ensure that I'm on the same train. We'll find a moment where we can get rid of the guy.'

'That last part won't work Father. It's a train exclusively for Germans, you can't come along. Trust me; I know what I'm doing.' Baltus wasn't happy about it but didn't pursue the matter.

Every time he saw his daughter he feared it would be the last. This Sjoerd Colijn was sharp; he wouldn't be fooled by a young maiden. The terrible finale was coming closer. What made it worse was that he couldn't shake the thought of him with his beautiful daughter in the rail compartment.

In Boston, Ted Bates had turned his attention to his own future. 'The year 1943 shall bring me back to life.' He really didn't know what was inspiring him. Ted resolved to read more about the war, in which the Americans were becoming more embroiled. 'And I'm going to train again,' he promised himself. From the turn of the year every other day, by good or bad weather, Ted went out to breathe in the fresh air from the ocean or the Arnold Arboretum. Sometimes he went over the hill to the stately white house where he met an older gardener. Around the house, little girls played as if there was no war, and there was a dark little boy who Ted thought couldn't be older than about six. 'I saw David grow from about that age.' Ted realized that he loved that boy as if he was his own son. He missed that child who by now assuming all had gone well would now be an adult.

Ted tried to no longer be dejected but looked with hope to the moment when his shop bell would tinkle and in would walk David. 'Why should I worry if I haven't heard any bad news?' he told himself bravely. Meanwhile, he enjoyed the sounds of the well-dressed children playing. As always, he continued on his training route around the house. This was where he would frequently meet up with the pleasant gardener and they would greet each other.

Boston 1943

Abdel Amini had taken up residence in Hillside and walked over the hills around the house with his friend Nabib. Winter was passing. Nabib indicated towards the yellow daffodils. 'Spring,' he said pleasantly but much too loudly in Abdel's ear. Nabib had difficulty exercising control over his voice. He couldn't express himself well in long sentences. His crooked mouth, a result of his hemorrhage and five year coma, made it hard to say a single word clearly.

'Sun.' It was splendid weather indeed, with the clear blue sky reflecting tin the ocean. Abdel Amini, who in Boston also wore his white suit and scatter cap even for relaxed occasions such as this, carried a couple of large rolls of paper under his arm.

The two settled on one of the white benches alongside the path which wound through the grass. There Abdel unfolded the drawings for his friend. Nabib couldn't take his eyes off them. A reproduction of sunflowers by Van Gogh spoke to him the most. 'Flowers. Pretty.' On the other canvases stood images from the Grand Masters. In the margins of the papers were dimensions. Nabib had a keen eye for art; this was something you had to feel above anything else. Abdel Amini made his decisions based on intelligence. 'We can buy several works,' he said to Nabib knowing, however, that the meaning of these words would elude him entirely. Whenever Abdel had to make a cumbersome decision he spoke with Nabib. He didn't know why exactly. Was is because simply speaking out loud helped you organize things in your mind, or did the childlike and uncomplicated answers of Nabib really play a role in his decision-making?

'Brown, yellow or white, Jew, Christian or Muslim, we all have the same eyes and brain. So why must we all think so differently?' he asked out loud. Nabib sat up straight next to him and looked attentively at Abdel Amini. He smiled at something. 'Pretty paintings, Nabib?'

'Pretty,' Nabib nodded with uncontrolled fervor. He looked again at the Van Gogh.

'We can buy them,' said Abdel Amini again. 'They don't belong to that Dutchman, but he's offering them to us.'

Between the big rolls of paper was a newspaper. Abdel Amini leaned against the backrest of the bench, crossed his legs over each other, and looked at the front page. He read a short article which continued on page four, so he thumbed further. He held open the paper with both hands so he could read on. 'Jews can buy back their own property. European escapees who had to leave their things behind at the beginning of the war can buy them back on the international art market. Some Nazis, such as Goebels, have taken possession of such art. They collect these stolen works of art and offer them to others to buy.' Abdel Amini inquired of Nabib, 'Propaganda or truth?' Nabib didn't answer. He had no idea what his friend meant. Abdel indicated toward the large images which Nabib now had on his lap. 'Stolen.' Abdel Amini said. Nabib looked at them again.

'Not good,' was all Nabib said. He gave him the rolls back and, with an angry expression, looked in the other direction.

Abdel Amini had his answer. Nabib's motives were as simple and pure as an innocent child. The two friends walked good-naturedly back down the hill in the sunshine. A sporty, but much older, man in a tracksuit passed them. Nabib waved at him. Abdel Amini halted for a moment, held onto Nabib's sleeve, and looked directly at him. 'I don't know how you manage it Nabib. You are right. And you've saved me, as always, from making a big mistake. I do not have to buy this stuff. It's stolen goods; with strings attached. Once this war's over the owners wouldn't be knocking at the Nazi's doors, but at ours.'

Amsterdam 1943

Heinrich had now been billeted for almost two years in Amsterdam. The Germans had commandeered an old existing barracks in the Mauritskade. The barracks, a large brick-built building of three floors, was populated by two hundred German soldiers and a handful of collaborating Dutchmen. The Germans were to keep order in the city and they did this with a firm hand. They considered the Dutch Resistance to be a minor irritation. The Dutch royal family stayed in Canada. The Dutch resistance kept the communication lines open to England, as from there Dutch Prince Bernhard was commanding them. The Germans, however, felt invincible. They considered their biggest threats to be far from Amsterdam.

The German occupiers could move freely within the city. Some soldiers had Dutch girlfriends. His colleagues were well aware that Heinrich had a Dutch girlfriend but they had never met her. They also weren't aware that he'd known her for more than ten years, from a long time before war had broken out.

Thanks to his length of service Heinrich had an executive position, so he got to hear things that he generally hid from the young soldiers. The Germans had been there long enough to build up a network of Dutch drivers, business partners and informants through which they could keep things under control. Sjoerd Colijn was one of these business partners and informant at the same time. As had others in German service, Heinrich had been informed of the existence of his hideout.

In his free time he visited Margaret as much as he could, especially now that in just over four months she would give him his first child. As he secretly continued to call on his much younger girlfriend and stayed overnight, they would talk until deep into the night about their situation. As far as Heinrich was concerned, there was no reason to suspect that they would ever need to be apart again. The Netherlands, in his eyes, would always be part of the German realm. The proud mother and father actually thought that, for them, the German occupation was a stroke of luck, although Margaret did feel the disapproval of her neighbors. Courtship with a German was one thing, but to be pregnant by one was much worse.

For their own security, Heinrich and Margaret kept each other as informed as possible. In a way this meant that Heinrich could watch the security of Jonathan and his family from behind the scenes. With any luck, it wouldn't be much longer now before the need for security was done away with.

After the curfew, the streets of Amsterdam were peaceful and almost deserted. Germans were still allowed to roam the streets, even wearing civilian clothes. This enabled Heinrich to walk through the streets to visit Margaret as soon as he had heard the terrible news of the plot Sjoerd Colijn had forged with his superiors.

Nervousness making him short of breath, he told Margaret, 'It'll happen within the next month or two. Sjoerd Colijn will be making his way to Geneva with some paintings. He's going on a regular transport but will be secretly transporting other pieces stolen from rich Jews; these belong to some of the most influential, important Germans who want to smuggle these out of Europe. He's also taking some of his own paintings, no doubt also stolen from the church, or from Jews, who knows? There's little we can do about that, but what really concerns me is that I suspect he's going to use this opportunity to hand over the Jewish family in the basement to the Germans. I'm not sure how he's managed to organize it all without incriminating himself. I'm afraid that he's probably arranged for himself to stay in Geneva, and perhaps from there get out to Britain or America. It wouldn't surprise me if by that time he has complete ownership of all Jonathan's riches and intends to take it all with him.'

Margaret looked pale and took hold of Heinrich's hand. Heinrich shook his head. 'It seems to be a done deal. One way or another, Sjoerd Colijn will be leaving the country; and probably with that special case I told you about.'

Margaret looked shocked. 'Together with the paintings?' she suggested.

'That's right. What a sly little man.'

'There's even more to his plot.' Margaret paused while, in her mind, all the pieces dropped into place. 'What do you think about what will happen with his wife, Huigje, and his son, Harm?'

'Well, they're not going with him.'

'Exactly. Naturally that's all part of the set-up. Huigje stays here and he pins all the blame on her. He's going to create the illusion that he knows nothing and that Huigje has hidden the people in the basement. In the meantime, he'll be safe in Geneva. He'll be well out of the way, but should anyone question him, he'll certainly put Huigje in the firing line.'

Night fell. Outside it was pitch black so that the English bombers had no reference points to help them get a sense of direction. Margaret had dense blinds at the windows and her room seemed cozy in the candlelight. Heinrich bent over the table while cogitating. He tried to figure out in his mind how the coming months would play out. He pictured the long train with goods wagons and roomy sleeping compartments taking Sjoerd Colijn along the Rhine to the south. Meanwhile, in a humble district of Amsterdam, Germans would be invading a small and wet basement. 'Perhaps I can be of some service,' Heinrich mumbled. 'What can I do?' For a long time, the only sound was the ticking of the clock on the stone mantelpiece. It was already late but no one thought of going to bed.

With his head between his hands Heinrich leaned on the kitchen table. The face of this old German looked different than usual; bleak and tired. He tried to think and listen to Margaret at the same time.

'You must know that a bond has developed between Huigje and Jonathan's son,' she said in an even tone, but with a definite implication that this was significant. 'It was so strange that Colijn knew about them but seemed to not want to do anything about it. Now I get it. It's all part of his plan. In one foul swoop he also gets rid of Huigje and David. That's his revenge. That why he could talk so easily with me about them. Every moment he must have been thinking "my time will come." Huigje comes to life with David. She gets color in her cheeks. And suddenly gets courage and a lust for life. That couldn't have escaped Sjoerd's notice. Of course, he never mentioned it to her. He was busy concocting his own secret plan. One way or the other we must put a stop to him.'

Heinrich looked up. 'We?'

'Yes, of course, 'we.' Don't you see this puts us in a lot of danger? What will your German friends say if Colijn involves me in all this? They know you have a Dutch girlfriend. If anyone finds out it's me then it brings you into danger.' Margaret shivered even though it was warm in the room. 'Perhaps we wouldn't be able to see each other anymore…or worse.'

Heinrich's thoughts had already stepped in that direction. 'And what would become of our child?' he wondered out loud to himself.

Margaret didn't want to think about it any longer. She stood up and starting pacing up and down the room. Heinrich came and stood by her and rested his hands on her shoulders. Margaret said, 'If I've got this all straight, it will happen this way; Sjoerd will reveal to your German bosses exactly what's going on. Or maybe he'll get a friend to do that so he can really stay out of the picture. Maybe he'll name Huigje and myself as the perpetrators and deny all knowledge himself. That's exactly how he is. All neat in his black suit, always with that hypocritical face. As if he's innocence itself. That's how he manages to deceive your friend Jonathan also. It wouldn't surprise me if he already has all of Jonathan's assets in his possession. If not, they soon will be. Meanwhile, all his financial problems are solved, as are his problems with Huigje and David.'

'And what about his son, Harm?'

'Sjoerd Colijn would not have wasted a moment's thought about him. He presents himself as a decent man, but he hasn't a shred of feeling.'

'If you're right, then he's the devil himself.'

'He wouldn't say that. He thinks he's an exemplary Christian. All Jews are guilty in his eyes for the death of Jesus. He sees their religion as false. Huigje's destiny he also would see as a just penalty for her sin. Her friendship and feelings for David he would consider as adultery. He'll see what happens to Harm as a consequence of Huigje's actions, not his own. You'll not see any signs of shame in him. He'll be walking about upright, full of self-confidence. Meanwhile, he's busy carving out a new future for himself and no doubt expects to have God's blessing on his plans.'

Heinrich nodded. He didn't know the man, but it would be as Margaret, rich with life experience, predicted. But how could a man who called himself a Christian invent this new life at the expense of the lives of innocent people. 'A new life,' Heinrich mumbled out loud.

'With a new woman,' Margaret added.

'What makes you say that?'

'Simple. Why do you think he's taking his secretary Brenda with him? You don't think he's bought a return ticket for her do you? He's no doubt got the idea she'll want to stay with him when he settles abroad.'

'Yes, certainly a secretary would give in to all that money and luxury.'

'Don't count on it with Brenda,' Margaret answered violently. 'Brenda's a wise girl. I don't fully understand her yet, but I think she's got her own agenda. Brenda is not someone who would be controlled by another; certainly not by a man like Sjoerd Colijn.' Margaret hesitated. She'd agreed with David not to tell Heinrich anything about the plan they'd forged in the book cave. But now things were different. 'As a matter of fact, Brenda is the most important link in the escape plan which has been prepared.'

'Escape plan?' An amazed Heinrich looked at Margaret. He was deeply offended that his open-hearted girlfriend hadn't mentioned this to him before. It wasn't long before he was ashamed of himself for that reaction. Looking at her worried face he realized that it wasn't out of mistrust that she hasn't told him. 'I hope it can be implemented rapidly.'

'The problem is, it's not supposed to be going ahead for a couple of months yet.'

'Why in two months?'

'Because they plan to escape in the cases in which the Germans think the paintings are.'

'The paintings Sjoerd Colijn is transporting.'

'Yes, the consignment leaving from The Hague. Brenda's arranged the details. Sjoerd Colijn has left her to organize everything. He trusts her. I don't know what she had to do to get him to. A clever woman can have any man wrapped round her little finger. You know that don't you?'

Heinrich didn't react to that. He thought about the days he'd spent with Jonathan and the Palestinian in Geneva. Jonathan had a good nose for business, but not a very good imagination. 'An escape in painting crates on a German train; Jonathan couldn't have come up with a plan like that.'

'He didn't. He doesn't even know about it yet. The idea is all Brenda and David's. The two creative youngsters took the matter into their own hands.'

During the battles that raged on several fronts in 1943 a change came about. Around The Netherlands the story began to circulate that the

Germans had given up their attack on Leningrad. Germans also heard such tales, but they imagined it to be simply propaganda.

Abdel Amini had heard from his friends and business associates that Churchill, Stalin and Roosevelt had met with each other in November in Tehran. Churchill and Roosevelt had met on a prior occasion in Casablanca, where they had agreed that if the Allies stayed strong together it would result in the unconditional surrender of Hitler's Germany.

Daily life in America was much different to that in Europe. Increasing numbers of American women found work in the factories, and this made for huge advances in their emancipation. The war mainly affected the families of the American Military. Others saw little of it. In Boston, Abdel Amini listened to the singing of Frank Sinatra who was making a conquest of millions of hearts. Besides the news of the developments of the war, the American newspapers discussed other matters which were making significant differences to America. For example, 'The American Dilemma,' a paper about race inequality by Swedish sociologist Gunnar Myrdal, was causing a lot of controversy. In Los Angeles and Detroit, young black and Latin-American men were frequently coming to blows with the white military.

Events which wouldn't be general knowledge for a few years yet were also taking place behind the scenes. In a couple years' time, nuclear weapons which were being developed would be tested in the Alamagardo Desert. Abdel Amini followed the scientific research and development of these weapons with interest.

David and Harm were more interested in what had happened over the last ten years with respect to the development of Colossus: The Giant Brain. The first electronic, mechanical computer was used in 1943 in Buckinghamshire, England, to decipher German codes. In Boston, the Mark 1 belonged to Harvard, whilst in Pennsylvania there was an entirely electronic computer that weighed more that twenty-seven tonnes and could calculate eighteen thousand times faster than its predecessors.

In contrast to how he was at home, Harm chatted with David often at the book cave. He couldn't talk enough about what he'd read in the books about technology. 'To hear him speak you realize that these books are already out-of-date.' David told Huigje. 'The books are quite old but that's not what I mean. Harm is enthusiastic about applications for technology which don't even exist yet. According to him, times are coming when every child shall have a radio. He talks about invisible particles that are shot against a screen and, as a result, when this war finishes, we in The Netherlands will be able to see what's happening on the streets of New York. It sounds like nonsense, I know. But if you hear him talking about it you nearly start believing it yourself. He reckons one day you'll be able to see each other as you talk to each other on the telephone, even if you're in another city or country. He says it's all just a question of getting the right technology. Machines will come that can think for you, make your food warm without fire, that can answer the telephone for you when you're not home.' Huigje burst out laughing at these crazy ideas.

In America, the elegant white mansion that stood on the sloping hillside had been almost completely restored by Tannous and Abdel Amini. This was now the base from where Abdel Amini worked. He and Tannous had managed to get two of his daughters into Harvard; the others had married American boys. Tannous found it unfortunate that they weren't Muslim boys, but the girls were without question very happy in their marriages. 'The girls are just as clever as their father. They've made a good choice,' laughed Tannous.

The two younger daughters played well with Jassar, the only son. The two young ladies with dark eyes would walk him into Boston and would sit and study under the chestnut trees while the five-year old would amuse himself playing in the grass.

The family had had their first summer in the mansion. Tannous decorated the house and Nabib was round about every day; either in the garden or the sheds behind the house. Many people in Boston knew Nabib better than they knew the patriarch of the family. The large figure of Nabib bent over a delicate flower was notable, and he always, in his own way, chatted with everyone who passed by. 'Good morning,' he would say much too loudly, even if it was afternoon. Good weather or bad, he was always in a good mood: that brightened people up if it were cloudy or made them even livelier if it were sunny.

The surroundings also did their bit to improve the mood. The inhabitants of Boston saw how, over time, the splendid mansion had been brought back to its former glory after being empty for a while. To bring it back to that standard required taste and love. You even felt as if you were younger if you walked past there, with the fresh ocean air, the sloping lawns and the breeze rustling the leaves on the trees. The crisp white mansion made the place complete. In fact it was so glaringly bright it appeared like an over-exposed photo.

Abdel Amini also loved the surroundings here which often put him in mind of Tel Aviv and the Mediterranean. But, just as his daughters were occupied with their studies, Abdel Amini was intensely occupied with his work.

Abdel's study in the mansion had been decorated with Oriental art: meaning there were many geometric patterns in the rugs and on the wall-hangings, but no portraits or pictures. He would have gladly surrounded himself with such works of art, especially European art from earlier centuries. Even though they weren't in his house, he wondered at the genius workmanship that he'd observed in the sculptures and pictures of Leonardo da Vinci. That's why he'd taken his friend to Rome before the war. Enthusiastically, Abdel hoped that one day he'd be able to return to Europe and show Nabib the Hermitage, The Louvre and, for something completely different, the Nile Delta. In his house, though, Abdel Amini didn't feel at ease to have such portraits and statues about, as he tried to carefully avoid anything he that that the Koran probably prohibited.

Due to the backdrop of the typical house of the Southern States of America, Government representatives and business contacts all felt entirely at home in this traditional American home. For the Sabagh family it was the other way round. It was the mosaics and tapestries and colors, along with the smells from the kitchens that put them at their ease.

Initially Abdel Amini didn't know what to do about the offer of Jonathan's house. 'Buy it, otherwise it could fall into someone else's hands,' advised Tannous. She was right. It was her counsel that gave him the push to do it. If Jonathan were ever to come back to America, he could consult with him about the mansion. No one else would get their hands on it until that occasion.

Not that it had been in any way a hardship to take it on. The family enjoyed seeing how their children had developed over the spring and summer. The space and quiet did his daughters some good, as well as his son. Spring and summer had been spent playing carefree. The first autumn had now enveloped the mighty abode and, once inside, the family felt that the house was as cozy as a warm jacket.

The same chilly autumn brought no thoughts of comfort for the family in Amsterdam. The nights drew in earlier and that made the environment in the basement stuffy. Until now, they hadn't really felt threatened; but now there was an atmosphere of fear in the home. The occupation had lasted too long. On the street-side of the basement, where the two sleeping rooms were, you could often hear marching outside. Then there would be a call, some shouting and then sometimes running and shots firing. It was scary to hear it without being able to see exactly what was going on.

Margaret and David kept themselves occupied with the escape plan. Although they sincerely hoped the escape would be possible, it didn't help their disposition to become any more cheerful. 'Maybe we're going to end up locked in here for our entire lives,' feared David.

'You mustn't talk that way,' answered Mother when she heard him. 'Why don't you go outside and try and work out some aggression. It's dark out there but be careful.'

Hidden by the high fence, shrubs and steps which led to the floor upstairs, David would sometimes go and have a work-out if he got angry. Margaret had given him a skipping rope which continually got caught in the branches. He used two heavy black bricks as weights.

That evening it was dark quite early. David had to stop his exercise as the air was heavy, as if there was about to be a storm. Sweaty, he hung around the table waiting for the fresh rain to start pouring outside the book cave. His wet hair dripped on the table as he made a paper airplane from a page of newspaper. Esther was already asleep in one of the bedrooms. Mother had found a crossword puzzle in one of the papers that Sjoerd Colijn had used to plug a hole in the wall. One of the candles went out. In the flickering light Father had fallen asleep, stretched out in his usual chair. David heard him snore softly and looked at him; his mouth wide open and his head resting on his chest. Absent-mindedly, David threw his plane and it landed in one of Mother's flower arrangements. He thought about how long life would remain this way if he didn't make an effort to do something. A small smile crept across his face at the thought that they might be out of here within two months. He and Margaret thought that they stood a good chance if they could reach the farm in North Holland.

That was the difficult part though. They would have to make it to Purmerend in one night; it was perhaps about twenty-five kilometers away. First they'd have to get out of Amsterdam. That they'd do during an air-raid alarm, no one would be on the streets then. The distance was the next issue. If they could travel about five kilometers per hour, they'd make the farm in about five hours, although that wasn't really realistic. David reckoned it would be more likely to take about seven or eight hours, even with little Esther in mind that was feasible. 'To be honest, even for Father and Mother it's a considerable distance,' David had said to Brenda and Margaret.

'And give consideration to the fact that Margaret will be about seven months pregnant by then,' Brenda had reminded him. Margaret wanted to escape with them. She had no other choice. She had become a part of them. In her mind she had already said goodbye to her house and belongings. It was really a work place, not a home. Everything there seemed to be breaking at the lightest touch. The house had given up, and so had Margaret. That evening as usual, despite the rain, she dressed in an oversized man's overcoat and surreptitiously sneaked food to the family again. To the neighbors it must have seemed as if she was visiting the Colijn family, or possibly that she was having an affair with Sjoerd, although, they wouldn't think that this time. Sjoerd and his family weren't home. Thanks to the key that Huigje had given her, Margaret could still get in unhindered. She went through the narrow hall to the kitchen. There she went down a little staircase with hand-rails on each side down to the swampy garden. Then, in the pouring rain, she opened the shutter and clambered in. Because of the rain it seemed even darker in there. Having to keep the window closed only added to the disconsolate and distressing environment. Outside the wind howled and the rain persevered. Mother shivered. It was the sort of evening families everywhere would be cozying up to each other.

Jonathan hadn't seen Sjoerd Colijn for three days as he was out of town. In the dark bedroom, Margaret and David once more talked through every detail of each step of the plan that David and Brenda had put together. 'The time is getting closer. We must be a vigilant. Father will stay ignorant of it otherwise he might talk to Colijn. He still talks to him regularly, but only about money and other things he considers as important,' whispered David after they'd run through the plan.

After a while they went back to the living room so that they wouldn't disturb Esther's sleep. In the living room, the conversation with Mother turned to food. His father sunk back in his chair again, half lying, half sitting. In Amsterdam, food was more often exchanged for other goods than bought. Every day a man brought eggs to Margaret's door, along with a little something else from his secret allotment in South Amsterdam. This time it was green beans. 'What people can't get hold of they steal. At the beginning of winter, people started to gather wood for their stoves from the park,' Margaret said while sitting at the table in almost complete darkness. She then told about a family who had almost choked to death trying to use coal in their stove.

At that moment they heard a noise crackle outside. It wasn't often that there was anything to hear.

It couldn't be Sjoerd or Huigje. They were gone for a week. 'They're not due back for another four days,' whispered Margaret knowingly. The conversation stopped and everyone in the book cave pricked up their ears.

Mother stood up quietly and went to the shutter to see if she could see where the sound came from. There was still a noise out there—as if someone was shuffling across the little garden. In the fading light of the single candle Mother stumbled over Father's legs. 'Shhh,' hissed Margaret automatically without realizing that this wouldn't make any difference. If they'd been discovered they may as well talk out loud.

Margaret also went to look out of the shutter. Mother wanted carefully to try and open it. 'I'll help you,' whispered Margaret. Jonathan drew in his legs and came out of his stretched out pose. He yawned at watched the two women.

The shuffling outside continued. It got louder. 'It's more than one person. That can only mean one thing,' David quickly concluded. At the same moment he realized that it was significant that Colijn wasn't home...or maybe, by some miracle, could it be him outside? Maybe with Huigje's father?

The noise stopped. Mother held her breath, listened and didn't dare to open the shutter. Father clung tightly to the armrests but stayed seated, also not making a sound.

The shuffling got louder again, now mixed with whispering voices. 'Who's out there?' called Mother in a shrill voice which, under the circumstances, was completely inappropriate. At that moment the shutter came crashing through the hole to a bang on the floor. Immediately a lamp was lowered through. A head with a helmet on followed. Outside a loud command was given. The family may not have understood the words but they knew exactly what it meant for them.

In the commotion, the benches were knocked over and Mother and Margaret shied away backwards, away from the hole. Mother again tripped over Father's legs. 'May I know what you're here for?' he asked wonderfully calmly, whilst advancing towards the first soldier who was poised, gun at the ready, for attack. Another soldier clambered in. Father asked the question in Dutch, even though he was fluent in German. But, language aside, the Germans had not come to engage in conversation.

From outside came the sound of more commands being given. David didn't know how to react, so he just stood and tried to assess exactly what was going on out there. It was all going too fast to be able to do something. All things considered though, what could he do against this group of uniformed men, all about the same age?

Feebly the whole family raised their hands, without hearing a command to do so, and shuffled to the same side of the table where the soldiers directed them. They stood all together in a heap before one of the book walls. The whole thing seemed to David to be rather disorganized and far from professional. It seemed like overkill. So much clamor, so many uniformed men and guns for such a little unarmed family. Would it not be likely to get out of hand?

Some command was called from outside in the garden and the many guns gestured nervously and clumsily for the family to crawl through the shutter. Without the opportunity to go and get any personal belongings the whole family pushed themselves through the broken window. Mother twisted free and called for Esther. She wrestled against the soldiers and ignored their threats and made for the bedroom. Before she could get there, a fair head appeared from the improvised doorway. The German, probably younger than David, grinned as if he'd made an important discovery and pushed the crying Esther to raise her hands also.

Without their coats, everyone was pushed outside into the tiny garden in the pouring rain. It was extremely dark out there and even the soldiers struggled to stop tripping over. On the staircase leading to Colijn's kitchen there were even more uniformed men, each with a weapon in their hands. Every soldier that bridged the gap to Sjoerd's house was soaked to the skin. The Germans called to each other and Margaret and David could only decipher a few of their words. 'Hold on tightly to my hand, Esther,' called Mother.

'Stay quiet. Just be calm,' Jonathan kept repeating to no one in particular.

It wasn't clear from the clamor whether the Commander really had control over the men. The young, inexperienced soldiers seemed to tie each other up in knots. And while they went through the small passageway in Colijn's house to the street they swapped instructions with each other.

'We've got to…' David couldn't finish saying what he wanted.

'I'm coming too…' said Margaret sadly, trying to make contact with David. The word 'escape' was avoided anxiously.

'As soon as we have a chance,' David roared.

'Me too. I have to come with you,' called Margaret though all the other sounds.

Sjoerd and Huigje would never have guessed from the appearance of their house what had transpired here. The door which led into the hall was carefully closed. Three Germans descended the front steps first, followed by the family, then the rest of the soldiers.

Jonathan stumbled as he stepped off the last grey step. Once on the street, despite the blackness, Margaret recognized the figure of Heinrich. With difficulty she suppressed her cries. Meanwhile, using body language, he tried to let Margaret know what to do. He nodded towards the corner. She understood what he meant. 'Run as soon as I say,' Margaret could just manage to let David know.

Suddenly Jonathan lurched forward into Heinrich's arms. There was some misfiring from the group of soldiers. Perhaps this was a result of their inexperience or their nervousness. Heinrich gave contradictory commands and, without knowing exactly what was wanted from them, the soldiers seemed to run chaotically at each other.

It wasn't clear if Jonathan had recognized Heinrich, but he clung on to him as if he would be able to rescue him. A couple of the uniformed men tried to drag him off. Then Jonathan started to kick and punch and even caught Heinrich full in the face. The whole group now dove on Jonathan.

'Run,' called Margaret as she put into action her own words. It escaped the notice of the soldiers trying to free Heinrich.

'Warten Sie!' called Heinrich to the two young Germans who went to give chase to the others. The confusion was enough for David and Margaret to get a good ten to fifteen meters away. Mother had instinctively reacted to Margaret's call and ran, still holding Esther by the hand, and she was about two meters behind them. David knew that he'd made a dangerous choice. He gripped onto Esther's other hand.

'Don't shoot,' ordered Heinrich, but nevertheless there followed a sharp detonation, probably from a small handgun. The runaways kept running and didn't stop to think about what was going on. The few soldiers who had started to give chase heard Heinrich's despairing call and hesitated, looking back to where the shot had come from. Without clear orders from their officer, the young men didn't dare decide for themselves what to do.

Jonathan then managed to shrug himself free. He knocked over two men as he headed in the direction of the two soldiers who were chasing his family. They stood up and went to catch Jonathan; two men held loaded guns pointed straight at him and at point blank range.

'Stehen, bleiben,' called one of them in a loud voice.

'Don't shoot,' resounded from the mouth of the older officer. The situation wasn't clear.

One of the young men, about three meters from Jonathan, called 'Halt!' and, while he was still running, pulled the trigger on his pistol.

Jonathan stumbled. Then ran a few steps. Then stumbled again. He ran towards the group that was waiting for him at the corner. The group also saw Heinrich running closer. All the focus was on Jonathan who fell to the ground.

At that moment, the group of escapees around the corner decided to run. The distance between them and their pursuers was about thirty meters. 'That should be sufficient,' hoped Heinrich. 'Warte mich,' he called to slow things down some more as the group of soldiers had more or less reached him. Heinrich bent down to where Jonathan lay on the street. The rain and darkness masked the tears that streamed down the old man's face. The young German who'd been knocked down by Jonathan rubbed at his uniform as if that was the most important thing here. 'Small children. That's all they are,' thought Heinrich angrily, yet saddened at the same time. The strong men had been sent to fight at the front. The old-timers and children had to do their military service in places like Amsterdam. Not all but many were from the province and were certainly not more than twenty years old. It was the most fanatical and stupid soldier who had fired the shot.

Heinrich wiped his face with his sleeve and indicated to the two soldiers to 'Sie bleiben hier. Und jetzt hohlen wir die andere Leute,' Heinrich ordered the rest.

As soon as she was around the corner, Margaret hid in the first doorway. She pulled on the cord that was dangling through the letterbox. It realized the latch on the inside of the door. She signaled for the others to come in. With a loud bang she closed the door behind them. The four fell exhausted onto the ground in the hall. Mother pressed her hand against Esther's mouth.

When Heinrich, breathing with difficulty, reached his men at the corner he knew that the set-up had worked. From the moment he knew that Margaret was linked with this group he knew that this was the only possibility. Margaret had always understood him. The younger soldiers thought the family couldn't be more than a hundred meters away. They had a child. And one woman was pregnant. They'd soon catch them up. Panting, Heinrich followed slowly behind the boys. He had to encourage them to keep going as much as possible. The further they got from Margaret's house, the better.

The escape of the Jewish family wasn't blamed on Heinrich too heavily. The young soldiers testified to how difficult the situation was in the dark night. To save their own skin and embarrassment they emphasized how the family had violently resisted arrest—and the death of the oldest escapee made this plausible. In the eyes of his superiors, Heinrich was simply too old for this kind of work. He was demoted and that suited Heinrich just fine. Had he not come back with at least one dead body, they perhaps would have been more suspicious about him. Jonathan had in effect saved him, as well as his own family, by sacrificing himself. It certainly wasn't an accident that Jonathan had fallen into his arms. That was as clear as daylight to Heinrich.

America 1943

In America, the effects of the war were now being increasingly felt. Ted had a stream of customers whose children served in the army. There were already some sons who had been killed in action in Europe. And still many more worried parents and young spouses hadn't heard from their loved ones in a long time. Ted Bates didn't feel alone anymore. The conversations in his shop lasted longer when he spoke about the Kerzner family.

'I carry a photo of my grandson close to my chest,' said an elderly grandmother who'd stepped in to buy a bulb. She cried softly.

'I have a young friend who is somewhere in The Netherlands,' said Ted. With a large handkerchief he swept away the tears on her face. Then he showed the only photo of David that he had. 'That's him, by the swimming pool. I was his coach when he lived here.'

With trembling hands she took the photo and looked at the lad on the starting block. 'A handsome boy,' she replied with a smile to the proud face of Ted Bates. She gave him back the photo. 'May God protect them, Mr. Bates. May God protect them.'

Ted didn't know what to say to that. 'Did you know that many Dutchmen are responsible for making America great? And that New York was initially called New Amsterdam?' He made these observations to try and get her talking on another subject.

Since that day she never walked past the shop without stepping in for a little chat. Ted then told her all the little bits of information about the small nation of Holland that he'd gleaned from David's letters. He kept them all in a small desk that was in the room behind the shop. Even though the conversations weren't always long, they always brought him pleasure.

He decided to take up his old hobby again. Sport wasn't the be-all and end-all; he became enthusiastic again about televisions. He read a great deal many more books about technology. 'It's for after the war,' he told the old lady and any other visitors who showed an interest. What exactly he was going to do with all that knowledge and apparatus Ted didn't know himself. For now it was a simple question of enjoyment. That was enough.

His window display was now full of devices that nobody had ever seen working. Ted had managed to get his hands on the 1939 Andrea 1FS, as well as the large cupboard with the General Electric model from the same year. The oldest model was the Baird T5 from 1936. Not that there were any transmissions at the moment. The apparatus symbolized Ted's hope that one day you'd be able to look through the misty lens into another part of the world. Perhaps Europe, where David was hiding himself somewhere…or perhaps had been caught.

Purmerend 1943

David wasn't sure how long they'd been sitting in the hallway, flat against the front door, listening for the quietest of sounds from the street. They heard the drumming sound of the soldiers' boots growing fainter. From then it had remained quiet. 'Let's go into the living room,' whispered Margaret.

She ran into the street to check that the blinds were covering the windows properly. Then she switched on the oil lamp and lit the stove. Large rolls of black paper hung behind the curtains to ensure that only the bare minimum amount of light shone through.

For David and the rest of the family it was a real experience to be in another room after years of being confined to the book cave. This house of Margaret's probably wasn't much bigger than the basement. It had the same layout as that of Sjoerd's. You came in by means of a small staircase. The, in the hallway, there was a coat rack fixed to the wall. Via a glazed inner door you went to a corridor without windows. The corridor ran to the back of the house where there was a kitchenette with a granite work surface. Through the kitchen door, down the staircase with metal balustrades, you came to a tiny garden where Margaret had put plants in tubs. To the left of the narrow corridor there were two wooden doors. The one nearest the front door led to the living room. The second door led to the bedroom, at the back of the house, nearest the garden.

The sad, wet family now stood in Margaret's living room and she started to take care of them. She draped Esther's clothes over a rack in front of her black stove. The little girl, wrapped in Margaret's dressing gown, curled up on an armchair. Esther was quiet but was shivering because of the cold. Margaret found dry clothes for herself and Mother. David shook his head. 'It doesn't matter about me. I'll soon dry out.'

'We have to leave here as soon as possible,' Margaret said suddenly, after they'd been just sitting in silence for about an hour. It really wasn't the time to stand still just because of what had happened to Jonathan; not that they knew exactly how he had fared.

'Best case scenario, the Germans have taken him with them and are perhaps nursing his wounds,' David suggested hopefully, although inside he knew better.

'I'm afraid we can't count on that.' Even in these circumstances Mother continued to remain rational. She looked at Esther who had fallen asleep in the chair, probably as a result of shock. Whispering she carried on; 'He could well be…dead. And, God protect him, if he's still alive then I doubt very much that the Germans will nurse him. Of course I don't know for sure what they're like but, if you believe the ghastly rumors, it can't be good.'

'We have to go on,' repeated Margaret. David was in agreement with her. Things had taken place differently to how they'd imagined but they had to be glad that they'd escaped and got this far. They still had a chance.

'There's one thing everyone will know now,' Margaret knew for sure, while her heart seemed to beat in her throat, 'I am now one of you. They'll be looking for me also. Fortunately they don't know that I'm Heinrich's girlfriend. And thankfully, Sjoerd didn't know that either.'

'We have to persevere with our escape tonight.' David gave no consideration to anything else. 'We have to try and get to Brenda's farm. Only this way can we get in contact with Brenda.'

'Can't we go tomorrow evening?' asked Mother with a glance at tired Esther.

'The Germans hadn't figured out tonight that Margaret is involved. But tomorrow they might. They might ask questions in the neighborhood. Or Sjoerd Colijn might come back early and direct them to this house,' replied David.

'You're right,' Margaret answered, unsettled. Gradually she recovered her calmness while she carefully looked through a slit in the curtains to outside. 'It's really pitch black out there. We couldn't have asked for a better night.'

'Then let's go in an hour. We have to whether we like it or not. The Germans will no doubt keep looking for us. Leaving it till later than that would be more dangerous.'

They spent the next hour going through the route that David had described. Everyone, including Esther who they'd woken up, had to learn it by heart. 'We'll stay together,' David said in English as Margaret also understood this. 'If we lose sight of each other then everyone has to make their own way to Brenda's farm. We'll meet together there and see if we can implement our original plan.'

Margaret improvised some dry clothes for Esther by cutting up her dressing gown into pieces using shears. Over the top of that, Mother put on her a jumper, much too large for her, that came down to her feet. She tied it with a scarf around her middle so that she would at least be able to run. A raincoat and hood was also cut to size to further protect the small child from the cold.

After an hour they carefully released the latch on the door and very carefully looked outside.

In the pitch black, the four moved hand in hand through the streets of Amsterdam; in and out of doorways and around corners, trying to make only a minimal amount of noise. The streetlamps had all been extinguished. It continued to rain. A single shaft of light that shone through an opening in a window glowed on the pavement.

David knew the route, through East Amsterdam along to the water at the lake IJ, from when he used to go bike-riding through the area. Margaret also knew the area well. Mother and Esther followed cautiously. It was going well. Amsterdam was dead quiet. The streets were deserted.

At the edge of the city, where the buildings stopped, the paths became overgrown country routes. These would lead them eventually to the lake. Again it rained harder and they felt the mud cling to their feet.

'Just a little bit longer and we'll be by the water.' David had cut a large chunk out of the blanket at Margaret's so that he'd be able to tie her to his back. That way, relying on David's swimming ability, they could reach the other side. David's love of swimming had come from his mother, who had passed on the same enthusiasm to Esther also. Margaret was the only one of the group who couldn't swim very well. This route through the water of Lake IJ had been chosen, though, as the safest route to the farm. 'They can't patrol this large expanse of water,' David had predicted.

If they stood still they could hear the water lapping on to the banks. The route through the city was the dangerous part. Nevertheless...

Suddenly David leaped quickly into the overgrown path along the side of the dyke. Margaret and the others followed him and pushed up closely to him. On the dyke behind them, a pocket torch flashed in the distance. The beam wasn't strong enough to reach the escapees. Already more lights were quickly becoming visible. It was dark on top of the dykes, but even more so at the foot, especially tight to the sides. 'Quiet,' hissed David, unnecessarily. None of the four moved, instinctively clinging to the side of the dyke for protection.

They waited to move until David gave them the order and then they slowly made their way along the path next to the dyke. The torches were coming worryingly close. The men who carried them were audible but they couldn't understand what they were saying. Certainly they were coming in their direction. After several short commands they heard barking. 'Dogs,' David heard Margaret's scared voice whisper.

It seemed as if the men were following the path that David and the others were taking. 'This path's a dead end,' David realized, now very afraid. He felt himself tense up and without thinking he froze with fear. If they stayed where they were the men with dogs would certainly catch them up. David had to think quickly. He summoned up as much courage as he could and jumped into the squelchy marsh. 'Run" he instructed the others, 'to the water.' Their wet feet stuck to the sucking floor. Reeds lashed against their faces. They didn't speak but they were no doubt audible to the men who were now accelerating towards them. They went in a straight line, directly to the water's edge.

Behind the reeds there was another expanse of twenty-five meters of grasslands. If they kept a distance of twenty-five meters between them and their pursuers they stood a chance, David knew. The men in the reeds wouldn't know where they were. When the men reached the grass, if the four weren't in the water, their silhouettes would give away their position. Although, even in the water they weren't yet safe.

'Are you still there, mother?' David roared behind him, no longer concerned about remaining inaudible. 'And Esther?' There was no answer. Margaret didn't say a word either; she was concentrating on keeping a tight hold on David's hand as she would stumble often.

After a number of meters they reached the grass. They had one chance. Hopefully they had been faster than the men. 'Where's Mother?' David hesitated before he left the cover of the reeds. As he moved crablike over the grass, he looked behind him and along the sides, but there wasn't anything to see. Margaret also reduced her speed. The mud was sucking at their feet, even pulling off one of David's shoes; not that he noticed. Margaret had already lost both of her shoes (they were only slip-ons) in the soaking wet marshlands. Her feet were bare but, with the cold and the adrenaline, she didn't notice either. Still no sign of life behind them.

David and Margaret reached the water's edge. The slope down to the water consisted of harsh basalt. David stood on the hard surface and stretched up as high as he could to try and see over the reeds. Someone was making their way through the reeds. Visibility was very poor. Something glinted in the moonlight. It was the shiny medallion that Harm had made for Esther. David felt relieved and became conscious of how rapidly he was breathing. He let go of Margaret's hand and indicated that he wanted to go back to the reeds. Margaret grabbed hold of him around his waist. 'Now you know that will help no one,' he heard her say.

More or less at the same moment, David untied the belt of the dressing gown that he'd tied around his middle. He had to choose. He took three or four steps backward. Margaret refused to let go of him. 'David, come.' Then he saw a light shining through the reeds. Mother and Esther were going to make it…Oh yes, they had to make it to the water.

Then suddenly shots were fired. Margaret pulled David back with all her might. They stumbled and rolled over and over down the sharp stones into the water. David's immediate thought was of Margaret's child. Instinctively David started to swim. Margaret clung on to him. Which direction should they go?

'Halt!' They heard the call amidst the sounds of dogs barking. 'Stehen, bleiben.' There were more shots fired. The slope was too high to see what was going on beyond it. David didn't want to swim any further. Margaret hung tightly onto his arm, trying desperately not to drown. He wanted to tread water until Mother and Esther came. Again, the shots fired.

Perhaps it was only a few seconds, David had no concept of time anymore, but those moments of uncertainty seemed to last for hours. Esther then appeared at the water's edge, calm and unhurried. Harm's necklace shone brightly in the moonlight. David wanted to call out her name, but something held him back. He gestured to the bank. Margaret floated next to him, resting on his hand, somewhere between dead and alive.

Two men appeared next to his little sister. David clearly saw one of them, in an almost reassuring manner; place a hand on Esther's shoulder. Then David ducked under the surface of the water so as not to be seen. He pulled Margaret under also. For short bursts of air he pushed her face about the water level. Wrestling with the water and Margaret's weight, David tried to swim as long as he could under the water along the bank; gulping at smatterings of air and exhaling under the water. Carefully he tried to keep Margaret's face just slightly above the water, so she wouldn't be noticed by the Germans. He twisted around to swim on his back, trying to keep his nose and mouth out of the water, but gulping down gallons of water. His legs and his one free arm burned with the exertion of trying to swim. He was impeded further by Margaret's clothes which billowed out and made for slow progress.

There was certainly no time to be frightened, and they couldn't talk about anything in the water anyway. David knew that this was what they'd planned for in the escape and he had to stick to that plan come what may. But the swimming was so much harder than he'd expected. In fact, he began to doubt whether he'd make it to the other side at all.

David now stuck his head entirely out of the water. Margaret's too. Air… they needed air. They'd simply die if they tried to stay under the water for a moment longer. David thought he heard more shots. It could well of been, although he couldn't hear anything clearly really. Not with the water lapping all around and a protesting Margaret clinging onto his arm. 'Perhaps if the Germans can't see us they'll hear us,' went through David's mind. As a gut reaction he dove under the water again, pulling Margaret with him. He couldn't stay under long. Excessive anxiety and speed means too little oxygen. David's powerful legs kicked hard to keep his body, and Margaret's, above the surface.

He reassured himself that he was still alive. Although he figured if he had been shot he wouldn't feel it anyway in the icy water. Why was he so tired? The distance he'd swim today was nothing in comparison to the distances from his training days.

A noise! Down again, quick. This spell under the water was much too short. It wasn't possible to breathe quietly anymore. In fact, he couldn't make his body work properly anymore. David struggled without real control. He stroked at the water with his free arm. Air, he had to have air, at whatever the risk.

David just didn't have it in him to dive anymore. If there were still armed guards out there then all was lost. But, for now, they were still alive. All was quiet. Where was the wall? Impetuously, David looked all around him, impeded by the swell of the water, waves, and a forceful wind. There was a dark line. Was that the wall? The opposite side, perhaps? No, impossible. They'd not been in there long enough for that. This must still be the side where Esther and Mother were lost.

David hitched Margaret up again. As long as her head stayed above water she had a chance. Her body felt slack, it didn't move. She didn't kick her legs at all anymore.

David peered all along the side. He dared to come further out of the water. Clearly he could see now all the little gulf along the water's edge. Esther and the men were definitely gone. David held the head of the lifeless Margaret even further out of the water. 'Margaret,' whispered David. 'Margaret!' She couldn't hear him.

Where had Esther gone? 'She can't have been shot. My sister must still be alive, she must,' David told himself. What about Mother?

After a breather, David again started swimming. This time, on his back, he swam directly across lake IJ. He'd abandoned the idea of using the belt to try and help Margaret across, and so kept tight hold of her instead. Strangely, David wasn't tired anymore. The uncertainty about Esther, Mother and Father kept his mind active. Even more disconcerting was the thought that he'd now been swimming for half an hour to try and preserve the life of this woman who had sacrificed herself to try and save his family; a woman who was carrying a child and who wasn't moving at all any longer.

A bizarre thought took hold of him while he swam. 'If something happens to the mother, how can I save the child? What if Margaret's dead?' Dead. That macabre word sang out with every stroke. 'Dead, dead, dead.' What would he do when he reached the other side? If he reached the other side. Where was the other side?

But David's sense of direction was excellent so he ended up in exactly the spot that he'd intended when the escape plan had been concocted. There was a boat launch which gradually sloped into the water. David no longer had any concerns about being discovered, but chose this spot to get Margaret cautiously out of the water. From here, they had to transverse more grass and marshlands to get to Brenda's farm. As he looked at her lifeless body he felt that this was going to be impossible.

'But at the farm, with some warmth, perhaps she might come back to life,' David wished enthusiastically. He had no choice but to try and carry her. And if it became light on the way, they'd just have to find somewhere to hide out. They'd just have to carry on further the following night. He hoped that, at least, it wouldn't still be raining.

One thing was for sure; there was no way back now. For now and for eternity, Amsterdam was gone. Somewhere in that city was Father. David pushed hard to get his and Margaret's body to the jetty. Nearby there was a wall with a large iron plate over it which they crawled under and sheltered from the rain. An unexpected patrol would also be less likely to spot them there.

David continued to lie there, trying to regulate his breathing so it was quieter. His body supported Margaret's and he tried not to put any weight on her abdomen. 'A doctor,' thought David. 'I have to find a doctor.' At that moment Margaret groaned and spewed water into David's face. Immediately David was relieved to realize that he'd managed to keep Margaret and her unborn child alive. With hope in his heart he dared to believe that the three of them could continue further. They had to.

Lying next to her, David gently stroked her hair. They must have lain like that for some time, wet, but protected from the rain. With all they'd been through, as well as the cold, Margaret could only say a little. The first thing she did say was, 'Exhausted. But we must carry on.' She was right.

Things had certainly not turned out the way they had expected when they'd made their plans. At least it wasn't raining anymore. Not that it made much difference, they were still wet through. Without any of the provisions they'd planned to bring, without passports, drenched and barefoot. It would definitely be better if they didn't encounter anyone, not even Dutch people. All would be well if they could just reach the farm by daybreak. With all the doubts that persisted, this was their only goal.

Margaret gradually seemed to improve on the way. Perhaps the walking warmed her up. That, in turn, gave David more hope. He supported her on his arm and focused on getting to the farm. If they could just make it there, they would have survived the first part of the plan.

A light shone in the distance. It was moving. And it appeared to be coming in their direction.

During the week that Sjoerd Colijn and Huigje weren't at home and the family had escaped, Brenda had been sent to The Hague. From there she was to organize the export of paintings, sculptures and other treasures. In fact, she was to travel with Sjoerd Colijn, in one compartment.

Days after the escape, Brenda was contacted by Sjoerd Colijn. It was Huigje, not Sjoerd, who told her of what had happened. Sjoerd Colijn listened without saying a word. Huigje didn't know many of the details. The family had escaped. The basement was empty. The shutter which you had to crawl through to get in lay in pieces on the ground. No one in the neighborhood had any information. No one even knew that there was a family hiding there, so they weren't missed. 'If they have escaped then, it must have happened at night. Otherwise someone would have seen something,' Huigje speculated. 'The neighbors did say that they heard Germans in the street after the curfew. But that happens often.' Huigje put forth great effort to control the tears.

'I'm sure that's it. By day the neighbors would have seen,' endorsed Brenda, nodding. 'It can't be any other way.'

Sjoerd Colijn muttered something about how lucky it was that they weren't at home if they'd been picked up by the Germans. 'They must have come through our house. All our interior doors were open. And the staircase to the garden is damaged. How in heaven's name would we have explained that we didn't know these people?'

Sjoerd Colijn's observations made Brenda think. She found it strange that Sjoerd Colijn and Huigje hadn't been questioned by the Germans or the NSB. But Brenda didn't pursue the matter; she thought it judicious not to ask.

For a week, so many questions burned anxiously inside Brenda. She had to wait until it wouldn't arouse suspicion before she could get to her home for the weekend. There, at the farm, David and Margaret would be waiting for her with the answers.

David and Margaret would have to wait for two months at the farm to come back in line with the original escape plan. Brenda was going to hide the pair in one of the large cases which housed the paintings that were being transported to Switzerland. 'Some of the paintings in the crates have come from some of the largest European museums, others from private collections. Some of these paintings are more than four meters high. Under no circumstances is the wood of the crates allowed to touch the painting. For this reason the crates are much larger than the paintings themselves. Two people could easily fit in there,' Brenda said, trying to put Margaret and David at ease.

Netherlands—Germany—Switzerland 1943

The time came eventually for the two to be hidden in the pitch black beside the awesome canvases of the Dutch masters. 'Nobody knows for whom these are intended,' Brenda had said. 'Some Germans suspect that Goebels himself is bringing them to a foreign country for his private collection. It's not going well for the Germans on the Eastern Russian front, especially after Himmler's losses in Africa. Rumors had it that the Allies had pushed far into Italy. No German wanted to talk openly about the situation, and certainly not about the objects d'art that the Germans were trying to smuggle out of the country, the intention being to live there once the war was over. The German officers weren't to do anything like that; they were supposed to sooner commit suicide. However, no one believes that, even though the Fuhrer seemed to be crazy enough to order such a thing.

Brenda was the one who had come up with the idea of using the painting transportation to enable the Jewish family to escape. Where better could they go than Switzerland? For the implementation of the plan they were entirely dependent on her. They'd discussed all the details in the book cave but, at the end of the day, all the real work rested on Brenda's shoulders. Sjoerd Colijn, secretly and at great cost, had bought some of the paintings. As his secretary, Brenda had to have access everywhere, and so had to have the trust of both the Dutch and the Germans.

Brenda had other reasons why she was glad that the other two would be on the train with her. Hopefully then she wouldn't be alone as she implemented the other parts of her plan. If it became necessary, she could even hide with them in the crates.

With skill and hard work, Brenda had fixed two wooden planks inside the crate which the two would be able to sit on. Ricardo would have been proud of her work had he lived to see it. She also ensured that there was enough food and drink for two nights. Ingeniously, the crate had a hidden door which could be opened from the inside but was invisible from the outside. 'This is also to my advantage if I must hide too. No one's going to look for me in a case which looks like it can only be opened by prying open the sides.' All the crates lay together, and some were filled with marble sculptures which weighed heavily. 'So the weight of two people won't be noticed,' she concluded.

So far everything had gone smoothly. Sjoerd Colijn had coordinated everything with his contact and, as a result, Brenda had the use of a large German car to get to the station. Brenda had used this to smuggle David and Margaret easily, avoiding the customs officers, into the bleak hall where the crates were stored, ready to be transported.

The shelves inside the crate, Brenda's father's idea, worked perfectly. Although Brenda's father agreed with the escape plan in theory, he wasn't happy with Brenda's plans. 'Revenge is never a good motive,' he had said. Things were always black and white to this farmer with his simple ideals. It is written 'you shall not repay evil for evil,' but did that still apply in these treacherous times? Wouldn't more lives be lost if this evil man were allowed to carry on? Would they be forgiven for what they were about to do if it were for this motive? Brenda had always denied that revenge was her primary motive, but there were motives when even she doubted that herself. Having said which, foremost in her mind was stopping Colijn from carrying on doing the things he did. She didn't know fully all that he was up to, but she'd clearly seen how he treated his wife and son, as well as the Kerzners. She saw how he had deceived everybody and had likely betrayed the family.

They didn't have proof of that but Heinrich strongly suspected it. At the farm she'd gone over and over it. 'But it was he who'd taken the family into hiding in the first place,' Father Baltus had said, not under-standing.

'He doesn't have anything more to gain from their staying with him now. He's completely milked Jonathan dry,' Margaret said icily. She hadn't a shadow of a doubt that Colijn was responsible for the betrayal of the Kerzner's.

'Strap yourselves in tightly,' instructed Brenda before closing the im-provised door. 'Then you'll not roll around here and there when they load the case.' The gap between the boards was minimal. In one parti-cular place, a knot had been knocked out of the wood. It was too little to let much light in but it was good enough to serve as a spy-hole. It also let in valuable fresh air to breathe.

David had managed to have a good look at the warehouse. It was crawling with Dutch workers and German military in working clothes. He also saw the train which consisted of dark green passenger cars with rectangular windows. After these came the neglected brown goods wagons. Colijn had reserved one of the luxury carriages for the journey for him and Brenda to share.

David estimated that they'd now been underway for about two hours. He suddenly began to panic. 'This was a crazy idea. Everyone's trying to get out of Germany and get to safety in Switzerland.'

At first the two didn't dare to even whisper to each other, even though they knew they were the only ones in the goods wagons and that their voices were likely to be drowned out by the clamor of the worn out steel wheels on the iron tracks. Every time they went over a crossing or junction, there was an almighty din and the carriage shook so much they felt sure that it would collapse.

'Try to sleep,' David said softly, finally daring to loosen his straps in the dark. 'You could sit on the floor with your back against the sides.'

'It's okay. I'll just sit for a while.' David found it difficult to understand Margaret. It was difficult for them to move in such a tight space. During the time on the farm, her pregnancy had become rather visible; her belly seemed to grow daily. David didn't know what the wise thing was to do: to talk about the risks and the future of the child or to just stay silent. On the farm in the grassy polders of North Holland, Margaret had felt the movements of the child grow stronger and stronger. Even David had felt a tiny foot kick against Margaret's abdomen. Obviously, he'd not felt it as strongly as Margaret had, but it moved him nevertheless.

On the other hand, there was still the gnawing uncertainty concerning Mother and Esther. Father was dead, Brenda had found that out. But here was a new little life, safely waiting in the womb until the time was ready for him or her to see the light of day. He or she was blissfully unaware of the evil in the world. The world keeps turning. 'I can't believe we're on the way. Perhaps I'll give birth on a mountain in Switzerland,' David heard Margaret say to herself, as if she'd read his thoughts.

'Love is between people. It doesn't distinguish between countries,' David heard Margaret whisper. He had learnt much from her at the farm and he gladly listened to her. It added to what he'd already been convinced of through the reading he'd done in the book cave; reading books such as The Torah, the rest of The Bible and The Koran. Love is universal.

'What will love mean, though, if I've lost Father, Mother and Esther?'

'We don't yet know how our adventure will turn out. Don't make the same mistake as many Germans, though,' warned Margaret. 'It's fair enough to hate criminals, but don't tar all Germans with the same brush. No doubt that's what the rest of the world will do.'

David knew that she was right. He though felt that Jews, Muslims, Christians, all had the same father. 'I don't understand it. We have one history, the same forefathers and the same God. What divides us? We've all got dark pages in our past. How many innocent women and children have been killed through the course of the centuries? All in the name of God: Jews against Gentiles, Catholics burning Protestants alive, eye for an eye and tooth for a tooth. God cannot be pleased with all this bloodshed, spilled supposedly in his name. Really it's people who are responsible for it. Without their so-called Fuhrer, no doubt the Germans would probably be a loving people.'

Margaret looked at him concerned. 'What's worse is that, at the moment, the German people believe that they are showing love by behaving in this way.'

David had a somber face. 'They think this is doing God's will? That just doesn't make sense to me?'

'Maybe there is no God,' suggested Margaret.

'If that were true, then surely there would be no love of neighbor either, you would say.'

Across from David, on the other side of the case, Margaret was being rocked rhythmically from side to side. As they put some distance between them and the house, David began to feel freer. The train, which stunk of the animals that it transported, was now in Germany and would travel for two days along the Rhine to the South. Would the two dare to stay in the box for two days?

Margaret tried to repress the thoughts of what Heinrich had told her. He had seen with his own eyes the removal of the Jews from Amsterdam in cattle carriages. He was ashamed of these contemptible actions; to see people treated like cattle. Where they were taken, he didn't know for sure. A colleague had said that they were all taken to be destroyed but that seemed inconceivable. Margaret smelled the reek that reminded her of the cows on the farm. She decided not to tell David what she thought. Not only it was it not necessary, but she was also starting to get a light, cheery feeling. It came as her faith increased in the hope that this plan might actually work. Perhaps soon she would be able to enjoy a walk in the Swiss countryside.

'David, can you hear me?'

'Yes…Margaret,' he stayed quiet.

'I believe we might just be saved,' said Margaret with a trembling voice. In spite of the loss of Jonathan and the sorrow of the previous months, there was also a possibility of joy. It was the same feeling of gladness, mixed with tension that David also felt. Eventually he got the feeling that he wasn't just on the run, but that he had the situation under control. Nobody had discovered them. They were practically free. It wasn't likely that a worker would come along now at this late stage and open up all the cases. Minute by minute, as they got closer to their destination, the fear which they'd felt too keenly for the last few months seemed to disappear. The euphoria of freedom suppressed the uncertainty of the future. David heard himself let out a deep sigh.

'We're going to make it, Margaret. Us and the baby.'

Happiness suppressed all negative emotions. It stayed virtually pitch black, but in David's head the light shone brighter with every second that the wheels ran over the tracks. He seemed to feel and hear every bump on the tracks. Fantastic. Freedom. As he'd never known before. Also, although he could hardly move in the wooden box, David felt as though his body had never been stronger. Happiness and strength; they always went hand in hand. 'If I swam now I'd win every medal that there was.' He could no longer smell the stench of the cattle that had long since penetrated into the crate made from freshly hewn wood.

Feeling lightheaded, David cautiously dropped to the ground and crawled along the rough floor to Margaret. He leaned softly against her. He put his face against the smooth, tightly stretched material over her stomach. So he stayed, lying against her, without either of the two of them saying a word.

He looked at her, even though he couldn't see a thing in the dark. 'When I'm in America, I have to become a doctor. I have to understand this,' he thought. With a broad smile on his face that he couldn't control, he felt himself become cheerful. A shaft of light shone through onto his face. It wasn't so remarkable that he should feel this way after all the anxious moments they'd been through recently; that he should feel more free locked up in a case than on the farm, with its green meadows and blue air, a case on a German train, at that. So trapped and yet so happy.

What was that strange shaking? Was he mistaken? No, this was something different. Now he heard a strange noise also; Margaret was shaking with laughter. That they weren't there yet they both keenly realized. It made this moment all the more remarkable. It was a real release of pressure. Tears of laughter streamed down their cheeks. In such a bizarre location, they seemed far away from all the misery. And nevertheless they had to keep their wits about them. 'We're not there yet.' But the exhilaration was too great. 'I'll never forget this moment my whole life,' hiccupped Margaret.

David saw a collection of images in his mind; Mother in the huge gardens, the green grass rolling down to the ocean, his old coach standing at the edge of the pool. How old would he have been then? Eight? He remembered the moment he had touched the side in the fifty-meter freestyle and realized that he was first. Father with his large pipe in the large lobby of the hotel. In his chair in the book cave. The musty smell of wet paper. The shot. And Huigje…he'd hardly thought of her since the flight from the basement. Why had all those memories of her on the edge of his bed stayed in the deep recesses of his mind? On the other hand, why was he always thinking about the curvaceous figure of Brenda?

For an hour, or maybe even longer, they lay there saying nothing, each with their own thoughts, David's head on the belly with child. They still had far to go.

Brenda had to spend time cooped up with Sjoerd Colijn in their compartment. 'Our room,' he called it. It was truly luxurious and quite roomy for a train, with enough space for a bed, a small table with two antique chairs and even a wooden writing bureau. On the left hand side were the huge square windows through which you could spend most of the day looking at the Rhine. On the opposite side was a door leading to the narrow passageways. All the windows had drapes: dark red drapes with gold cords and tassels. The bed knobs on the iron bed were also gold-colored, as were the corners of the bureau. The compartment really made an impression on Brenda. She never saw a room such as this, let alone on a train. She didn't know such things existed.

Under the desk stood a black leather case that Brenda hadn't seen before; it had two heavy straps around it, each strap having a separate lock. She knew it couldn't have clothes in it because she had packed his clothes herself. No, this heavy case looked more like it must be transporting money. That fit in with the character of her cunning boss.

Brenda understood that German officers were also traveling in such comfort in other compartments along the same iron tracks. The light was subdued in the private compartments, even throughout the day. That made the room almost cozy, were it not for the fact that she could feel Sjoerd's eyes on her body all the time, whether she stood or sat. It made her more nervous and anxious than she had expected she would feel, but she had to play the game. She knew what was awaiting her. Sjoerd Colijn was expecting the price to be paid tonight.

Brenda couldn't say that her duties as a private secretary were difficult. Even though she'd not really had any formal training for it, she was earning five times the going rate. She did her work well. Reluctantly, she'd always done the book-keeping for the farm, always accurate to the last cent. Here the figures and the countries where the money was going to and coming from were different, but that was all; the principles were the same. Brenda saw how Colijn was paid for all kinds of services he performed for the church, although Brenda wasn't aware of what services he actually did. He got a lot of money from inheritances from people in the church who had died but were finding it difficult to locate the beneficiaries because of the war. And then there was the money which had come from David's father, as well as from other Jewish refugees who had knocked at the church doors for assistance. Sjoerd Colijn was already a very rich man by the time he had employed Brenda. To look at his simple home and the lifestyle of his family, you'd never have known it. As a matter of fact, even Huigje knew nothing about it.

Colijn had terrifically well-funded accounts in the Netherlands, Germany and America. To the outside world it was invisible, but to Brenda it was now very clear just how much money was involved. She had especially noted the large amounts that were being transferred to an account in America. 'Whose account are these amounts being paid into?' Brenda sometimes asked.

'That doesn't concern you,' Colijn snapped.

Money also came into Colin's account from somebody in America;

someone with the name Sabagh, who had taken over Jonathan's mansion when Colijn had offered it to him. Part of the capital that Colijn had put together with Sabagh's money came from David's father. Seven-figure numbers had been transferred into Colijn's accounts. Brenda also saw the private contracts that Colijn and Jonathan had signed, and she'd previously told David about them. 'I don't know how much your father still possesses in America. On paper here it seems to me as if he's bankrupt. I think he certainly has more debts than property. Everything has been transferred to Colijn.'

That was no surprise to David, he suspected as much. 'What can I do about it?' He'd answered with a note of disinterest in his voice. 'It's Father's money. I've tried to talk about it with him. It's not made a scrap of difference.'

Brenda had read a clause in the contracts that stated that everything would revert back to Jonathan after the end of the war. Now, as she busied herself with paperwork so she wouldn't have to talk to Colijn, she realized that this clause would never come into effect. She was more convinced than ever that Colijn must have had a hand in the treason. Or perhaps he'd left it for his companion, Herbert de Jonge, Huigje's father, to handle. That idiot would do anything for Colijn. That way the sly man would keep himself above suspicion and out of the firing line.

Colijn was certainly in league with the Germans, of that much she was sure. A great deal of money was coming in from German accounts and making its way to American banks. Brenda suspected that it was to purchase weapons, or possibly to pay for American spies. As soon as she could find out where the money was going she would be able to confirm her suspicions.

Colijn wasn't mysterious at all about his dealings with Abdel Amini Sabagh, Jonathan's former business partner. The Palestinian business partner had taken over vast amounts of American property, the mansion in Boston being at top of the list. 'Sabagh probably isn't aware of what this has all cost his friend, Jonathan. He hasn't seen the private contract between Sjoerd and Jonathan, unlike myself,' thought Brenda.

Brenda had certainly become a lot wiser in the time that she'd been working for Colijn. Some things, however, she had understood from the very first moment; in particular, Colijn's innuendos and his true intentions toward her. It wasn't for nothing that she was getting paid more than her role was worth. For much less, Colijn could have gotten a well-trained secretary, albeit without such round breasts and shapely legs. He had chosen her because, from the very start, Brenda had played along with his sensual game. 'Well you look the part,' were the first words that Colijn had said to her the minute she walked through the door for her interview. 'I hope that you can do more than just keep the books.'

Brenda accentuated her voluptuous figure and looked directly into his thin face. 'I don't know what you mean, but, I'm young and I can learn a lot,' she lisped with her full, red lips. The simple insinuation was enough to arouse Sjoerd, and he was sold before he even knew it. Brenda had him wrapped around her little finger, just like all the boys in her village.

For the months that followed she worked hard to keep him at bay, despite his vulgar remarks about Huigje and a man's 'needs.' His lust-filled glances confirmed that she was right to.

In the softly lit compartment, she leaned over the wooden bureau, faking interest in the customs documents. Meanwhile, Colijn couldn't take his eyes away from the contours of her buttocks. 'Men aren't automatically interested in your hips, you know,' she heard Margaret say. 'It's all down to the way you move them.' Brenda felt beads of sweat appear on her forehead.

'This is noble thing to do,' she tried to reassure herself. 'For Huigje, for all the innocent people that Colijn and his German friends have hurt. Not to mention all the money that he's stolen. A night of sacrifice in this compartment with one bed. It's a must. There are worse things than this. Stay strong.' But she felt herself become sick.

Brenda had more or less promised him this night, it was the only way that Colijn wouldn't have dismissed her before the travel started. He wanted to collect the full price on the second night as well. She was planning to use the improvised pistol that her father had made on the second night. She couldn't do it on the first night, because Colijn's German friends would notice that he was missing from the dining car at breakfast. It would have been difficult to keep him hidden after breakfast for another day and night.

In Amsterdam, the war was taking its toll on the country to a greater extent every day. There was hardly any food and the people were on the brink of starvation. It was necessary for Huigje to fend for herself for the last few months. The young mother came out on the street as little as possible. It seemed as if all the neighbors were looking at her, judging her, as if she was contaminated. She felt more alone than ever. Cold and anxious.

She thought back to the week that David and his family had suddenly disappeared from her life. On one evening in that week she had gone with Harm and her husband to visit one of the elders from her church in Durgerdam. 'You just pay attention to looking after the child,' Sjoerd had said suddenly, as if he had ever worried about whether Harm was being looked after. Then he went deep into conversation with the elder about God's will. Huigje had no desire to go there. She would much rather have sat and talked through her problems with David; Sjoerd knew that's how she felt without having to say anything.

The elder's wife, with her deep wrinkles and grey hair tied up in a top-knot, was lovely and seemed to mean well. She sat bolt upright at the dinner table and seemed to follow the discussion between her husband and Sjoerd as they justified the German occupation and their treatment of the Jews. Huigje couldn't bear to listen to them. But the old, balding man with the weak face and sunken eyes continued to talk about man's fall into sin and God's judgment. The man spoke at length about everything from Moses to Calvin to Luther, only to Sjoerd and completely ignoring his wife. There seemed to be no end to the evening so, when Huigje finally suggested that perhaps for Harm's sake it would be better if they left, Colijn for once didn't get angry. When they eventually got home, Huigje promptly put Harm to bed. It was already extremely late but she still wanted to visit David. Maybe he was still awake.

She returned to her house dazed and confused. Colijn was sitting at the table reading a newspaper. He did nothing more than raise an eyebrow as he saw her bewildered face. 'They're gone. How can that be? Where have they gone? They're gone!'

Provocatively slowly, Colijn folded up the newspaper. 'So you can see for yourself how untrustworthy and how ungrateful people can be. They must have thought they could find somewhere better to live.' Caustically he added, 'and you'd become so friendly with them.'

Not only was the book cave now empty, but Margaret had also disappeared from the neighborhood. She had rung her bell once, but no one had opened up. Most of all, Huigje wanted to speak with Brenda, if she came to visit for work. She waited for a light to come on in the room. But ever since the family had disappeared, Brenda too seemed to lose her cheerful disposition. She didn't have much to say.

Huigje was an intelligent woman; perhaps life would have been more simple and satisfying for her if she were less so. Now she saw through everything and became aware of tensions and plots that were going on around her, but was aware that she was being kept out of the loop. 'I don't have anyone anymore,' she said to herself on disconsolate days like these.

A large, bolted book cupboard stood in the corner of the room. Only Brenda and Colijn had the keys. Brenda would come and organize stacks of papers around the clock. They would do all their work at the dinner table in their small house. Brenda would push aside the flowered, woolen tablecloth to make room for the papers. It was clear to Huigje that Colijn had other ambitions with all his money.

Weekly, Colijn would give Huigje the rations coupons for herself and Harm. Other than that, she had no dealings with him.

'This is terrible.' Brenda looked up when she heard Huigje gasp. Huigje's fragile shoulders shook in the cheap dress. Brenda had never seen her in anything else, though Brenda thought that in a suit she'd be a very elegant young woman. 'Nobody can tell me what's happened to David and the others. They must have been discovered and were picked up, because all their things have been left behind. At night I can't sleep and by day I just become more tired.' Brenda had to agree that she'd never seen Huigje looking so bad. She was always much thinner than her, but now her cheeks had become very drawn, and you could see all the sharp bones protruding from her pale face. Brenda felt deep compassion, but of course she couldn't say anything. It was much too dangerous. 'How could the Germans have discovered that they were there?' Huigje cried, glancing at the door through which Sjoerd could walk at any moment.

Brenda felt her pain but the whole situation was so precarious. One mistaken word from Huigje could shatter the whole plan. 'Can't you get any information from your church?' asked Brenda, keeping the conversation going against her better judgment.

'Ha…the church!' Huigje shivered in her thin dress, which seemed to be even more disheveled now that Huigje had given up looking after her appearance. The contrast between her clothes and Brenda's new clothes, and her fresh complexion, was immense.

Huigje saw that Brenda was distancing herself from her, and she understood why. Clearly she had seen how Brenda played and flirted with Sjoerd Colijn. Often she traveled with him on business and that was becoming increasingly common. Perhaps Brenda saw a future together with Sjoerd. If that were the case, it was logical that she'd keep Huigje at a distance, but Huigje did miss her former confidante.

'There's nothing that the church can do for me,' Huigje sighed. 'Sjoerd has said that I mustn't interfere. If I inform the church I'll be directly going against his orders.' She looked so sad and alone. Brenda felt compelled to do something. 'I'd hoped to have a friend in you,' whispered Huigje, almost begging, in spite of everything.

'I am your friend, Huigje. More than you think.'

Huigje did not answer. 'You just want Sjoerd,' she thought. 'I don't understand why. He's an animal; a rat, a deadly rat. People on the street won't even look at me because of my sneaky husband. What do you see in him? Status? Money?' She suspected that Sjoerd had much more money than he let her believe. Yes, that had to be the reason. Oh, she understood why Brenda had created the distance, but she did wish that things could go back to how they used to be. Huigje admitted, 'I've lost David and Margaret. You're my only support.'

'I'll not let you down,' was the only answer that Brenda could muster. Huigje didn't understand what Brenda was trying to say, but that was how things were these days. Ever since she was a child, life seemed full of riddles and pain. Even caring for Harm was increasingly difficult now that he was getting bigger and no longer had David to talk to.

David and Margaret guessed that it was late in the evening. Even though the goods wagons were linked to the luxurious carriages, they decided that they now dared to get out of the crate. They figured that no one would want to travel all the way down the train, crawl and squeeze past all the other crates, just to get to their compartment. 'We have to get out of here for a little while to stretch our legs,' David said. 'It's not good to stay cramped for forty-eight hours. Perhaps we'll have to run when we get to Switzerland and it'll be so difficult if we've not even moved around for a couple of days.'

Margaret agreed with him. It was thanks to him that they'd even made it this far.

They crawled on the straw, and probably manure, that covered the floor. Above the large, sliding doors were windows with iron bars. Moonlight shone through. In fact, one of the sliding doors was broken and stayed slightly open, allowing the night air to come in. It wasn't cold, just fresh, which the two appreciated after being shut up in the stuffy box. They got a hunk of bread each and a piece of cheese made from the milk from Father Baltus' cows.

David continued standing. He stretched from side to side; he wanted to make sure he stayed fit as he had tried to do in the little garden in Amsterdam. For a little while the two enjoyed their relative freedom and the hope of reaching Switzerland. So far everything was still going to plan.

'You don't have to expect that the officers will be poking into the case with swords or anything to see if anyone's hiding in there. That's what they did in the middle ages, into carriages full of hay. They're not able to shoot either. Their officers won't be happy to see bullet holes in their Breughels or Rembrandts,' Brenda had tried to reassure them. It sounded logical enough. 'At the station on our side there will be soldiers watching carefully to check that no one tries to sneak onto the train. They're not interested in what's already on there. In fact, they're not allowed to know what's on the train already. It wouldn't help morale if the soldiers knew that the German officers, heads of government and their allies are bringing their valuables out of the country in case Germany loses the war.'

'The greatest danger is in Switzerland, then,' remarked Margaret.

'I doubt it, said Brenda lightly. 'It's not German territory. Switzerland has not been occupied. Of course, its borders are closed except for money and securities. Because of the value of the transported goods there will be Swiss guards. The Swiss have to be sure that no paintings are stolen. That's their only task. They've got no interest in the people that are on the train. In the carriages there are people who naturally must have authorization to pass the border; their papers are thoroughly checked. I expect you'll be held at the border for quite a while when they do this. But I believe no one will check the goods wagons.'

If Brenda was just being optimistic to hearten David and Margaret they didn't know, but it did help them in any case. They felt so calm now that they didn't even bother to whisper. 'I feel deliciously relaxed,' Margaret called to make sure she was heard above the clamor of the train.

At that moment, the door that connected them to the next carriage was flung open with a bang. Margaret and David froze with fear.

In the doorway stood Brenda; her face wasn't clearly visible but her feelings were. Panic. David had never seen Brenda like this. Immediately he rushed over to her before she'd even stepped foot in their compartment. Panting, she let her head fall heavily onto David's shoulder. 'What is it?' David asked, almost shouting, with concern. 'Are you wounded?' She couldn't say a word. Simply she shook her head, much to David's relief.

With one arm around her waist and the other hand stroking her hair, he moved her further in away from the door. Margaret also rushed forward and supported her on the other side. 'What's the matter, my dear?' Asked Margaret, caring as always. 'Come on dear, tell me everything.'

David fully expected a German soldier with a gun to storm in at any moment. Brenda was behaving as if she was running away from someone. She was breathing heavily as if she had just run the whole length of the train. David estimated that to be at least one hundred meters. 'No one knows where I am,' she gasped as if she understood David's concerns. That, in any case, was reassuring. The heavily damaged interior door swung to and fro as it had done for the entire journey so far. Nobody was coming.

For the first five minutes, Brenda could hardly get a word out. In the half-light, leaning against David, she cried and cried, while he continued to hold her steady and stroke her hair. He looked at her face with an expression of questioning and comfort.

Suddenly, Brenda dropped to the straw. David looked over at Margaret who was watching them from a distance of a meter or two. How could she remain so calm?

Eventually Brenda sat up. She took a couple of stumbling steps in Margaret's direction. She left David behind and, without anything to lean on, she jolted forward. Astonished, David watched Brenda cling onto Margaret's neck and push herself up against her.

She seemed to whisper something in Margaret's ear. 'He wants....' was all that he heard her say, the rest escaped him. Not that Brenda said much more because Margaret had quickly got her hand over Brenda's mouth.

'Don't worry. I understand already.'

Their voices became even quieter, Brenda wasn't crying any longer. She was breathing deeply with her back to him, leaning on Margaret. They were in a strange, cramped position with Brenda's head on Margaret's belly. Margaret withdrew to the furthest corner of the carriage with Brenda, gesturing that David was not to follow. 'What's this all about?' He asked. He was given no answer.

After a little while, he saw Brenda and Margaret come away from the corner. Brenda swayed and shuffled through the movement of the train. Her breathing and movements were back to normal, back to the Brenda he knew. Back to the woman he longed to hold. Back to the woman he dreamed about in the book cave, on the farm, or actually everywhere.

She dropped down beside him on the ground and unexpectedly kissed him on the cheek. Fortunately, due to the dim light, she couldn't see how he blushed. Even with a kiss like this he could feel how full her lips were. He didn't understand what was going on. He got another kiss. 'Thanks, darling.' Brenda had called him 'darling!'

Margaret came over to them. She had something in her hand that she'd fetched out of their traveling box. 'Stick your arm out,' she instructed without explanation to David.

David didn't understand what she wanted and hesitated. Then, as Margaret grabbed hold of his left arm, he realized that she had a knife in her hand. 'What are you doing?'

'Work with me now, and don't ask too many questions.' The knife was razor sharp. Therefore, it only took a moment for Margaret to accomplish what she wanted. With the knife she'd cut off his sleeve. She nicked the top and then ripped it into two strips. David and Brenda leaned against each other. They were surprised but said nothing. David felt Brenda's hand next to his. That gave him an extra feeling of security and rest.

'Give me your arm,' David heard Margaret order again, in her strong Amsterdam accent, leaning against one of the posts supporting the roof in this juddering carriage. Automatically David rose up his other arm. 'No,' said Margaret. 'The arm without the sleeve.' David put down his right arm and lifted up his left again. Margaret grabbed tight hold of his arm and lifted it straight up. Suddenly, he felt warm blood trickle down his arm. Astonished he realized that Margaret had cut a gash in his arm. Instinctively, he wanted to withdraw his arm. He couldn't, Margaret still held his hand tightly.

He felt Margaret soak the cloth in blood by pushing it against the wound. 'What are you doing, Margaret?' Brenda gave him an answer. She took hold of his face in her hands and twisted it to face hers to kiss him on his bewildered mouth. She kept him like this with her hands and lips until he heard Margaret say, 'That's it.' Margaret let go of his hand at that same moment, and a fraction of a second later Brenda released his head after pressing firmly on his lips one last time. In the dark she looked at him lovingly.

'I wonder if she'd noticed how I'd been looking at her at the farm?' David asked himself. It was getting darker. David saw her large eyes stare at him meaningfully as she stood up.

'Come on, come on,' he heard Margaret say. What did she have in mind for them now?

Brenda also gave Margaret a little kiss and she disappeared through the wooden door with one of the two cloths in her hand. She didn't say a word, but she had regained her confident, athletic step. 'Now what was all of that in aid of?' David really wanted to know from Margaret.

'I'll tell you when you're old enough,' Margaret teasingly answered.

David had stopped bleeding. In the dark Margaret tried to make David's arm as clean as possible using the other half of the sleeve. Then she finally revealed why she had done all this.

Sjoerd Colijn sat straight up in the chair and played with the gilded knob on the wooden armrest. The train had made a stop and he'd managed to get off at the station and stretch his legs for five minutes. Now the train journeyed to Basel, to cross the border there. Sjoerd Colijn was very pleased with himself.

He thought about the last conversation he had had with Huigje's father in the little church in Durgerdam. He could still feel the wooden pews. Herbert de Jonge always sat uncomfortably on them; the wooden benches were always too little for his large frame, and the edge of the bench cut into his buttocks. There wasn't enough room to fit his legs between the rows so he always had to twist round to sit at an angle. The backrests dug precisely into his shoulder-blades.

It was in that same cold, dreary church with its pale, white walls, that the two had secretly forged their plans. This was where they came up with the idea of arranging the basement in Amsterdam. The church books and prohibited literature had to be stored somewhere, and Colijn had the idea to stack them to divide the basement into little rooms. 'We shall have God's blessing,' Colijn knew for a certainty. 'It's all in the scriptures what the penalty for their unfaithfulness would be. And then there was what they did to Jesus. It's entirely in God's hands.'

Colijn let Herbert think that it was he who had brought the library into order. He was serving the church and thereby helping him; Sjoerd Colijn could make good use of those strong arms.

He remembered the early days, seeing Herbert's fine daughter, Huigje. She was slightly built and, like a child, was a little frightened of him. That attracted him to her more. In the beginning he felt much more powerful than Huigje.

However, that had all changed, but at least now he had his Brenda. Now she seemed to gladly want to do the things that he had in mind. 'Not in your home,' Brenda had resolutely said. That implied a promise; a promise of another place. That place was now, in this luxurious compartment.

Colijn liked the woody interior of this carriage. Especially now, as night was falling, the shimmering lamp gave off a warm, orange glow.

'The war could still last a long time,' Colijn had told the curious Herbert in their last conversation together. 'And while it lasts I can't develop myself here.' Herbert didn't understand the words exactly, but his did understand his intention.

'You want to leave here?' He muttered.

'Yes,' Colijn answered so sharply that it echoed through the empty church. 'You may as well know that everything's now arranged for me to leave. I'll come back when the war's over.'

'How?' Huigje's grumbling father wanted to know. 'And what are you going to do with me?'

Colijn revealed a great deal of his plans and told of how and why he also traveled with Brenda to Switzerland. 'All the funds from the church are in my name. Sooner or later someone is going to question that. I'm going to take the funds from the church with me to safety.' But that wasn't everything. Colijn leaned further into Herbert and continued. 'More importantly, I have to make sure that I take over all of the money belonging to the Jew in the basement. All of that is in America. Here in Holland there's nothing more I can get from him. And there's also his case: It's full of gold and gemstones. It's much too risky to try and sell them here. In Switzerland it's possible for me to sell them, or perhaps use them as security.' Sjoerd Colijn had arranged his affairs well before he left.

Five years it had cost him, and now he was rich. So rich that Brenda would stay with him. Herbert de Jorge couldn't stop him. 'When I'm established in America I'll bring you over, as soon as it's possible,' Sjoerd Colijn promised his worker.

'That will only be possible if this war ever stops,' muttered Herbert.

'Perhaps it won't be so long before it is over. Since America, Canada and Russia have become involved, it's really only a matter of time. Believe me; it took Hitler three years to prepare for this war; to build ships, airplanes, tanks. Well, now the allies have had over three years to build their arsenal. I reckon they must now be ready to attack.'

Herbert couldn't follow what Sjoerd was saying about the war. He just stared at him, trying to figure out how he would get through the coming times without his friend. 'There's nothing for me to do anymore', he observed with consternation. Herbert de Jonge had need of a plan maker, an organizer. Herbert thought about the blessings they'd had. The Jews in the basement had certainly been a gift from God, so the Bible and Sjoerd had said. 'We set up the basement together. I thought that maybe you'd got another project for the two of us.'

'You're going to be busy enough.' Colijn looked at him seriously and thought about how he was going to phrase what he was about to say. 'The church is going to be breathing down your neck when they realize that I'm gone and so is all their money. You have to work hard to cover my tracks.'

'How?' Herbert was scared at the thought of the impact of Colijn leaving, and seemed shackled to the wooden benches.

'Simple. All the evidence will point to me, but I'll be gone. That means you're in the clear. So what you need to do is bring the evidence to the attention of the officials. Then you'll become a hero, not a victim.'

Herbert slid restlessly back and forth on the uncomfortable seat. He muttered, 'what will you be doing in the meantime in America?'

'First of all I'll sell my paintings and the jewels from the case. If it's all worth what I think, I'll start my own business, a company which makes products that will make peoples' lives more enjoyable after the war. Something technical. Cars maybe, or radios, or televisions. Before the war, German companies like Telefunken and Loewe made such things. Once the Allies have freed Europe, that sort of apparatus will really be in demand.'

Herbert de Jonge didn't know what sort of apparatus his friend was going on about. But he saw the same twinkle in Sjoerd's eye that he always had before embarking on a plan that would make them rich. Herbert heard Sjoerd say, 'Look, when I'm in America I'm going to buy a huge house. As soon as the war's over I'll get you over. Then I'll make you the foreman in my factory. And here's something else to interest you: with my money, you'll be able to get any woman that you want.' Sjoerd had already got Brenda in mind for himself; things always turned out the way that Sjoerd predicted.

Herbert was confident that things would work out just as Sjoerd planned. He pictured the two of them revolutionizing America with the television, not that he knew what it was. At no point, though, did it even cross his mind to ask what was to become of Huigje or Harm. All he thought about was that black case of Jonathan's. On several occasions he Sjoerd had broken it open. The gold and jewels in there shone amazingly. A note was inside which indicated that the contents really belonged to Jonathan's son. It instructed him to do some good with the contents, together with another boy who also had such a case. Well, hopefully Sjoerd was going to do something good with that money now. Herbert hoped that the Germans had shot not only Jonathan but the son also. That would save Sjoerd from a great many problems.

Now, weeks later, Sjoerd smiled as he compared the cold of that white church to the warmth of this comfortable train compartment with its deep red upholstering and wooden furniture. This was a new beginning; a new beginning with a woman who truly captivated him.

He was still waiting for her after she'd left so abruptly about an hour ago. She'd certainly been gone a long time. Still, no matter. She couldn't go anywhere. That was the beauty of this plan. Brenda had promised him so much; now she had to make good on those promises.

Brenda Baltus took hold of the door handle, took a deep breath and stepped into the compartment. Sjoerd Colijn was sitting in the chair closest to the door. He looked at her, smiling. 'You're back.'

'Naturally.' Brenda only stood in the doorway for a moment. Then she swayed her hips as she walked across the carriage, and Sjoerd was captivated by her torso.

Brenda was practically perfect. All the boys in her village admired her hourglass figure. She couldn't take a step without being ogled. Well, they could look all they wanted, she decided what happened. That's the way it had always been.

She took a small step forwards and her knees touched his. Sjoerd Colijn stuck out his hands and let them follow the form of her hips. Brenda bent down towards him, her firm hands sliding over the man's thin shoulders. She could sense his nervousness and impatience. 'We have the whole night, Sjoerd,' she said, but he didn't hear it. As far as he was concerned, the moment had come.

Brenda felt Sjoerd's hand go higher and higher up the inside of her thigh. She wanted to vomit. It would be dangerous if Sjoerd picked up on her panic and hysteria. Beads of sweat broke out as his hand traveled further up. 'Please God, let it work out as Margaret has predicted.'

Suddenly, Sjoerd withdrew his hand in fright. He raised his hand and with the other pushed Brenda on the bed. 'What is that? Blood?' He screeched. Now it was more important than ever that Brenda didn't lose her head.

'You have to continue to play the game you've been playing for months,' Margaret had said. 'You really have to imagine and believe that it is your time of the month. If you don't, he will sense it and be suspicious. If you can pull it off, he'll be just as scared of it as any other man.'

'Your blood!' Groaned Sjoerd Colijn, still with his hand outstretched as he sat back on his chair.

'Sjoerd, I am…' She didn't say any more. Her voice trembled, but she tried to give the appearance of being a woman of the world. 'But surely that doesn't make any difference to us.'

'You are unclean!' There was such disgust in his voice, and his eyes were watering. Brenda had to put forth a great effort not to show her sense of victory and relief. Her sweat, her trembles, the fear in her voice. Surely Sjoerd had seen them all but had provided another explanation.

Colijn stood up. He knocked the chair over to the ground. 'Here, look,' he shouted as he thrust his hand up to Brenda's face. 'Your blood. You're unclean. And you said nothing about it, you bitch!' Ten Brenda felt the slap of his bloody hand against her jaw. Brenda thought of tomorrow evening. It wouldn't be like this tomorrow. Then she'd be able to shoot him down.

After he'd hit her, Brenda cried even louder and tried to plead with him. 'That only happens once a month,' she stammered sincerely. 'It's just nature. I am a healthy woman. That's what you want isn't it? A healthy woman? This doesn't have to stand in the way of our love.' She played the scene exactly the way that Margaret had instructed, trying to believe the things she was saying. Tears rolled down her cheeks. 'We can go further another time. I want to be with you, Sjoerd.'

Her words, which even she didn't know where they were coming from, made Sjoerd Colijn slowly calm down. 'I've been waiting for this, Sjoerd. No, I didn't say anything. I didn't want to miss out on this evening.'

'Okay, she couldn't change her body clock,' Colijn considered, frustrated. 'But she could have said something.'

'I think that this is the last day of my period. If it's not possible now to do anything, then perhaps tomorrow?' Brenda tried to summon up all her pity and conviction to add weight to her words. 'Not today, but tomorrow. I know almost for certain that the bleeding will be over by tomorrow.'

Colijn looked at her. He was on the bed and was surprised at her. 'If you're not better tomorrow I'll beat you, you rotten slut.' Brenda again tried to summon up courage. She'd not be beaten once more. She'd shoot him before that happened.

The next day, the train traveled along another section of the Rhine. On the slopes on the other side of the river, farmers cultivated the grapes from which wine would be produced.

David and Margaret dared to come out of their dark shelter but, nevertheless, kept themselves hidden in a corner behind some crates containing life-size sculptures. From there they could see through the half-open door, and they saw villages speeding past. If the train slowed down as they passed a station, the two withdrew back into the dark corner.

Sometimes, when they stopped at a station, they heard sounds and fragments of conversations and commands in German. At a couple of stations, someone had tried to close the door which, because of its age and state of disrepair, wouldn't remain closed.

Brenda also managed to spend the day fairly carefree. Eventually, Colijn had seemed to come to the realization that every woman was indisposed in this way, and that Brenda had no control about it coinciding with their trip. The two of them had breakfast together in the dining cart and she had placed her hand on top of his. They'd had an enjoyable conversation about the cultivation of grapes and how wine had been made for centuries. The Romans were responsible for spreading wine-making across Europe and for the introduction of vines on these sunny slopes. There was even talk of wine-making as long ago as the Old Testament.

The train was now close to Basel, the last stop before Switzerland. As had been planned before, the last two wagons were uncoupled and three more were added. Brenda had wisely put her friends in one of the first few goods wagons so that they wouldn't be taken away with the back carriages.

Eventually, the evening crawled closer. David and Margaret knew what Brenda had planned for tonight. Between Basel and the border, the customs authorities would do a check. After the border she would strike. There would be no more controls after that. The dead body of Sjoerd would not be discovered. By the time he was missed, they would all be far away from the train. That's the way it had to be.

'He has to die', Brenda had concluded with moist eyes. For months she had suffered making that decision. David wanted to react but father Baltus held him back.

'There's no point trying to talk her out of it. Brenda always does what she wants. It's much better if you just try and support her. That's what she had a real need of.' That was the very reason why Baltus had made the pistol for her. He tried to engineer it so it made as little noise as possible. It only worked at very close range, as the aim wasn't good.

Now the evening fell and the moment came closer, David and Margaret both fell quiet. It was impossible for them to be of any assistance. Of course, they'd agreed to hide her though as soon as she'd done it. She would have to choose her moment. No doubt that would be late in the evening, or deep into the night, so that she could make her way to the back of the train without being noticed.

The tension was unbearable.

Brenda didn't know what to do for the best. She didn't know whether to let Colijn drink a lot of wine at the dinner table or not. She didn't know how he would react: With alcohol in his veins he might be even more violent and cumbersome. On the other hand, she had to keep him in the dining car as long as possible. She maneuvered matters so that it was already late when they went in to eat.

'Tonight is our night,' she whispered to him at the dinner table, scared about the hidden meaning behind the words.

'You mean you're no longer…'

'Don't worry. Like I said, tonight is our night.' Brenda lifted her glass in a toast. 'To us, Sjoerd. To our future in Switzerland.'

'In America,' Colijn corrected her. Brenda didn't know if alcohol made Colijn more violent, but it certainly made him more talkative. She listened as the candle flickered and he went on and on. 'America. That's where our chances are. You don't know the half of how rich I am.' Brenda did, however, have an idea about that but she wisely kept her mouth shut about what she discovered from the accounts. 'We have to go back to our room now,' she heard Colijn say.

Brenda poured another drink into his now full glass. 'You want this, don't you?' she said as Colijn took a couple of gulps. Thus Brenda tried to stretch the evening out for as long as she could. For some time he kept insisting that they now go back to their carriage, each time sounding more annoyed than the last. To try and stretch things out any longer would be dangerous, Brenda realized.

For the whole day Brenda had managed to keep her nerves in check. Now that it was evening and the two went through the doorways from one compartment to another, she struggled to continue to keep control of her emotions. It was as well that the train rocked them from side to side and threw them of balance. 'If I stood still he'd see how much I was trembling,' Brenda thought to herself. As they walked along, Colijn said this and that to her. She didn't hear a word.

Then they arrived at their compartment. Sjoerd held the door for Brenda to go through first. After he followed her in he dove on the bed. Lying on his back he kicked off his shoes. All the time he kept his eyes on Brenda and a smile on his lips. It was going to happen now. She had no more chances.

Brenda had to concentrate hard so as not to faint. 'Strip,' she heard Colijn stammer. She was frightened that he would see how nervous she was. That didn't happen. Dutifully she removed her woolen jacket and repeated what she had heard previously.

'You strip too, Sjoerd.' She realized that if he were naked, she'd keep the upper hand; he wouldn't be able to run after her in any case. Colijn indeed untucked his shirt and started to undo the buttons, still lying on his back. The knitted vest became visible.

Panicking, Brenda realized she'd forgotten about the gun. As she undid her blouse she tried to nonchalantly wander over to the little cupboard. She managed to get the gun without him noticing it. She went over to him on the bed and, as she lay down, she pushed the gun against his side. 'Hey, what's that?' Colijn said as he pushed her back.

Brenda didn't dare to pull the trigger; then there was a struggle, and Colijn got shot in the knee. He rolled back onto the bed and Brenda beat him about the head with the weapon. Sjoerd Colijn's body slackened, and he lay in an unnatural pose on the bed. 'He must be unconscious. Or dead,' the thought occurred to Brenda.

The gun which her father had knocked together could only be loaded with one bullet at a time. It was too risky to go in search of other bullets. She dare not lose sight of Colijn. She toyed with the idea of smothering him with the pillow, but she didn't dare do that either. 'He's not worth it,' she muttered to herself, not realizing what a strange thing that was to say. She wondered what she would do now.

Sjoerd Colijn stirred. Dizzy, he tried to sit up. He was like a boxer, trying to get up after the count. Now that the threat of the assault had gone, Brenda regained her characteristic confidence and poise. She raised her arm and knocked Sjoerd unconscious again with the handle of the gun. 'This is revenge,' she said aloud. Sjoerd fell back on the bed.

It remained quiet in the compartment. Apparently, no one had heard the shot. This part of the plan appeared to have been successful. Brenda pulled Colijn's legs so they were stretched out on the bed. 'I have to improvise something. The others are waiting for me. They'll be so worried.' Once more, she thought about suffocating him. 'I can't kill him in cold blood,' Brenda knew for certain. But she knew she couldn't simply stay there until morning when he would be discovered. 'I have to think of something new.'

Every time Sjoerd stirred she whacked him again with the barrel of the gun. 'Perhaps I'll accidentally strike him dead,' she thought. A wave of nausea passed over her each time she hit him. It was already the early hours of the morning when Brenda realized she had to get away now.

She tore a towel into strips and tied a piece tightly around his inanimate face, drawing it so it was especially tight between his lips. Using his shoelaces, she bound his hands to the iron bedstead. They were so tight that they cut into his flesh, but she couldn't take the chance that he might not be dead and may be able to loosen himself.

Before it really became light, Brenda left the compartment. If their maps and calculations were correct, they must have been traveling through Switzerland for some hours now. She hurried to the goods wagon where Margaret and David had spent a sleepless night.

It was still fairly early in the morning when the train came to a halt in Bern. On the platform were security guards, but they stood with their backs to the train. They would prevent anyone getting on to the train. There were goods onboard that were too valuable to risk any unauthorized persons boarding. Whoever wanted to get off the train seemed not to interest them one bit.

David carefully glanced along the platform, but no one seemed to be looking in their direction. So it was that the three managed to disembark unseen. Their clothing suggested that they were just some of the many travelers and free people that were walking along the platform.

Switzerland 1943-1946

It would be three years before David and Brenda would succeed in travelling together back to America. 'I have so many plans,' David made clear, 'for Ted Bates' shop.'

'Plans, but no money,' Brenda would tease.

'No money, but a fantastic idea,' replied David. 'And a lot of good training,' he said as he thought of how much he'd learned from the books in the book cave. 'At Ted Bates' shop there's a notebook of mine containing all my ideas about television. I've got a lot to add to that book. In my head I've drawn up a complete business plan involving display equipment, computers and satellites.'

'Well, then!'

Margaret also had plans of her own but no money either. 'As soon as the war's over, I'm going to Heinrich, even if that means going to Germany.' No one knew how long that would be.

The threesome successfully kept themselves by working on farms, although that wasn't possible for Margaret for long. Two months after their escape from the Netherlands she gave birth to a little boy. She named him after David: 'Little David.'

For three years the three labored in barns or farmhouses in the Swiss valleys or mountains. Roomy homes were made out of natural stone blocks with a lot of granite and woodwork, especially in the carved wooden verandas around the houses. The three dark winters with the deep snow was an experience for them. Through the winter they smelled the cows in the barn mixed with the smell of smoke coming from the woodburning stoves. In summer, David and Brenda enjoyed the fresh air high on the Alps, where they took the cows to graze. By day you could hear the lively ringing of the cowbells. In the evenings, David and Brenda tried to learn what they could of the Swiss version of German from the locals. David also tried to help Brenda get mastery over the English language, which seemed entirely strange to Brenda.

At night they all slept together in the straw, where David thought back to Huigje and forgot about his desires for Brenda.

Food and lodging was free with their employment. This meant that David and Brenda could save their meager wages, so that in 1946, with the help of Ted Bates, they had enough to pay for their travel back to

America. In the middle of the summer, they said farewell to Margaret and little David and crossed the ocean over to Boston.

Argentina 1945

A year before Brenda and David took a ship to America, before the capitulation of the Third Reich, a fleet of twenty submarines, mainly with German officers on board, sailed south. By Cape Verde, the Atlantic archipelago near Africa, they met up with another group of submarines. Not knowing what to do, they pulled back to the American coastline. On board one of the submarines from Operation Ubersee Sud, Sjoerd Colijn had managed to secure himself a place, thanks to his German contacts and his money. He was in one of the vessels with the German officers with a large amount of gold, setting sail for South America. Other officers scuttled their submarines.

The first to arrive in Argentina was on July 10th of that year, it was rumored among the crew that Hitler, Eva and Greta Braun and Martin Bormann were on board. The second submarine arrived in Argentina on 2nd August, after she had torpedoed the American battleship, USS Eagle 56, even though the war was already over.

After Brenda's attack, Colijn couldn't walk and could only stand with difficulty. Because of his damaged skull, he could hardly even talk. Still he managed, along with fifty highly placed officers of the Third Reich, to find shelter in a place called Rio Negro, a desolate region of Patagonia. It was here that Sjoerd Colijn met the ugly Croat, Divo Krlea. He, just like Sjoerd and the German officers, was trying to figure out what he was going to do with this new 'world peace.'

Boston 1946

Excitedly Ted Bates waited in the sunshine, leaning against the wall of the simple, bleak, grey, flat-roofed passenger terminal. He stared out at the ship that brought David and Brenda growing bigger by the minute as it came nearer. Ted Bates ran up the steep ocean wall with his hand to his forehead, trying to keep the sun out of his eyes. Around the edges of the white steamer, under the three black chimneys, you could see people lining the railings, they looked like little dolls. The captain let the horn blow loudly as if to invite a welcome. Of course it was impossible to recognize David from this distance, but nevertheless Ted waved exuberantly. He caught sight of a child.

'Will I recognize him straight away?' Ted had wondered the minute he'd read that David now had enough money and was on his way back to Boston. 'How much has he suffered since the time I saw him last?' In Ted's mind, all he could see was a boy of about twelve. 'How old are you now?' Ted screwed his eyes up as he tried to calculate. 'Twenty-two, maybe twenty-three...twenty-four?' Against his instincts, Ted forced himself to try and look out for an older chap.

David hadn't inherited his father's physique. He wasn't particularly any taller than other young men, but his muscular body, broad shoulders and firm chest made him stand out from the rest. His hair was dark blond with golden highlights. His eyes weren't dissimilar to Brenda's, but where hers were pure blue, his had a flash of green in them. However, David had inherited his father's carefree eyes which always seemed to radiate happiness. When Ted Bates saw David, he wouldn't see anything of his tall, skinny father in him. His father always wore jackets that hung off his shoulders. Ted Bates could only ever picture Jonathan wearing his grey striped, double-breasted suit, with the rigid-collared shirt that left a gap all around his neck. Ted expected David to be a sporty young man wearing a casual shirt with short sleeves on this summer's day.

His expectation was true to the reality. Along with his white, short-sleeved shirt David was wearing some pleated trousers that he'd bought in the city special for the journey. His heavy, old shoes, which had served him well on the farm, Brenda had cleaned well for the occasion and had bought him new laces for them. 'You have to arrive in America clean and tidy.'

With the breeze lightly blowing through his hair, one arm on the railings and one arm around Brenda, David searched along the ocean wall. Together with Brenda, with her blond hair and bright blue eyes, they formed an attractive couple. The sun-drenched, carefree holiday that they'd had on board, lying in their swimming costumes next to the pool, had bronzed their skin. Three weeks in to their journey, David had come to know Brenda in a different way; not that he hadn't thought about Huigje and wished that she could have seen this.

When the awesome steamer had docked, two gangplanks were raised to allow the passengers to disembark. It was incredibly busy on the dock, so busy that Ted struggled to see over the shoulders of all the other people. He kept trying until a hand grabbed hold of his shoulders and wouldn't release them. A strong, manly voice behind him said, 'Ted…Ted Bates!' Ted twisted himself around and looked into the green/blue eyes of the broadly set, bronzed young man.

'What a man you've become, David,' Ted whispered.

Ted stuck out his hands and pulled David into him. Then came the tears, and David comforted Ted, as if their roles had now and forever been reversed. As if he were a child, the older man shook as he cried on David's firm chest and David felt his shirt become wet.

Over the top of Ted's head, David glanced happily and timidly at Brenda. She didn't do or say anything until David slowly loosed Ted's grip. She just watched the scene around her as parents greeted their children, business men shook hands, and the porters busied themselves with cases and trunks.

Eventually Brenda went and stood right next to the two men. Ted Bates gratefully accepted the white handkerchief that she offered him. 'So you must be Brenda?'

'Indeed, Mr. Bates. Brenda Kerzner.'

'Kerzner?'

'Well, sort of…I will be very soon!'

Boston 1946-1951

Ted Bates had dragged his bed down to the little room behind the shop and slept there. The upstairs rooms he'd given to his two young guests. It wasn't long before Ted and David were getting up early again and going back and forth to the open-air fifty meter swimming pool. Throughout the day, David and Brenda helped Ted in the shop or perhaps took deliveries to people in the city. In the evening, the three would sit together in Ted's little room and talk, or if it were a warm evening they'd lounge in the garden. They would summon up all their old memories and also talk about their future, near and distant, in Boston.

'I've saved your notebook, David.'

Brenda knew immediately what Ted was talking about. 'Let us see it.' Before the war, David had used the thinly ruled notebook with the black and white photo on the cover to record his swimming times and training record. If you turned it over, on the side with the dark blue cover, you could see where David had written all kinds of notes about the things that fascinated him; the television, for example. In the back there was also a clipping from a newspaper article about how John Watson, from IBM, had started off as an accountant and a sewing-machine salesman. There were also notes about the calculator that Howard H. Aiken had produced, which could multiply numbers with twenty-three digits in four seconds.

'In the meantime, in Pennsylvania now there's the ENIAC with its eighteen thousand tubes which works a thousand times more quickly than that,' Ted took pleasure in telling David.

David took hold of the notebook and opened it out on the table in the corner of the room. He reached for a pencil and wrote: 'July 1946, Chapter 2. Sooner or later, television is going to conquer the world, the result of which will be world peace.'

Before very long, the conversation turned to the painful subject of David's family. What had become of Mother and Esther? The Red Cross, as well as other aid organizations, had been unable to trace them. At this moment, war criminals were being tried in Neurenberg. Atrocious depositions were coming to light about what had happened in the German camps. They were worse, much worse, than anyone had imagined.

And then there was Jonathan's legacy, that was another story. Only the stately, white house testified to their past glory. There was now a large, foreign family living there. They'd restored the house splendidly and the gardens were beautifully tended, just like formal gardens in a park. Brenda thought the house was lovely, but it made her think of the awful contracts that she'd witnessed. Suddenly she grabbed on to David's arm. 'David, David. We must warn that man as soon as possible. We have to warn the man who's living in that beautiful house.'

David didn't understand what on earth she was going on about. 'Warn him?'

'The contracts!'

'My dear, what do you mean?'

'The contracts with Colijn. Colijn means to take everything from him, just like he did with your father.'

David didn't really have an appetite for that subject, but Brenda found it important, so they took a little walk and sat on a bench on the grassy hill. There Brenda revealed all the details of the accounts and contracts that she'd seen at Colijn's. David tried to throw her off course by saying, 'let's forget about it for now. We'll discuss it tonight with Ted, if that's okay with you?'

It surprised him to hear her say, 'Okay, tonight then.'

After discussing the matter with Ted, Ted said, 'really, all that that man has bought via Colijn, from your father, really should have been passed on to you.'

'What does that matter? Without Mother and Esther, what does it mean to me?'

'Well, you're going to need some money if you want to realize your dreams about television.' Ted Bates was serious. 'I can already see a shiny sign, above a modern building, saying "Ted Bates Company."'

'Ted Bates Company?'

'Obviously. But of course it will be our business together. With so much money you'll obviously be the company director.'

'You mean this, don't you?'

'Of course I do…of course, even without the money; you're welcome to be a part of this business.'

Brenda had been listening for a while. She wanted to bring the conversation back to its original subject. 'Look, I don't want to interfere with your business, but that aside, would you please, just once, go and talk with the man on the hill?'

'But why? Why?' Both men said.

'Well, firstly, it seems logical that the man will be able to tell you something about your father's capital. He has done business with Colijn, who was acting on your father's behalf.'

'And secondly?' David wanted to know.

'And secondly, we have to warn him.'

'About what?'

'About Colijn, of course. Haven't you been listening to what I've been telling you?'

'Why would we go and warn a complete stranger? Perhaps he's a bad person too. He does do business with Colijn.'

'As did your father. And he lost everything to him. I have seen the contracts.'

'And then what?'

'Well, I don't know. We just ought to warn him, that's all. What do you think, Ted?'

'I know the gardener.'

David laughed and slapped his hand down on the table. 'What's that got to do with anything?'

Ted Bates shifted uncomfortably in his seat. He raised a finger and pointed it at David. 'Now look, their old gardener is an invalid and a close friend of the owner. He's a happy person and well cared for. Someone who looks after his friends like that cannot be a bad person.'

'Hmm.'

'And something else. I regularly see the older sisters in the garden watching their little brother, Jassar, play. There's something good about that. They're a peaceful family and I wouldn't like to see them duped.'

'You know,' Brenda interrupted. 'We'll call by tomorrow and ask the man some questions. We'll do our duty and warn him, and we'll just see what happens from there.' She theatrically placed an arm around David's neck and pulled him in to her. 'And you never know, they might invite us in. And then I can see where you grew up.'

'You always get your own way, don't you?' David sighed and kissed Brenda's face.

Abdel Amini was at home in a large room which had been arranged as a living room; he was alone in the enormous space. In his mind he thought back to earlier times. He would much rather, a thousand times rather, be in his old Jaffa. But considering the problems with the Jews and the other expected problem in the Middle East, that just wasn't an option for his family. As he looked out of the terrifically huge windows over to the ocean, he could imagine the warm summers by the Mediterranean Sea. Abdel Amini paced up and down the room with a letter in his hand. He looked perplexed. Aimlessly he wandered about the room, alternating between looking at the letter and then at the ceiling. The room was bathed in light and you could see tiny dust particles lit up by the sun's violet rays above the expensive pieces of furniture.

Deep in his thoughts as he was, Abdel Amini didn't hear the doorbell, or one of his staff announce that he had some visitors. He was too busy trying to make his decision. A single decision now could mean either good or bad for the future. He knew that a good decision now could mean that he could take his ease and do nothing in the future. When was it time to invest and when was it time to get out quickly? To know when to do each of those was an art. Abdel Amini had thought that it was now time to withdraw from the war industry. His reasoning was straight forward: Initially, the government needed weapons, tank and airplanes. Abdel's capital grew as the bombs dropped on Germany. At the moment, they had sufficient amounts. When he was confident that the Allies would win the war he withdrew from his investments. His expectations came true. Whereas Boeing had once had fifty-five thousand employees, now in the summer of 1946, they only had five thousand. It was being speculated that recreational aviation would be the next boom, but Abdel Amini calculated that that would be some time yet before it was profitable.

Now he was presented with a new opportunity. He had to make a choice. Should he make a small investment? The proposal in the letter was obviously such a good one that Abdel Amini wondered why he doubted still. 'We stand at the beginning of a new era,' the letter started. 'Television will conquer the world.'

'There are two people here for you, love.' It was the gentle voice of Tannous which broke Abdel free from his contemplations.

'Two people? I wasn't expecting anyone.'

'Two youngsters. They live here, in the neighborhood.'

'Ah.' Abdel walked over to a dark brown bureau with copper decorations and placed the letter on top of a tray of paper. 'Let them in, Tannous.'

Flying in a propeller aircraft wasn't the most comfortable means of transport, thought Sjoerd Colijn. In his condition, however, it was the best way to travel from Argentina to New York. Fortunately he still had the wealth, despite the enormous losses that he'd suffered, to purchase first-class tickets. Happily he was screened off from economy class. In fact he'd bought the most expensive tickets available to allow him to have the most legroom, which was also required for his tall employee, the Croat, Divo Krlea.

Of course, due to his handicap and the worry about his large financial losses, Colijn didn't travel well. As the plane flew over Brazil he muttered heavily and moved restlessly. 'You'd expect better from a commercial flight these days,' he winged, not expecting a reply.

Divo Krlea muttered something stupid which Colijn couldn't understand. He didn't bother to get an explanation; to talk was too much effort. Divo Krlea was here for his brute strength, not for his business instincts. Instinct had told Colijn that, now that Divo Krlea could no longer use his strength for the Croatian Fascist Party, he would be able to make good use of him. In the meantime, Divo helped him with his luggage as they went from plane to taxi on their way to New York.

Divo Krlea squinted at Colijn. A beaten, flat nose and a mouth with several front teeth missing made his shaved head look even more hideous. He was head and shoulders above everyone, had a frightening presence and looked as strong as a bear. Various travelers recoiled as they passed him and looked up at him. The suit which Sjoerd insisted Divo wear didn't make him look any more respectable. Divo scarcely fit into the seat on the airplane.

Since the war had ended Colijn had lost a lot of money. He hadn't been alert enough to foresee the fall and sell his shares in the collapsing industries, and the bad phone lines to Argentina had compounded the problem. By the time he did manage to sell them they were practically worthless. It wasn't simple to live a comfortable life in Argentina without spending a lot of money. The mysterious trip to Argentina by submarine had taken a large chunk of Colijn's finances. Still, there was enough left to establish himself in New York and to take Divo Krlea with him; sufficient to live, but not enough to invest in the new economy. The paintings which he'd bought with Jonathan's money gave him no solace. They'd been so contaminated that he'd had to sell them in Switzerland for far too little money. As for the money from the Dutch church, which he'd embezzled long before he went to Argentina, it was now worth nothing due to the enormous rate of inflation.

Internally Colijn grumbled on and on about the vicious world he lived in. God had promised him blessings but, as usual, His ways had proved to be unfathomable. Other families who once had similar capital as Sjoerd had managed to remain rich. But that was nothing more than a small piece of the pie that Colijn had taken from his Jewish partner, Jonathan. Thankfully he still had the case. And, because of that, Colijn grinned inwardly.

The seat on the plane where Colijn sat was big enough, but he was still in pain. 'Where is the case?' he snapped at Divo Krlea.

The Croat gestured forwards. 'By the toilet.'

It had taken Colijn six months and a large amount of money to bribe the customs officials to allow him to seal the case and carry it on with him. This and Divo Krlea were how he could feel secure that no one would tamper with it. The presence of the trunk and the Croat may have put his mind at ease but it didn't stop the pain in his hips. Every day, at least twice, Colijn thought back to the cause of that pain. The pain that got worse and worse.

'That stupid bitch,' flashed through his head, stabbing it with pain every time he thought of that angry night on the train from Amsterdam and Switzerland. Colijn had never been able to get rid of that nightmare, and when he awoke he always wondered why this happened to him.

'Why?' He asked, not realizing that he'd asked out loud. Divo Krlea looked at him, not understanding the question. Sjoerd Colijn thought further. He could think of absolutely no reason why Brenda should have turned on him in 1943. Deep humiliation hurt him more than the bullet which had made him invalid. To fall out of love was one thing; but to bring him to this situation, where no woman would ever desire him again, was another. 'Why?' Sjoerd Colijn muttered again with an expression of pain on his face.

'I don't know,' answered Divo Krlea, shrugging his shoulders.

Colijn looked at him. 'You don't know anything,' he snarled viciously at him, as best he could with the limited amount of oxygen he could force from his lungs. 'But you will be able to help me,' he thought to himself as he contemplated revenge and secretly promised that Divo would play a part in it. A malicious smile played on Colijn's lips. He'd find Brenda, bring her back, and then they'd ensure that she would suffer for the rest of her life the way he had suffered for the past three years.

But first he had to invest the treasures from Jonathan's trunk. How exactly he was going to do that, Colijn didn't yet know. What he did know was the phenomenon that television was to become, according to the son of Jonathan who seemed to know all about it. The boy was right: In the coming decades everyone would want such a thing in their home. Although he did have some money to invest in them, it wasn't going to be enough. He had the trunk full of gold and jewels. It perhaps wasn't a good idea to sell them, but surely any bank would be willing to use them as security.

'What are we going to do in New York?' grumbled Divo Krlea beside him.

'That depends on how my business partner reacts. I've written him a letter.'

'What about?'

'I want to set up a company, a factory. But it's not possible on my own.'

'Why not?'

'Because I need more money.'

'That's no good. Then you'll have to share.'

Colijn sighed, making a strange sound. 'Well, we'll see about that.'

'And what will you make in your factory?'

'Televisions,' answered Colijn briefly.

'Much too difficult.'

'Technology is where the money is,' Colijn whispered in a crackly voice with great effort.

'I understand that. But how are you going to be able to bring your televisions to the man on the street? Surely that's the tricky part.'

Colijn waited to catch his breath again. 'I'm going to find someone who can help me with that. What I need is a good business plan.' Then Colijn twisted angrily this way and that in his uncomfortable seat, a sign that the conversation was now over. The plan flew on, and Colijn hoped that, despite the pain, he'd be able to sleep.

Hand in hand, David and Brenda walked in the sunshine along the gravel path around the mansion. They passed benches that looked out towards the sloping lawns. They took deep breaths of the fresh, sea air. Brenda's face turned towards all the things David pointed out to her; the window of the room he slept in as a child, the tree that he'd built the tree house in, of which he'd been so proud. On the driveway stood a Ford motorcar, still glaringly clean although it was so old. David had a lump in his throat. 'As a fourteen year-old boy, I dreamed of the day when I'd be able to drive this car.' Brenda heard the nostalgia in his voice.

They pulled on the shiny, gold-colored bell-pull beside the door. David stepped back and could still hear the ringing behind the heavy, front door. A dark-skinned man in a white suit with gold-colored buttons and epaulets stood before them and allowed them entrance.

Ted Bates had been right. The house was beautiful and looked almost majestic, however there was a peaceful, warm, inviting atmosphere within. In the centre of the hallway was a large staircase with robust wooden balustrades. It was grand, but not flashy. Somehow, you felt at ease there. Poking his head through the carved wooden rails at the top of the stairs was a little boy; it had to be the boy that Ted had mentioned. Brenda gave him a little wave, but he pulled his head back and disappeared.

Brenda was open-mouthed at all she had seen, and actually David wasn't any less astonished. The house was completely as he remembered it but every corner had been beautifully restored. In David's memory the house was old with creaky floorboards and loose banisters which wobbled if you leaned on them. That was all different now. The house was like new; all the wood was gleaming white. The decoration, on the other hand, was completely different with lots of dark red, black and copper. Or was it gold? 'Gorgeous,' Brenda whispered in complete admiration. Without realizing that this was not the way the house looked when David had lived there she said, 'your mother had taste!'

'This wasn't done by Mother,' he just had time to say as they were shown into the living room.

Before them was an older man, slightly balding, in a spotless white linen suit. He gave a little bow, a nod of the head really and said, 'good afternoon. What can I do for you?'

Brenda walked closer to the bureau and stuck out her hand to shake the man's. 'My name is Brenda. We've come to tell you something important, a warning. This is David.' She pulled David forwards. 'David Kerzner.'

Abdel Amini's jaw almost hit the floor. 'Kerzner. Of the family Kerzner?'

David stepped out from behind Brenda and also shook Abdel's hand. 'Yes, sir. I am David Kerzner. I actually grew up in this house,' he said as he gestured around the room.

'That's…that's…' Abdel stammered while he tried to think of what to say and glanced down at the letter on his desk. 'That's…a coincidence.'

'A coincidence?'

'Ah, I mean…let's say, unexpected.'

David got the impression that the little man was shocked and was trying to get control again. Brenda always reacted far quicker to situations than he did and was far more spontaneous and impulsive. Without waiting for Abdel to say anything further she said, 'he's the son of Jonathan Kerzner.'

'Yes, I know… I mean, I know Jonathan. And that he had a son. And that's you?'

'Yes,' said Brenda, before David had chance to open his mouth. 'Yes, he grew up in this very house. That was his bedroom, up there.' She pointed upstairs.

'I understand that,' stammered Abdel Amini.

'Perhaps we've offended you. Perhaps we should have written you a note first?'

Abdel Amini responded by a reassuring gesture. 'Ah no, my girl. That's not what I mean.' He paused before he proceeded further. To David, he seemed a bit too smooth. 'No, my child. I'm so happy that I've met you. It's…' Abdel Amini was unsure about what he wanted to say. 'It's…'

'It's a very pleasant surprise, is what my husband's trying to say.' A slim, tanned woman in a long, dark dress which reached the floor, slid up to Abdel. She proudly stood beside him and slid her hand onto his arm. Pleasantly she said, 'I am Mrs. Sabagh. My husband has been rather surprised. You'll probably understand why if you know more of the background. Won't you please sit down? I'll ask if the tea's coming. You have to know that my husband has always looked out for you. For your father, mostly. Please sit and you'll be astonished at my husband's reaction.' Tannous turned around to face Abdel. 'You talk so much about Geneva and Jonathan and now you seem not at all glad. What's the matter, darling?'

Abdel Amini took his wife's hands off his shoulder, turned and walked towards his desk without saying a word. David and Brenda watched him, as did Tannous, waiting for his reaction. They didn't take a seat as Tannous had requested.

Abdel Amini fetched the letter from his bureau and walked back across the living room. For a moment or two he stood still, firstly looking David in the eyes, then turning his head round to see the concerned face of Tannous. Finally he met eyes with Brenda, as if this only had something to do with her. 'I'm sorry, young lady. I don't know how to say this.' He handed Brenda the first page of the letter, which David estimated to be about six pages long. Most of it was irrelevant to her. With a short, stabbing motion he indicated which paragraph to take note of. 'You see, my girl,' he continued softly. 'Jonathan Kerzner is dead. David's father died in the war. I've only known that for about a week, thanks to this letter concerning a business proposal from a mutual acquaintance.'

Brenda felt a chill down her spine as she recognized the signature of Sjoerd Colijn. 'He lives, then,' she mumbled unintelligibly.

David broke through the awkward silence. 'I know that my father's dead. He was shot during our escape from Amsterdam. He saved our lives by doing that. It's a long story.'

For a short time, the four looked at each other in turn, not knowing what to say. Eventually, Tannous insisted more forcefully that everyone take a seat. 'You've all got so much to tell each other.' Abdel Amini folded up the letter and put it in his inside pocket.

They moved to sit around a square coffee table which wasn't above knee height. Brenda couldn't wait to sit down, and in her haste she kicked Tannous' legs. She waved the page of the letter that she still had. 'This is exactly the reason why we've come today. I thought that if Colijn was still alive he'd be doing business with you. I just knew it.' Brenda held on to one of Tannous' shoulders. 'I was this man's secretary. This is exactly why I've come to warn your husband.'

Abdel Amini settled himself into an oversized armchair which was much too big for him. 'I know, my girl. Now don't upset yourself.'

David looked at the man beside him, the small, dark man in the white suit. Why in heaven's name would you wear a suit around the house? And why would anyone choose to do business with someone like Colijn? David had doubts about this man before they had come here, but he had let the feelings of Brenda and Ted overshadows his intelligence. Why should they warn this man who was now living in David's father's house? There was something nagging at David in the back of his mind. Was this man really as gracious as he seemed? Or was that just the normal way of a successful business man? Could he really be trusted?

'Are you really Jonathan's son?' the man asked.

David was hurt by the question but answered, 'yes, sir.'

David found it surprising that Brenda didn't distance herself from Abdel at all. Unasked, she began to tell all about Sjoerd Colijn, the farm, the book cave and their escape to Switzerland. Everything. Not always in a logical or chronological order. No one else could get a word in. Perhaps she said too much, especially towards Tannous, she spoke of how he, David, and his family had ended up in the book cave. Tannous listened attentively, her hand over her mouth, gasping with shock at what they had been through. Abdel's reaction was much the same as David's; he didn't have much to say.

Eventually, Brenda seemed to come to the end of her tale.

'Tell me again, slowly, from the beginning. When did you go to Jonathan's house?' Abdel asked Brenda.

'I didn't go in his house. I worked next-door. I've said this all already.'

'I thought that you worked on a farm?'

Brenda rocked impatiently back and forth on the armchair. 'That was before. Before I worked in Amsterdam. For Sjoerd Colijn.' Brenda addressed Tannous directly. 'Your husband's money is the issue here. He has the same contracts with Colijn that Jonathan had. I've seen them with my own eyes.' Impetuously she gestured towards Abdel Amini. 'I've a feeling he doesn't believe me. I feel like he's almost laughing at me.'

Abdel Amini did indeed laugh a little now and then. 'Now, now. It's not as bad as all that, my girl,' he reassured her. He tried to soothe her, and sure enough, by the end of that summer afternoon, calm was restored in Brenda's excited mind. Even David and Abdel were now talking more after drinking copious amounts of tea.

In the end, the afternoon was used to tell each other all they possibly could in such a short time. All? As spontaneous and excitable as Brenda was, she hadn't said a word about her attack on Sjoerd Colijn. For this reason, David wisely decided not to mention it either.

Abdel Amini also didn't seem to reveal all. By the end of the afternoon, David was convinced of that. He hadn't fully let on about his dealings with Sjoerd Colijn, past or future. He also seemed to ask too many questions about a black leather case, and became quite unpleasant about it.

'Does David know anything about that mysterious case that Sjoerd had?' Abdel tried to find out. 'I just can't believe that his father never spoke about it.' It seemed clear that the older man didn't trust David.

'Why would my father talk to me about it?'

'Out of interest.'

'Mr. Sabagh, I've already told you three times that I don't know anything about that trunk. It wasn't until after the war, when Brenda told me about it, that I even knew of the thing. Believe me; we were concerned with far more important things. In any case, everyone who travels has a case. I don't see why you're making such a fuss about this one.'

Brenda understood why. 'There weren't any clothes in that case. It was too heavy. Perhaps there was money in it.'

Now it was David's turn to laugh. That's why Abdel was so interested, why there were so many questions. No wonder he was curious. Money.

Little matters were concealed but not entirely washed away by the tea and fond memories. David and Brenda didn't get to find out much about Sjoerd Colijn, but they heard a great deal about Jonathan, and that felt good.

Finally, as it got closer to mealtime and the sun began to set, David and Brenda began their walk on an almost chilly evening. It wasn't the white-suited servant who showed them out, but Abdel and Tannous themselves who waved them off.

'Did you hear what they said?' Asked Brenda when they had walked far enough along the gravel to be out of earshot. 'We've been invited to come back again with Ted.'

'Yeah, I heard them.'

'And that we should drop by more often.'

David shrugged his shoulders. 'Yeah, I heard that too. And that we should keep our diary open in 1954, eight years away, for his son's sixteenth birthday.'

'Perhaps that's an important milestone for people from the Middle East,' wondered Brenda.

'It seems a bit ridiculous, if you ask me.'

'We will still go there again, though?'

'I hope so.'

'You sound enthusiastic.'

David came to a halt at the end of the driveway and looked at the lights shining within the stately house. He nodded towards the house. 'I'd gladly like to see the rest of the place, as Tannous had promised.' Brenda also turned to have one last look at the large windows in the half-light.

'We'll go at least one more time,' said Brenda, but as she did David felt her shiver. With one arm around David, and the other pointing forward she said, 'look there.' A hunchbacked man slid around the edge of the house. They both felt an icy cold. 'I'm…I'm frightened David. Do you think he's a thief?'

Strangely enough, David had the same anxious feeling. 'It's probably the gardener.'

'I don't know. He hasn't got a hump has he? No, I've got good intuition for things like this. This man is in danger. Mortal danger.'

The next day there seemed to be an abundance of sunshine and the butterflies danced about their garden. That day a remarkably well-kept, old car stopped in front of the door to Ted Bates' shop. It was the Ford Art Deco that was parked on the gravel drive outside Abdel Amini's yesterday.

The man in the white uniform with the gold epaulettes who had let Brenda and David in yesterday entered the shop. David was behind the counter trying to work his magic on a broken radio by trying to replace some of the components.

Although he recognized the man, David was surprised to see him holding out a set of keys between his thumb and forefinger. 'I'm to deliver this to you, sir,' the man said formally before David could ask him what he was there for.

'Keys?' Asked David.

'The car,' answered the Arab servant in remarkably good English. 'Mr. Sabagh wanted you to know that this was never included in the sale of the property and therefore belongs to you.'

David walked around the counter and stood by the man. 'Pardon? You mean that Art Deco is for me?'

'That is what my employer claims.'

David felt color rise in his face. 'But that's crazy. I can't believe it.'

'Mr. Sabagh expected that you would react this way.' He had lowered the keys but now held them up high again. 'Weren't you always crazy about this car before you went to Amsterdam?'

'To be honest, as a boy I used to dream about being able to drive this car.'

'Mr. Sabagh said something along those lines.'

'Your Mr. Sabagh can't possibly know what I dream.'

'He must have learned it from your father,' answered the servant.

David couldn't resist taking the keys for the beautiful machine. David wanted the car so badly. He repressed the question as to who he had to thank for it, his father or Abdel Amini. But that afternoon he simply enjoyed his drive with Brenda along the coastal road.

During the war, as a young mother, Huigje had come to see in the book cave the illustrated Catholic women's magazine. She copied the characteristic pictures of models smoothly. And if no one caught sight of her drawings, she would draw them naked.

Immediately after the war, Huigje got to hear of how women around Europe were becoming more emancipated; wearing the same clothes as men and even smoking cigars. She found out about a French car engineer called Louis Reard who wanted to show off his latest design in Paris with a woman in a bikini. They couldn't find a model that would be willing to wear such an immoral garment. Huigje wanted one thing; to learn to draw, better yet paint, slim women. She had to go to Paris.

Abdel Amini was enjoying the sun and the fresh, ocean air. 'If I sit here I feel like I can forget about the world and just let it pass me by,' he had told Tannous on similar occasions. This time is was the five-page letter that commanded his attention. 'I have a dilemma,' Abdel mused.

Sjoerd Colijn had put forward a good business proposal. He must really say yes, but he didn't want to. It was a yes and a no simultaneously. Something told him that he had to do this with Sjoerd, but why? It was pretty certain that he would lose money on this venture; exactly as the spontaneous young blond woman, without reservations, had warned him.

The idea of television for the people was a good one. Still his instincts told him that he had to count on it being a loss. Instinctively, Abdel took a walk around the gardens. Such walks in the past had always helped him with tricky situations like these, especially with the help of Nabib.

Inadvertently, Abdel found his friend who was dressed in his usual blue overalls. He released his hold on the wheelbarrow and walked over to the path where Abdel was. 'I have a problem,' Amini groaned.

Nabib laughed. The word 'problem' meant nothing to him. 'You, friend,' said Nabib softly.

Abdel Amini took the letter from out of his inside pocket. 'I have the opportunity to participate in a good idea. A new product that, according to my business partner, will take over the world. Television. I agree with him on that one. The annoying thing is that we have to invest together. I would rather do it alone. Otherwise, later we will be eating out of the same bowl.' Nabib listened to him, as well as to the gulls cawing above the ocean. 'The problem is…' Abdel Amini struggled to get things clear in his own mind. 'Hmm…what really is my problem?'

'Will he eat all your food?'

Abdel Amini looked surprised at his friend. 'Something like that. Yes. That's also, in fact, what the young woman meant.'

Ah well, if that's all the problem was, the solution was simple as far as Nabib was concerned. 'Then you can have my food.'

Abdel Amini looked up with big eyes. Nabib hadn't helped him yet…or maybe he had. The sun's rays burned down on him and he smelled the freshly cut grass. That was a good idea. Abdel patted Nabib on the shoulder and walked back to the house in a more cheerful manner than he had left it, crunching the gravel underfoot. There, waiting for him at the door was Tannous. 'And?' Tannous asked gently as they crossed through the door together.

'I have the feeling that I'm going to have to pay for my meal, but I won't get to eat anything,' he answered enigmatically.

Tannous looked at him, not understanding him at all. 'Ahh, maybe you can have the leftovers for a knock-down price,' she teased.

Abdel Amini came to a grinding halt in the middle of the hallway. Tannous had to stoop a little bit to get a kiss on the forehead. 'That is a lovely woman.'

It wasn't more than three years before David opened his first factory in America. 'Ted Bates Company' was emblazoned in gleaming characters on the gable. Three American experts had invented the transistor which, according to David, would enable the development in this field to accelerate.

The Ted Bates Company was one of the first factories that abandoned the use of radio bulbs and replaced them with transistors. The company was way ahead of its time. The devices, especially radios, became smaller. Unlike the televisions which increased in size exuberantly, until they were almost impossible to lift.

The factory was festively opened by none other than the mayor of Boston, who told his true tale of the discovery of the microwave to amuse the public. 'The microwave was discovered in 1945,' burgomaster James Michael Curley began to tell the public. 'One Percy LeBaron Spencer discovered that a bar of chocolate in his pocket had been melted by an electronic tube from a factory radar.' Mayor Curley carried on predicting a golden future for the Kerzner family here in Boston, one of the richest cities in the country. David thanked all the people present, the Mayor, and also Mr. DuMont, who had done everything possible to produce a television network.

'Ted Bates Company provides the glass and other components for the new apparatus by DuMont, who have always been ahead of their time, technologically speaking,' David explained in his interview with an audience of office and sales staff and production workers.

In the years that followed, Ted Bates opened more factories and sales offices along the Eastern Coast of the United States, such as Washington and New York.

New York—Boston 1951

Sjoerd Colijn had lived in the district of Manhattan for almost four years now in the same hotel. He had a living room and bedroom on the tenth floor; the luxury of the lift and the telephone made life relatively easy for him and brought the world to him. Like a dog, Divo Krlea brought the newspaper to him every evening as if he had no other job for him. It was four years ago that Sjoerd Colijn had, for the first time, frankly said to Divo, 'sooner or later I'm going to get trouble from my partner. I want you from time to time to keep an eye on him, so that you're prepared if we have to make the man disappear.'

Divo had easily found the large house in Boston and was even more delighted to see the tall, slim, dark-skinned woman that he hoped one day to be his. Sjoerd Colijn didn't interfere with the details.

For four years, Sjoerd Colijn had kept Divo busy with little jobs like putting pressure on people who wouldn't pay up, or making reluctant bankers see 'reason.' Meanwhile, Sjoerd never asked questions about his visits to the whores of New York or queried the results of his violent games. Sometimes, Divo even brought some of those women back to the hotel for Sjoerd, and Sjoerd prayed that God would forgive him.

'The one who pays gets what he wants,' was the tenet that Divo lived by. And he wasn't wrong.

It was evening. Divo Krlea knocked on the door and came in, as usual, with the folded newspaper under his arm. By this time, Sjoerd Colijn was sitting in a tailor-made wheelchair that he could propel using his own strength. 'It's going better for you,' said Divo Krlea, and he was right about that too. Colijn could walk, albeit with difficulty, and could now talk more and more easily, since a little aid was introduced which amplified his voice. The two men had gotten to know each other better and knew what they meant to each other.

'How's it going with the Palestinian?' Asked Divo in his hoarse voice, with genuine interest.

'It could be better,' answered Colijn honestly.

'It's been a couple of months since I had a good look at the house. Certainly it's time for me to pay them another visit.'

'That's for sure. And be sure to report back to me about the woman.' The two men had a common interest in Tannous; inaccessible until now and probably a thousand times cleaner than the prostitutes that they were used to. After his nocturnal visit, Divo Krlea had described her from top to toe, and anything that he'd forgotten, Sjoerd simply imagined. Abdel Amini was his prey: A descendant from an inferior and unbelieving race who in the bible, more than three thousand years ago, had given their women to the believers.

'Give me the paper, then.'

Divo Krlea did as he was told, then pulled up another chair and began looking at the sport pages in another newspaper. Colijn was only interested in politics and business. 'According to McCarthy there were fifty-seven communists and two hundred and five sympathizers working in the Ministry of Foreign Affairs.'

Divo muttered something unintelligible.

Colijn turned the page to the foreign news. 'Ah, South Koreans fear an invasion by North Korea. I promise you, if there's a fight, China, Cambodia and Vietnam are going to participate.'

'There can't be too much fighting for them with their funny slit eyes,' the Croat stated positively.

Sjoerd Colijn read further and Divo Krlea concentrated on the basketball results. It was quite some time before Sjoerd Colijn reached the business pages. Until that time it stayed relatively quiet in their hotel room, just the sound of the rustling newspaper pages. As soon as he began to read the business pages, however, he beat the centre of the page loudly. With difficulty he broke the silence with his mechanical-sounding voice. 'Look at that. More than seventy-five million people have seen their first trans-continental broadcast. This is the beginning. Now we're going to start making a profit.'

'Seventy-five million people,' was Divo's reaction, who wasn't sure if he believed it or not.

'A profit is sure to come. I know it,' cackled from Sjoerd's throat.

'And once you've got your profit, you can get rid of your partner.'

'That's how it'll be. However, for the time being we still need his money.' Sjoerd Colijn turned another page. 'More about the broadcast...'

Suddenly Colijn stiffened. Not that he made any noise, but it was so dramatic that Divo immediately looked at him in surprise. Colijn held the newspaper out before him. 'Good grief...What...what have we here?' Divo Krlea looked on patiently, waiting for the answer that Colijn would supply himself. There's a whole page devoted to the Ted Bates Company. Look at the photos.' Divo did his best, but couldn't really see anything from his position. 'Can you see that? That's the people I told you about!'

'What people?'

'That woman. The one who wanted to shoot me dead,' stammered Colijn. The Croat whistled through the gaps in his teeth and stood up out of his chair to come and have a better look. 'And it wouldn't surprise me if that man standing there is Jonathan's son. It certainly looks like him.'

In Boston, Abdel Amini held the same newspaper in his hand. He called for Tannous. 'Look at this, dear. Our young friend is in the newspaper.'

Tannous came closer and, with her straight back, elegantly sat next to Abdel on the arm of the chair. 'Let me see…Ah, you're right. How wonderful. What do they write about him?'

'The article's about the broadcast that went out to seventy-five million people and the companies that cooperated together to make that possible.'

'Read it to me.'

Abdel Amini took his glasses out of his top pocket to be able to read more accurately. 'Ted Bates Company was the Supplier behind the Scenes,' read the subheading in the business pages. And what followed what an extraordinary, heart-warming tale about a quickly-growing, young company. They'd already had a vision of what would be in the future while the war was still on. In fact, in simple terms it had already been planned out in a notebook by a boy of fourteen. Abdel read it out, unable to stop tears filling his eyes:

Four years ago, the promising swimmer David Kerzner returned to Boston from Amsterdam, where he had suffered greatly. The first thing he did was visit the little electronics shop of Ted Bates. There he retrieved and added notes to a notebook that he'd left behind seven years prior. The notebook contained his first pen strokes about the future of television. He noted his dreams which he has now come to realize.

David Kerzner predicts, just like the pioneers at DuMont, that within ten years every home will own a television. More importantly though, the young man wrote that 'television will change the world. There's a real chance of it honestly partitioning the wealth and resulting in world peace.' Currently only five percent of households own such an apparatus. The young man foresees that by 1955 this shall be fifty percent, from coast to coast. Seventy-five million watchers were able to see the broadcast by President Truman in September. This constitutes a threat to Hollywood, who could never dream of reaching such a number of people, but is an exciting development for politicians who see the advantage of reaching such a large portion of the population.

Kerzner jumped at the chance to become part of the market, especially as his company was one of the first to start using transistors instead of radio bulbs. His company has grown at a rapid rate, but, wealth is not the motivation for this young entrepreneur. David Kerzner acquired great knowledge in pitiable circumstances during the war. He studied a diverse range of subjects; theology, technology, economic studies. That's how his vision matured. Television would be a way for people to have insight into the difficult circumstances others were living in. In turn, this should motivate the world to work for equality; it could encourage tolerance. Broadcasters such as NBC, CBC and DuMont will not only broadcast entertainment shows, but also news items highlighting, for example, the horrors of war. This way, perhaps politicians will be able to avoid war at all times. 'Then at last maybe we can have the world peace that everyone desires,' David Kerzner told this newspaper. When we asked the young entrepreneur how pictures could be transmitted from Europe, China or Africa, he simply laughed. 'For that we will use satellites which circle the earth. But I can't tell you any more about that because I don't want to give anything away to my competitors; RCA, Zenith and Cobagh.'

David Kerzner has started out on his career as a remarkably wise man. 'My wife and I started working in Ted Bates' shop in 1946. It went very well, but there wasn't enough turnover to contemplate opening any factories. Then, six months later, we were suddenly paid one hundred thousand dollars into our account. In fact, I still get a monthly allowance from the same account. It came from Switzerland. We suspect that it was an inheritance from my father. However, due to the banking secrecy laws in Switzerland we aren't able to trace it. My father lost his life in the Second World War, as did six million other Jews. Probably then, he must have arranged these funds before the war. For one hundred thousand dollars, four years ago, you could build ten houses; therefore you could also build a factory. We've been very lucky. There must often be other entrepreneurs with even better ideas, but no capital.'

The young man is now twenty-seven. What does he expect from the coming fifty years?

'There are only a few people who believe me, but I believe that by the end of the twentieth century, every house around the world will have a television. As well as being able to see people all around the world, you'll also be able to talk to them on the telephone. And … in twenty-five years' time, we'll land on the moon!'

That last remark we assume to be a joke but, going by this young man's track record, you never know. He could be right. Kerzner suggests that we meet together in twenty-five years' time. He'll bring his notebook, where he's written all his predictions, and we'll see who's right.

Abdel Amini put the newspaper down on his lap and looked up into the face of Tannous. 'That David and his notebook!'

In New York, Sjoerd Colijn also laid the paper on his lap. 'That notebook. We have to have it.'

Divo Krlea muttered that he'd already thought as much. Sjoerd Colijn recognized the same agitation that he felt in the eyes of the Croat. 'And what's more,' he whispered, even though there wasn't anyone else in the room that could hear them. 'That man and woman.' Colijn looked at the harsh figure of his co-worker and thought carefully. 'Do what you want with the woman, and then kill her, in the same way as she wanted to kill me.'

Huigje had been living in the mill in the village of Durgerdam. She no longer lived there but continued to use it as a studio. Now she was living in the home of Elsbeth and Jennifer. The two spinsters had died six months ago and had left her their house in their will. 'This house isn't going to go to the church,' the two had told her when they were on their deathbed, saying their farewells.

The proximity of the church would prove to be a blessing to the sisters in their later life. Huigje held to the belief that it gave the two oldsters some hope and comfort. Perhaps, then they'd be able to just pass away peacefully.

That same peace and security Huigje missed on a daily basis, but especially on a Sunday. Then all the churchgoers would pass her door, and not one of them would say a greeting to her. In that church-going village, Huigje was in the minority, and she felt alone because of it. That held her back from crossing the little bridge and visiting the church. Actually, she only felt contempt for the people there.

Nobody spoke to her directly, not even to ask where her father was. For a while now, he hadn't been seen at church on Sunday. This was a cause of gossip which Huigje found out about through the children who spoke to Harm. Some suspected that her father had been arrested by the Germans, or were convinced that he wasn't arrested by Germans, but by Dutchmen, and he was now imprisoned in a Dutch jail. Others were under the impression that he'd fled to Argentina, or was now living in America.

'Child, let them think what they want,' recommended Elsbeth and Jennifer graciously. 'Leave the past behind you.' And gradually, Huigje learned to do just that.

It didn't help matters as she developed into an accomplished painter and began to dress rather eccentrically and headstrongly.

'Why do you never go to church, Mother?' Goodness. Harm didn't speak much but, when he did, it was always about a difficult subject.

'I don't have the need,' Huigje lied.

'It hasn't anything to do with Betsy, then?' Was Harm starting to grow up and be aware of things that had nothing to do with technology?

'What do you mean, Betsy?' Huigje pretended incomprehension.

'Well, she wears trousers. And she smokes; even on the street!'

'Is there something wrong with that?'

'No, but I don't see any other women wearing men's clothes and smoking going to church.'

Betsy was so different from Elsbeth and Jennifer, although they dressed flamboyantly too. Betsy usually wore tight trousers and a jacket. Her hair was closely cropped which looked like more of a man's style than a woman's. Betsy claimed that she was truly emancipated, and she had an opinion about everything. She was almost forty, but the strange thing was, she seemed less lively and less highly spirited than the two spinsters were even in their last days. The two were strictly religious but nevertheless very tolerant. Betsy, on the other hand, seemed to live in complete freedom but was extremely hard-hearted towards the church and, in fact, anyone who didn't agree with her point of view. That did cause Huigje some concern: Harm must never be like that.

'Could you see me wearing long trousers and going to church?'

'Ach, as long as you don't start smoking!'

The large factory of the Ted Bates Company began to be enveloped by the darkness of night. The white walls became bleak, being poorly lit by only a few lamps. The two-story office building that was attached to the factory had its own entrance. A little step led to a double-glazed door. Beyond that was a reception desk, which wasn't manned at this time in the evening.

David was working this night in his office above the entry. If you walked out from his office, along the hall, you would find a gallery from which you could see the production staff. The factory was designed so that office staff and production staff couldn't see what each other were doing.

This night, most of the production staff were still there. Overtime had become the norm since the sale of televisions had increased so much. David had seen a dramatic increase since the positive publicity in the newspaper article about him. That was September, and now that October was nearly over, they had to think about the increase that was sure to come up to Christmas. Of course, David had worries. Many sets had been sold, but there were many customers who were failing to make payments. In particular DuMont was struggling with their arrears at the moment, but of course the salary costs continued.

David now sat at his desk, bent over some market analysis. The company of the already legendary DuMont had used too much of its capital. DuMont didn't only sell televisions, they also produced programs for the viewers to watch. However, their programs reached too few people as they transmitted on an unfavorable frequency. At the moment, they were still the fourth largest network in America. The question was could they stay that way? Shareholders were starting to mutter and grumble. They felt that DuMont was too busy with too many different projects; production and sale of televisions, production of programs, as well as the transmission of them. More and more shareholders wanted to split the company up and sell parts of it. One anonymous shareholder had leaked to the press that this was likely to happen. For David it was essential that the sale and production of DuMont televisions remained intact.

Ted Bates Company provided many of the components. There was a danger that this part of the company would be bought by someone else too. Would the new owner want to continue working with David's components?

Another file lay beside the report about DuMont. David stood up, walked to the other side of his office, poured himself and glass of fresh water and sat down again. He opened the file marked 'Competitors' in large, black letters.

NBC and CBC were described as 'exhausted.' David comforted himself that he wouldn't have to battle against them; they were too large for him to be able to conquer. Fortunately, making and transmitting programs was their core business, not the production and sale of televisions. Zenith was a large manufacturer: David could see the possibility that they would want to take over the factories and sales offices of DuMont. But he was doubtful that DuMont would want to sell to their largest competitor. There were also other interested parties around the corner, like the Dutch company Philips, and then there were smaller companies similar to his, Cobagh for example, who also subcontracted to make components. David didn't know much about Cobagh except that, if DuMont were to transfer to them, he would be put out of business.

David sat and thought, with his elbows on the desk and his head in his hands, while it became fully dark outside. The sounds in the factory escaped his notice.

Suddenly David shot out of his chair, aware of a strange smell and warmth under his feet. At the same moment he heard cries coming from the direction of the factory. Alarmed, David ran out of his door and along the hall to the gallery. A large part of the factory was enveloped in smoke, only the high ceiling being visible. He could hear the sound of people choking as they tried to make their way out of the building.

In a flash, a large section of the gallery became seized by flames. At that moment a large man started running along the gallery in David's direction. 'It's alright,' David called to him. 'Look after the people downstairs. It's only me up here.' The large man didn't seem to take any notice and continued running at David, ignoring the flames licking at his feet. Now the man was almost where David stood. David gestured at him to stop but the man brutally barged past him as if he wasn't there.

David's head flew against the wall and for a few seconds he couldn't see anything. Thankfully, David regained his senses, gave his head a scratch and stood up. David figured that the man, who must no doubt work for him, must be in a blind panic. All the other offices accessible from the gallery were locked so David realized the man must have gone into his office. If the fire increased any further he would be trapped in there.

The gallery and the hall filled with smoke; the same suffocating stench that had broken David out from his thoughts earlier. Quickly David ran to follow the man, feeling the heat of the flames as they consumed the woodwork in the gallery. He noticed that the staircase was in flames. The only possible place to go was his office, behind the man. There was the only window.

David rushed to the door of his office with one hand over his mouth. The smoke had filled his room. Through the smoke and darkness he could just see the man even though he was only a couple of paces away. The wall set alight and the red glow made the image of the man clearer. That's when David realized something strange was going on.

The huge man leaned over David's desk and opened the drawer with one hand and took something out of it with the other. It was so odd to see him doing this rather than be anxious about saving his life. The man had something wrapped about his face to keep out the fumes. He raised his right hand to look at what he'd found in the drawer and then laughed. Immediately then he turned to leave the office by the door that he'd entered it.

David was doubled over; there was almost no air at all. Now he had to try and think of a way to get out. This employee hadn't asked to be saved. At that moment, the other guy was on top of him and crashed something heavy on to David's head. David staggered. Without letup the man struck again and again. David instinctively raised his arms to fend off the subsequent blows. With his full weight and all the effort he could muster he dove into the abdomen of the man to try and knock him off balance. It didn't seem to affect the man at all.

David had to decide: keep trying to fight or get out of there. The man reached inside his jacket and pulled out something which had to be a gun. David threw himself on the floor and rolled over to the corner. He heard shots firing in his general direction. A large piece of the ceiling suddenly dropped to the floor right beside him. On his other side, David could see the legs of the man coming towards him. 'I have to get out of here,' was the only thought on David's mind.

This whole time, air was disappearing from the room. 'If I don't get a breath of air soon, I've had it,' David knew. He struggled to his feet and stumbled across the smoke-filled room until he got to the closed window at the back of his office. The office was now completely ablaze. In a last-ditch attempt David, seized the typewriter and threw it out the window. The fire raged with the influx of oxygen. David knew he had to go through the window of his first-floor office. 'It can only be about three meters up,' he thought. 'If I'm lucky, I'll land on my back and survive.' Without hesitation, David launched himself out of the window.

He was lucky. Under his window a car was parked which broke his fall. He landed on his back and slid down the car on to the bonnet. His burned body was pierced in several places by shards of glass, but he was alive. Employees ran over to assist him and drag him to safety. They'd been watching the blaze and had seen him tumbling from the window.

Later in the hospital, David realized that he'd effectively escaped death twice that evening. He was so lucky. His left arm had been broken in the fall, and several lacerations had required stitches. 'So, you're saying that you broke the glass and then jumped through?' Asked the two officers who sat by his white metal hospital bed. Brenda sat on the other side of the bed and listened to what David and the policemen had to say. 'There are other questions we'd like to ask you too.'

'Yes, of course,' David said. 'But can I ask why?'

The older man explained. 'Were you having any problems? Or did you have any enemies? I don't know what you suspect about it, but it's possible that the fire which brought you here was started deliberately.' David considered what they said and nodded. The agent took a notepad from his breast pocket. 'Let's hear your side of the story first, Mr. Kerzner.'

David told them all about the evening, his collision with the large man and the shots that he'd fired at him. 'Did you know the man?' The policeman asked.

'I thought that it must have been an employee from the factory. As far as I was concerned it was just a fire—you don't expect there to be any outsiders. But he can't have been an employee, it's logical that it must have been someone else. Someone I've never seen before.'

In New York, Sjoerd Colijn was sitting in his hotel room at twilight. He looked at Divo Krlea who stood before him, legs apart and hands by his sides. 'So then, that's everything.' He took the notebook out of the hand of the Croat. 'And the Jew?'

Divo Krlea shrugged his shoulders. 'There was a man at the office. He perhaps was the Jew.'

'Did you kill him?'

'I don't know. It was difficult to see clearly in the heavy smoke. I fired at him twice, and then I had to go.'

Colijn thumbed through the book, not really reading it, and thought. The Croat didn't move from where he stood and waited for his next instruction. Colijn slammed the book shut and looked at Divo. 'You have to go back. First look in Boston to see if the Jew's still alive. If he is, then get the woman and, if you don't get him at the same time, get him next.'

'Okay,' the Croat said without emotion, as if he was being given a simple shopping list. 'But I have one problem.'

'And that is?'

'Money.'

'We've already settled that.'

'Yes, but that was four years ago and now the work is much harder.'

Colijn hesitated for a moment. Then he reacted smoothly, 'that's true. Now they've had a warning. I will sort things out so that tomorrow evening I can pay you some extra. Then you can tell me if that is sufficient.'

The next day Sjoerd Colijn went by taxi to the bank, where the bank clerk wheeled him from the street to his safe-deposit box. That same evening, when Divo arrived as usual to bring the newspapers, Colijn gave him a rough diamond from out of Jonathan's black leather trunk. 'Find out how much it's worth. It should be sufficient. Do what you want with it, it's yours.'

In the German region of Sinsheim, a small borough between slightly sloping hills where grain was cultivated, Margaret and Heinrich were enjoying life. They rented a three-roomed apartment with a small balcony on the third floor of a simply constructed, yellow building.

It was impossible in the days immediately after the war to correspond with David and Brenda, but since 1951 it had become relatively simple. David had already given Margaret Ted's address in Boston. 'I don't know if we'll be living there, but we'll be somewhere in the neighborhood,' he'd said at their emotional farewell. 'In any case, we'll definitely be able to pick up any mail from there.' Letters took a long time to cross the Atlantic by boat. Things were greatly accelerated, though, with the introduction of the blue paper and stamps which indicated they were to be transported by 'Airmail'.

Margaret read that David and Brenda had married soon after arriving in Boston, also that they were living above Ted Bates' shop and that they were expecting their second child already.

In the first of the long letters that arrived in Boston from Europe, the situation was described of how things were now that the war was over. For the first time in his life, Heinrich didn't feel secure. There were still many fanatical Nazis, who accused anyone who gave themselves up to the Allies as traitors. Heinrich was pleased to give himself up to the Allies and had therefore become a target for these fanatics. He was too old to fight back against his deluded countrymen. But luck was on his side; just before his German colleagues were going to execute him on the 4th May, a group of Canadian military intervened.

After a while, Margaret and Heinrich learned from David's letters that Abdel Amini Sabagh was living in David's old home, which started Heinrich's correspondence with Abdel. In these letters, Heinrich was brought up to date about Abdel's son and what had happened to the black trunks that he himself had brought to Geneva. 'Our case is still waiting to be given to my son, Jassar,' Abdel let him know. 'Perhaps it would be better not to tell David anything about the other trunk that was supposed to be his.' Heinrich agreed with Abdel's suggestion. It wouldn't serve any purpose to tell him, it would only bring dissatisfaction.

David didn't often write to Germany but, initially, Brenda did. 'We've visited the house where David used to live. It's splendid. I naturally wondered if it would somehow work out that the man might be willing to help David. Or perhaps he might know if there were other properties that David should have inherited. But all in vain. My darling husband wants to conquer the world with his own strength.'

Every new letter that came from America to Sinsheim added another detail to the success of David's ambition to conquer the world. In a letter in 1947, Margaret read how one hundred thousand dollars had suddenly appeared in David's account and how, because of this, he'd been able to advance the business of Ted Bates. 'They don't need the money in the case,' Heinrich noted. He wrote as much to his Palestinian friend to try and put his mind at rest.

As time progressed it seemed as if David was really doing well for his family. He opened factories and shops all along the east coast of the United States and Brenda kept the readers in Germany aware of every development. Eventually, the letters between Margaret and Brenda became less frequent and mostly talked about Brenda's little one and Margaret's son, who had been named after David. Margaret told Heinrich about Brenda expecting their second child; about the attack on David's factory and David himself, Brenda hadn't mentioned a word.

The article about David and Ted Bates Company hadn't only been read by Abdel Amini and Sjoerd Colijn. The interview had far-reaching, positive consequences. 'Most readers would skip such stories,' said Ted Bates. And he was right: the average man on the street hadn't read it and, as a result, David was still largely unrecognized in Boston. However, the article had caused a stir amongst the people he did business with and his competitors.

Not long afterwards, David was invited to give a lecture at Harvard, and by the end of 1951 had been put forward as a candidate for Businessman of the Year.

On one particular day David, held up by the snow, hadn't arrived home until half past six o'clock. Brenda was dying to tell him about a phone call. 'Quick, now. You've got half an hour to get ready. We're being picked up for a television interview.'

At seven o'clock a large, black Cadillac stopped outside the shop. Ted Bates was going to baby-sit little Christie and they waved the two off. On the luxurious back seat, Brenda held on to David's hand and the uniformed driver slowly drove them out of Boston. The man looked in his rear view mirror at the couple on the other side of the glass that separated them and laughed. 'You should look forward to later too,' said Brenda softly. 'As we drive back tonight I'll expect you to show your gratitude for having such a clean white shirt to put on so quickly. That'll look great on TV.'

The car sped out of the city. David leaned forward and tapped on the glass. 'Where are we going to?' The driver seemed not to hear. David knocked harder and louder. 'Hello…can you hear me? Where are we going to?' Brenda pulled his jacket to pull him back. She gestured next to her, between the seats and the floor, where a fine, almost invisible, mist was being sprayed into the car. Almost at the same moment, David felt himself get dizzy. 'Hey…driver…don't you hear me? There's something strange going on here.' The driver continued to look right ahead without a hint of a response.

Brenda retched. The car drove along a lonely road through a wooded area which was free of snow, where little white lights marked the edges of the road. David began thumping as hard as he could on the glass. It didn't give way, just like the chauffeur. 'Give me your shoe,' he shouted at Brenda. She didn't respond. Instead, she slumped sideward and slid off the seat. He dropped one arm and tried to reach Brenda's feet. At that moment he understood why Brenda had apparently fainted. Rancid air burned in his nose and David could only just manage to get Brenda's stiletto-heeled shoe from her foot. With a mighty swing David beat the glass between him and the driver. It marked the glass but didn't break it. David felt his strength decrease dramatically. The next swing didn't affect the glass at all.

David fought desperately to stay conscious. He put forth extreme effort to try and crack the glass of the car door but he didn't even reach it. Before he could make the shoe reach the door his body gave up. Then there was just blackness.

In Boston, the winters are notoriously cold, especially when it's frozen and the sea-breeze comes in. This particular morning, frost had covered the windows of Ted Bates' shop.

Ted was worried. Christie had slept through the night without a problem, and she'd happily eaten her cornflakes without a hitch. But that wasn't the problem. Ted paced nervously in the kitchen where he'd put Christie in her high chair. The stove here meant this room warmed quickest. Any other day, Brenda would have stoked it up before Ted had even woken up and come through to the kitchen in his pajamas.

That was the first alarm bell. He waited for an hour and Brenda still hadn't come down. Something wasn't right. When he'd checked that they weren't still in bed, Ted wondered to himself as to whether he ought to call the police. 'They'll probably laugh at me. Young people do sometimes stay away for the night.'

It's true that did happen. You could also say it was fairly common, but not for David and Brenda. Therefore, Ted knew for certain that something was definitely wrong. First, he'd try and reach the NBC studios.

At roughly the same time in his hotel room, Sjoerd Colijn took his third phone call that morning. This time the large Bakelite horn didn't produce the voice of an investments consultant, but the gravelly voice of the Croat, Divo Krlea. 'We're at stage one.'

Sjoerd Colijn knew exactly what he meant. 'You have them? Both? Are they…?' Colijn searched for an alternative word to 'dead.' 'What kind of condition are they in?'

'They're alive. They're sitting here,' answered the Croat.

'What do you mean?'

'I mean they're still alive. You can see them if you want.'

Colijn, without anything to say, held the mouthpiece away from his nervous head. 'Are you still there?' he asked when he brought the horn back round to his mouth.

'Yes,' muttered the Croat. 'I'm waiting.'

Colijn's voice wasn't strong at the best of times, and his nerves didn't help. 'I'm coming to you,' he croaked. He felt his bladder press and felt desperate to go to the bathroom because of nervous excitement. 'I'm coming to you,' he repeated louder, his voice still shaking.

The Croat's ugly face contorted into a grimace. This wasn't according to plan, but he'd obviously done well not to kill the two yet. They were his boss's obsession. He had to see them, had to be there when he killed them. 'How are you going to come?'

'You just keep them alive. I can be brought there.'

'Travel isn't simple for you,' Divo growled.

'Don't you worry. I'm coming. Where can I find you?'

'Let me tell you,' muttered Divo, afraid to give any more information than absolutely necessary over the telephone.

'Then I'll see you there.'

'When?'

'Not today. Possibly tomorrow. Be careful now; make sure you look after them.'

'That won't be a problem.'

'Good, then,' Colijn sighed and put down the telephone. Then he said more definitely, 'you'll see me soon.'

The Croat was about to hang up, thinking about how he would organize the coming days. 'Wait!' The phone crackled loudly in Divo's ear. 'There's one more very important thing.' The Croat listened patiently. 'Don't talk about me. Don't say who I am. Leave that entirely secret. Do you hear me? Don't talk about my work. Don't talk about television.'

Divo knew exactly what Sjoerd Colijn meant. He promised he wouldn't say a word to the two prisoners. The smallest hint would be too much.

Brenda had recovered slightly and was sitting, half anaesthetized still, tied to a simple wooden chair, her back towards David who was a little ways behind her. Outside it was light. Inside the old barn without windows it was still dark, even though an open fire about six meters away from them did give off a faint red glow. A primitive chimney took the smoke out through the roof. Brenda estimated that it had been about an hour before Divo Krlea came back. The man was large and heavy. He looked like a foreigner. A large, faded, grey winter coat hung off his shoulders almost down to the floor. One side of the coat seemed shorter than the other; an optical illusion caused by his humped back. Dragging his feet, the man walked round to Brenda and she was surprised to see the man who stood, legs astride, before her. The crossed eyes, flat nose and crooked mouth with several missing teeth, seemed terrifying. Brenda felt her breath catch in her throat. There was no point calling for David. She'd been trying that for the past hour.

'What do we have to do for you to get out of here?' She could only talk with difficulty. It felt like she'd drunk too much brandy. It was, of course, a result of being drugged in the car. She tried again. 'What do you want? What have you got to do with David?'

Divo looked at Brenda. A scornful smile played on his lips. 'I know what you're thinking. You're thinking how you can get out of here. You're wrong. I'm watching you. With this eye I can't see anything.' He reached up to his left eye and removed the glass eye from its socket. He held it up to Brenda's face. 'But with my right eye I can see you just perfectly. Behave yourself, don't cause any trouble and if you're lucky, we can make love with each other.'

Brenda felt a sickening burning sensation rise through her. She anxiously swallowed, resisting the urge to vomit and looked at the man in his right eye, unable to hide her fear. 'I'm…I'm expecting,' she stammered.

'Four months, aren't you?' The man laughed, sordidly.

'How…how did you know that?'

'I know everything about you.' The man straightened his back. 'You behave for the next few days. The way you act will determine how you spend your final hours,' he said as he walked off.

He returned a little later with a crutch in his hand. He placed it next to the fire. Without taking off his coat he allowed his huge frame to fall to the ground in front of the fireplace. He lay there watching Brenda squirm in the tight ropes; he watched her movements with pleasure.

David still didn't move.

Ted Bates had turned the card over on the shop door to say 'Closed.' He had rung NBC, but they knew nothing about an interview. Now Ted dialed the number of the police force.

Sjoerd Colijn had rung the taxi company, where he'd had a car specially converted for him. Next to the driver a huge, steel chair had been constructed which could be swung to the outside. Colijn was able to wheel himself from the hotel to the car, where an attendant was waiting holding open the door. For short distances, for example from the chair to his bed or from the wheelchair to the car, he could just about walk with the aid of two crutches. The lid of the boot had been raised to that his wheelchair could easily be stored there. If he wished, Colijn could also sit in the back of the taxi without getting out of his wheelchair.

The taxi was waiting outside the front door at four o'clock, just as Colijn had ordered. The door at the curbside was pleasantly being held open by a heavily made up woman of about forty years of age, although she was obviously doing her best to appear younger. About half an hour earlier, she had met Colijn in his room, shook his hand with her own slim attractive hand with long painted nails, and picked up his cases. Colijn had observed already how she smiled at him with her narrow red mouth, without the reservation that women usually had for an invalid such as him. She wore a sort of uniform; scarlet red with a tight skirt which sat just above her knees and a jacket which fastened to the top with a collar which stood up.

In the hotel room, she lifted both the cases at the same time and walked to the door, giving Colijn the opportunity to see her dark nylons, the seam of which disappeared up the hem of her skirt. The skirt was tight around her hips and Colijn enjoyed watching them swing from side to side as she swayed out of the room. Her voice was low and husky. 'I'll be taking you all the way to Boston.' At that moment Colijn decided that on this occasion he would travel in the front of the car, next to her.

It was a full two hours before David began to recover slowly in the large, cold barn. Just like Brenda, he felt the ropes tight around his chest that fastened him to the chair. He realized that she was also tied, as he was, behind him. Their feet weren't tied, and David felt that this was good for them. The chair he was sitting on seemed so old and rotten it looked as if it could collapse at any moment.

Brenda sensed David recover. In the meantime, she'd been able to have a good look around the barn. They were sitting in front of the hearth, the fire in which had been roughly stoked in the middle. They looked at the tall, shoddily built barn doors, which hung crookedly in the doorways that had not been closed properly. The roof was made of roughly hewn pieces of wood, supported by huge, round beams covered in knots from where the branches had been lopped off. On one side, there was a hay loft piled high with hay.

The fire glowed in front of Brenda. Even though it was some distance in front of her, her face still burned. She could hardly feel her hands behind her back, though, because of the cold. She had complained of this to the man, but he didn't take any notice.

Later in the afternoon, it became a little warmer. Every now and then, the man went outside briefly, leaving the door open behind him. Brenda saw the snow.

Late in the afternoon, the man couldn't take it any longer. He'd made a decision. Without saying a word he stood up, walked to David and Brenda and checked the ropes which bound them. Afterwards, with uneven steps, he walked through the door. Brenda and David heard him start the car outside and disappear.

'What does that mean?' Asked David, twisting his head round awkwardly to try and see Brenda about five meters away.

'Do you think he might have decided to leave us alone?'

'I don't think so. We must try and get out of here, before he returns.'

'You're joking.' Brenda looked at the tight ropes around their bodies.

'We have to try something. That was the man who tried to kill me in the factory. He's not going to let us live this time. Try to kick your shoe to me.' Brenda looked at the one shoe that she still wore. 'If you manage to hook it on your toe, you'll be able to kick it high. You'll need to twist your chair round as far as possible to face me.' She tried jerking her chair around, the ropes painfully cutting in to her, making her feel as if she would suffocate.

When she was far enough around, using the ground she wiggled the shoe off her foot and hooked the ankle strap on to her toe. 'That's it now, now's your chance.' Brenda realized that she had one shoe, one attempt. She carefully swung her right leg back and forth and then gave a hard swing. The shoe dropped off too early and landed on the ground. With a lot of effort, the ropes embedding themselves further into her flesh, she tried to shuffle the chair forwards again on two legs.

'Thank goodness. Let's have another go.' She gripped the shoe between her toes. On the highest point of the swing she let it go. The shoe thudded to the ground, out of David's reach.

Seeing Brenda walking the chair on two legs had given David an idea. He swung his dilapidated chair the way Brenda had done. David twisted with all his force to try and separate the back of the chair from the seat. 'Hold on, love.' Eventually the back-rest and legs broke apart from the seat. He tumbled to the floor, but now at least he could stand. He walked over to the shoe, fell to his knees and with some contortion, was able to pick up the shoe. Using the sharp stiletto heel as a lever, he started to prize the ropes. It took him at least an hour, but eventually he worked the ropes. Partly stumbling, partly crawling, the exhausted David made his way to Brenda, bathed in sweat. The criminal who had abducted them was not back yet.

Divo Krlea didn't give them a moment's thought. It took him three quarters of an hour to reach the edge of the city and to find something edible. The small shops were now closed. The self-service shops were open—there you would walk around with a basket and collect what you needed, but people would see him and remember him. Everywhere where he went people took notice of him. Ah, what did he care?

However, he couldn't find such a self-service shop, and for this reason he stopped at a petrol station that had a small restaurant attached. The

Croat parked the car, which had far too little leg-room for him, and squeezed himself out. Dark was falling, and the snow in the parking lot had been cleared. The establishment was lit up with red lighting, and decorations hung in the window. He knew it was risky to go in, but he granted himself a bite. The job was nearly all sewn up.

At the bar, a woman in a white uniform with a pink apron passed him a plate with a hamburger with lettuce and ketchup. At the moment, two men of about forty stepped inside. Without taking off their jackets, they sat down at the same bar.

'A black Cadillac,' Divo heard the smallest of the two men say. 'With the driver bent over the wheel with a knife in his back.' Divo understood that the man he'd used to pick up his two victims had been found. He hadn't dared to let him live, afraid that he'd later be able to point the finger at him. The Croat finished the last few bites of his hamburger, ordered two to take away and reached into his pocket for some money to settle up. After a visit to the toilet, Krlea made his way out into the cold to get back in the car. He grinned. No doubt his two captives would have wet themselves by now. In the prisoner of war camps where he'd worked, he'd made people pee themselves from fear. The man and woman who he'd left in the barn were brave and calm, but nature will take its course. And to add to that discomfort, the woman was now tired and hungry. Divo Krlea knew that she would break when he returned.

Sjoerd Colijn ordered his chauffeur to stop at a motel between New York and Boston. There he took two rooms. However, the thin woman didn't make use of the other room. She wheeled him in his chair to his poorly arranged room, helped him from his chair and put Sjoerd Colijn on the bed. Without saying a word, she stripped right in front of him.

'What now?' Brenda whispered, although that wasn't necessary.

'Come.' David raised his arm, the blood from the friction burns that the ropes had caused appearing through his clothes. He put his arm around Brenda and drew her towards the fire. 'What do you think?'

'We have to make sure we get away before that man comes back.'

'In the cold?'

'What else…?'

'Would we survive that? You in the snow, with one shoe with a high heel? And me in my white shirt, which would look so good on the television?'

'We simply have to.'

'I don't know about that.'

'What then?'

David thought. 'We need a car.'

'That's a good one.'

David took firm hold of Brenda's shoulders. 'Listen. What would you think in his place?'

'That we'd be long gone and must have run far away.'

'That's exactly what we'll make him think.'

'What do you mean, David? Let's get going. Then we'll have a head-start. We haven't got any time to lose.'

David resolutely shook his head. 'No, we're not going. We're going to stay here.'

Brenda felt her heart beat in her throat. 'Stay here,' she moaned, short of breath.

David motioned upwards. 'Of course. We'll put a ladder up against that beam and hide in the hay. The man will look for us outside and we'll try and start his car.'

'Do you know how to do that?'

'What?'

'Start a car without keys?'

'No, we'll have to figure that out there. The key simply is to make an electrical contact. There must be another way to do that.'

'In the dark? Come now, David. Let's just go. I'll be okay bare-foot. We'll run. It'll keep us warm.'

'You're right,' David said to the relief of impatient Brenda. 'Put my jacket over your dress. Don't struggle.' With Brenda's hand in his, he rushed to the door. 'Wait.' He stood still at the large door which he'd pushed open. 'What...what if we just hide ourselves here and forget about the car?' Brenda looked at him. 'Listen, we could climb up there. The man wouldn't expect that and would look for us outside. He'll not be able to find us, and he'll not want to hang around for fear that we've called the police. He won't want to wait for them to arrive.'

Brenda thought quickly with David. His plan sounded absurd, but it was the best option so far. 'Come on then,' said David. 'Let's go back.'

Brenda let go of David's hand. 'Not yet.' With strength she pushed the barn doors further open. 'He has to think that we've escaped.'

'You're right.' An icy wind blew in. It was no weather for being in just a shirt or barefoot. It was now almost dark and was snowing still. David and Brenda walked back to the barn. David took hold of the wooden ladder.

'No ladder, you blockhead. He'll see it.'

They looked around. 'There.' Along one of the sides, there was a barrel. 'If I stand on it I can climb up. Then I'll pull you up.' David picked up two large pieces of firewood from beside the fire. 'You never know. If he finds us out, we've got a weapon.' Brenda took hold of a rusty iron staff which was bored though in several places with screws. David threw it up to the loft. Rapidly David jumped on to the barrel and, athletic as he was, had no difficulty getting up to the hayloft. Lying on his stomach, he reached down to Brenda and helped her to clamber up. Once up there, they huddled up close to each other pulling the straw completely over them, grateful for the protection from the cold.

Abdel Amini sat behind his large bureau and wrote, in English, a letter to his friend Heinrich. A small electric lamp with a transparent green shade shone on the paper: 'I don't know how you are faring, my old friend. Since I turned sixty, it seems as if all my questions from my youth have come back. Daily I ask Allah what we're doing this all for.'

'Here in Boston it's snowing. Not as bad as it had in '47, when lorries with shovels in front had to clear all the roads, but still… It's really cold and, different than earlier, I don't find I can keep myself warm by just keeping busy. Nabib tries to keep the gravel path free of snow. I often ask myself which of us is the happiest.'

'Since Churchill scared us to death talking about the "Iron Curtain" and my American friends find it necessary to have nuclear testing, I'm afraid that our children will roll from one war into another. Not to mention Korea and the hatred and animosity between the inhabitants of Palestine and Jerusalem. That doesn't bode well for our children.'

'I've learned to invest my money in weapons no longer. Do you know, good friend, it doesn't help anything. Satellites and those big, blue computers of IBM are what I believe in now. Are they a peaceful alternative? The businesses that I invest in get most of their custom from defense, just like Jonathan and I made our money in the past.'

'How is it going for your little boy? Jonathan's son is doing well. He has the business instincts of his father, but has a different outlook on life.

Perhaps he got that from his mother. The boy is far more idealistic than his father, which comes with youth anyway. He still thinks that television will improve the world. He believes it's going to prevent wars. Personally, I think it's only going to encourage them. Television will become just like tanks and guns in some people's hands. I promise you, it's going to be a powerful weapon. Television productions and studios are popping up in America like mushrooms. I sometimes wonder if money can be made there. We'll see what happens.'

'The world seems such a chaotic place. Evil finds a home everywhere, my dear Heinrich. But hospitality is to be found among your Christian, Jonathan's Jewish and my Muslim brothers. It's difficult to know how to bring up your children when you can't understand the world yourself. I hope, against my better judgment, that Jonathan's son's dreams will come true. Whenever I get the opportunity, I'll try to support him. Don't let him know that.'

'In the meantime, one of my business contacts is planning to undertake a similar project with television. I don't always understand this man, but... ach, I don't always understand David's plans either. David doesn't like to let you in to know what he's thinking—not like his lovely spontaneous wife who always lets you know exactly what she's thinking.'

'As we get older we seem to have more worries. It shouldn't be that way. We haven't found the answers that we've been looking for. I believe that I've reconciled myself to the fact that it'll stay that way, as has my friend Nabib, with his childlike mind. I hope all is going well for you, my friend. Can I invite you to come and visit in 1954? My son, Jassar, becomes sixteen then, old enough to stand on his own two feet. I think back with so much pleasure to that day in Geneva when I found out that my son had been born. So, health and Allah permitting, we'll meet up in 1954. "Deo Volente," as you Christians so nicely say. I have decided to give my son his case on his sixteenth birthday, the one that was put aside for him. I cannot wait to see what he does with its contents and its instructions. Make us happy by your presence, my friend. Again, please keep this secret from David. It would only cause him pain. Let me reassure you that David is going to be alright. He can make it without the case and without Jonathan.'

David and Brenda had been hiding for some time in the hayloft before they heard the large, uneven steps of the Croat returning. As soon as he saw the tall, barn doors open, he knew there was something wrong.

The two prisoners had gone. Divo Krlea now had deep regret about calling Sjoerd Colijn so triumphantly. He should have followed his instincts and killed the two of them immediately. Then their bodies would have been hidden deep under the snow by now, and he would be relaxing in his room, knowing that Sjoerd Colijn was happy with him. The Croat was angry with himself, but not for long. They were like wounded mice, they could try to get away, but the cat would always catch them eventually. Tired and anxious as they must be, it was an unequal fight which he would certainly win. It was just a question of when. The woman was brave; the man was strong and impulsive. But, a cat gets more satisfaction from quickly overpowering a healthy mouse.

With his crooked gait, he walked over to the fire, passing the broken chair and loose ties. He made no haste. Therefore, David and Brenda started to get worried that he might spend the night in the barn. That didn't happen. The Croat gathered what little he'd brought and in a relaxed manner went towards the door, as if he'd just decided to go away for the weekend.

He paused at the door. David and Brenda could see him, thanks to the flickering light from the fire, with his humpback silhouette in the long, heavy coat against the white of the snow outdoors. They didn't see that inside the man was laughing. Slowly, he turned himself round. 'The footprints come back.'

Brenda turned to face David. 'Our footprints, he's noticed,' Brenda whispered, knowing immediately what this meant for them.

David and Brenda watched the movements of the man in the doorway and saw how he looked around the barn. The man concentrated his gaze at the hayloft. Afterwards, he ran with his strange step to the ladder which lay flat on the floor. He seemed to be studying the floor. 'Perhaps he's going to walk past it,' whispered David. As long as the man stayed that far away, he wouldn't hear him. After a certain amount of reflection, Divo Krlea picked up the ladder with one hand and dragged it to the hayloft without any effort at all. He stood beside the barrel that David had used to climb up.

David stood up a little. 'We're not going to just sit here and wait for him to come and get us.' David didn't bother whispering anymore. 'He's strong, but we're fast, and there are two of us.'

'Wait…look.' Brenda grabbed onto David's arm before he stood up fully. The man fished something out of his pocket. 'A gun,' Brenda said, scared. 'A gun. I can see its shape.' David and Brenda didn't have any time to try and figure out what to do.

'It's definitely the same man,' said David, thinking back to the fire. 'There's no use us trying to run. The man has no scruples. He'll shoot indiscriminately.'

'He is half blind.'

'What did you say?'

'He can only see out of one eye.'

'And that one doesn't seem to see well. That's why he missed me at virtually point-blank range before.'

'Well, if he doesn't shoot straight, perhaps we can take our chances and run for it.'

'Where? Here on the hayloft? No darling, we'll wait for him. We'll wait for him and surprise him. He'll be expecting us to be frightened, hiding in a corner somewhere.' David tried to talk Brenda and him into feeling courageous. 'We'll show him. The person who strikes first always has the advantage.'

The man moved assuredly, at his ease. Soon he would be right on top of them. David and Brenda didn't speak another word. David seized the piece of firewood and Brenda took hold of the iron bar with the screws. She held it like a lance in her stronger, right hand. In her left she had the other piece of firewood.

They watched as he put the ladder against the hayloft. The ladder stretched four rungs above the floor which they stood on. The top of the ladder swung side to side with each step that the Croat cautiously took up the ladder.

'Patience,' David reminded his brave wife, with a finger in front of his mouth. The Croat was planning where he was going to look up there, but first he had to get up there. Then he'd look in the balcony, then in the hay. The two were unarmed. The cat would simply look through the straw until he found the two mice, probably sniveling in the corner.

His head appeared above the floor of the hayloft.

The Croat realized that he had miscalculated. Downstairs it was lighter. Up here he had to give his good eye time to adjust to the dark.

That cost him some time. His head twisted around from left to right. His one eye saw nothing.

The man put his foot on the next rung. He stepped up and now his upper body, with the grotesque hump, stuck up above the beam. While he carefully moved up again, David shot forwards with a savage cry. Without realizing his luck, David was on the Croat's blind side. The man turned his head to see what was going on, but it was too late. The large block of firewood crashed onto his head. David lost his grip on the wood and it dropped down, along the side of the Croat's body. The Croat lost his balance and, while trying to strengthen his grip on the ladder, shot impulsively vaguely in David's direction. David's leg collapsed under him. He felt no pain, but couldn't stand and swung to the side.

The man now seized the opportunity to hold the ladder more firmly with both hands to climb up faster. Brenda knew that he couldn't shoot and that this was her chance. She jumped forwards like a tiger, trying to use the pole as a lance. She only grazed the man's head. He now released the ladder with one hand so he could shoot. David had been right: he and Brenda were much faster. So much so that she was able to have another go with the lance before he could aim at her. This time she was successful. It stuck deep into his good eye. Brenda wanted to pull back her weapon to be able to use it again, but that didn't work out. It had sunk deeply into his flesh. The man screamed. Meanwhile David kicked against the man's hands where he had got hold of the ladder. The ladder moved. The man let go. Brenda pulled with full force at the lance which was still stuck.

The man, of course, didn't stand a chance at being able to shoot anymore, being completely blind now. He instinctively reached through the rungs of the ladder to put his hands to his bleeding eye. He desperately pulled at the stick but then couldn't let it go; the screws acted like barbed hooks. Brenda let go of the lance, which was in fact the only thing which was holding the man and the ladder to the hayloft floor. David's kicking had more of an effect now. The ladder slid sideways. As a gut reaction, David wanted to stop the ladder from falling but caught himself. David and Brenda realized now that the man was finished.

The ladder and the heavy man fell smack to the ground. David and Brenda looked down over the edge of the hayloft. By the flickering light of the fire, they could clearly see that the great man lay on his back, his limp legs folded unnaturally under his body. Both his hands were still around the rusty lance, but he no longer pulled at it. They felt sure he must be dead. The lance stuck out about a meter into the air. 'We have to help him,' whispered Brenda, her hand in front of her mouth in horror.

'Are you stupid?' Answered David, surprised to hear himself say that.

Sjoerd Colijn ordered the woman in the red uniform to drive slower on the dual carriageway so they wouldn't miss the small track. He'd spent the morning relaxing in the motel, now it was early afternoon. During the night it had again snowed. Today it was dry and the main roads were clear. After the night with that woman, Sjoerd Colijn felt as strong as if he were twenty again, not like a man who was an invalid. He was up to see the sunrise, and he enjoyed the meager breakfast more than the rich meals in his expensive New York hotel.

The confrontation that was awaiting him didn't excite him anymore. The hatred for David and Brenda and the desire for revenge had dissipated in one night. That's how powerful love can be…or whatever this was. Of course, Colijn's intelligence told him that this woman was playing some game. She was not pretty, but there were surely enough men younger than him, without handicaps, who could live with her. No doubt there was a reason why she had chosen him. That was it; Colijn felt that he had been chosen. She'd obviously planned to become his chauffeur, and after last night, also his lover. A fantastic mistress, who made him forget his misery and gave him hope for the rest of his life. Sideways, he glanced at her; she smiled back at him, not quite as happy and relaxed as Colijn himself.

Colijn's attention to the chauffeur was broken by a siren. A black and white colored police car overtook them. Sjoerd Colijn was on edge. A second car followed. He wondered where the track had gone to. He had familiarized himself with the area with the Croat on previous occasions, but then the area was green. It hadn't occurred to him that he wouldn't be able to find the track again between the white trees. 'Slowly, girl.'

A third police car overtook them. The car slowed down and the chauffeur slowly steered the car over a bumpy side-road to the right. Sjoerd Colijn felt how the big car juddered down the country road. He began to sweat. 'Straight on,' he ordered the woman, who looked at him in surprise because she didn't have any reason to turn. Colijn didn't say anything until they neared the turn for Lowell. 'Left please.' The woman obeyed and drove towards Lowell, looking for the centre. Sjoerd Colijn ordered that she turn the car around and they took the same road back again, this time trying several different side roads with only a few houses on them. With the weariness that had returned to his invalid's body, Colijn turned to his driver and asked, 'what do you think of it?'

'What do I think of it?'

'Yes, you. I'm interested in your opinion.'

The woman took her hand off the steering wheel and put it on Colijn's knee. 'I really don't know what you mean.'

Colijn didn't expect that response and so he gave the answer himself. 'I have been considering living closer to Boston,' he lied. 'To tell you the truth, I'm not impressed with it. Maybe you think it's strange, a little bit impulsive, but in the summer it looks really good. But now that I've seen the winter here, I don't want to think that I would end up here. I like New York better.'

'You're absolutely right,' the woman agreed with false enthusiasm. 'This environment is not for you.'

'Let's forget all about it and go back home.' The woman started the car and slowly turned the wheel.

On the way back, they passed a police car with two policemen standing next to it, talking to one another. Sjoerd Colijn looked straight ahead. This couldn't be a coincidence.

David and Brenda took the car keys out of the Croat's deep pocket and drove to Boston. Brenda was behind the wheel, David had both his hands around his painful calves. In Boston, she drove straight to the hospital. From the reception she rang Ted Bates and the police. The police confirmed later that the big man was dead. The lance had gone through his eye, into his brain. They had difficulty removing the lance, as one of the rusty nails had become hooked on his eye socket. Over the coming weeks the police were unable to track down who the man was. It did, however, become clear that this was the man who had killed the chauffeur who had picked David and Brenda up to take them to a television interview. That made David and Brenda's story to the police credible and the police realized that the Croat had been killed in self-defense.

Boston 1954

David had swam his lengths in the pool as usual that morning and now he walked in the sun with his grey, wool jacket over his arm. He was guest speaker at a seminar at Harvard. That afternoon, after the seminar, he would change, put on a tie and, because of Brenda's insistence, would put on his dark blue suit. There was no going against what Brenda wanted. That evening they were going to the birthday party for Jassar Sabagh. It had been planned a long time ago. Tannous was always dressed well; Abdel Amini would, as usual, wear his white suit. 'It doesn't show respect if you're not dressed well,' Brenda told David, and Ted agreed.

The Harvard business school is on the other side of the Harvard campus, on the river Charles. It is situated in one of the classical buildings which remind onlookers of England's Oxford and Cambridge. This was where David gave his speech.

He started by painting a picture of the changes he had seen around him since his escape from Amsterdam: skyscrapers, more cars in the streets, luxury shops for those who could afford them. To young people, these things would seem normal, as if they'd always been there. The impact of all these changes, even in their own living rooms, the students didn't realize. The dining table, which at one time was in the middle of all living rooms, had disappeared to make room for open-plan living. This was necessary to accommodate the new invention in the corner of the room: the television. You could see the shows and sports events that were being transmitted from your cozy armchair. Large fridges appeared in kitchens. More and more American children drank soda instead of milk. A culture developed where children could help themselves to any treat, without having to ask.

David predicted that in twenty years America would be full of over-fed, over-weight people. The world changes very quickly. These days, some could afford to go to England by airplane now, rather than by boat. Transistors and plastics had caused a revolution. Radios became smaller and sold worldwide in great quantities. Some predicted that, eventually, in the homes of ordinary people you would find more than one radio. And that later still, even children would have their own television sets.

After this introduction, David talked about his own choices and the history of Ted Bates Company. His listeners paid rapt attention while they sat on wooden benches. 'The market for television is exploding.'

However, David could foresee problems; growth doesn't necessarily mean gain. 'All the profit is invested back into new production lines or new factories.'

'Isn't that good?' A young person in a green blazer suggested at the back of the college hall.

'Yes,' agreed David. 'The developments are going quickly and you have to keep up. Sooner or later, satellites will be flying around the earth and they will send television images around the world. The Russians and Americans are in a bitter fight as to who will be first to accomplish space travel. What does that mean? The Americans will be able to follow the Olympic Games live.'

'Do you mean that Ted Bates Company will also have to invest in space travel?' Asked the boy at the back.

'Yes, indeed. Unfortunately, that costs us a lot. We ourselves don't have the amount of money for that.'

David showed the students how much it cost to build factories, sales offices, and shops in thirty American cities. 'And you also devote all your time to it,' David sighed.

'What about the competition, then?' Another boy wanted to know.

'They have to cope with the same problems. The rumor goes that Cobagh is going to struggle. Look at DuMont. Fantastic, innovative company, active on all fronts. Yet its shareholders and the banks warn them that their financial support is going to run out.'

'Does that have any consequences for Ted Bates Company?'

'Surely. We are one of their main suppliers,' replied David, frankly.

Just like a good farmer's daughter and housewife, Brenda sorted out the house in the time that David did his speech. David had brought an electric Hoover home from the shop. On the side of the apparatus, there was a big bag that collected the dust, which had to be emptied every so often. At the end of the hose you could attach a soft brush. Brenda used this attachment to remove dust from the photo frames containing the pictures of the children. She would pick them up one at a time and look at them. Christie was now eight and Klaas was three. 'I still have the same figure as I did before I had them,' she thought proudly.

It would prove to be an unusual evening. Between the hassle of everyday life and the rapid growth of Ted Bates Company, it sometimes seemed as if their history never existed; rarely did they talk about the past. One of the things they'd not spoken about was this long-ago arranged meeting with Sabagh. Brenda looked forward to it with eager anticipation, and she sensed that it obviously had something to do with the past.

Ted Bates was going to look after the children while they went up the hill to David's parental home. They would take the Ford Art Deco, which David had received from Abdel Amini on the day that they'd met for the first time. 'That car really is yours,' Sabagh had said. He was right, though it didn't feel comfortable to David.

What the evening was going to be about exactly, Brenda didn't know. But other subjects, like that about the car, would be sure to come up in conversation. Brenda remembered the first meeting and the things that Abdel Amini had said as if it were only yesterday. With Tannous, he had seven daughters and last of all a son who had become sixteen today. He lived in the beautiful house which at one time had belonged to David's father. It was bought through the mediation of Colijn. Brenda figured that Colijn couldn't be anything other than stinking rich by now. Inside the house you saw all sorts of servants who kept the mansion clean. By the looks of the garden, their gardener must have been at work twenty-four hours a day. 'Don't get a false impression from all this,' Sabagh had told Brenda when she'd been overwhelmed by the luxurious mansion the first time she saw it. 'I'm really not that well off. My gardener's richer than I am.' It was a mysterious thing to say and Sabagh seemed to take pleasure in repeating that sentiment from time to time. In subsequent meetings, he added a little smile and acted more secretively.

Brenda picked up a black and white wedding photo of David's father and mother that Sabagh had given her from the big house. She switched off the vacuum cleaner and the whining noise slowly died down. The obnoxious odor it produced also disappeared. She fell back into a comfy chair and bathed in the sunshine which shone through the window into the room. September, and still such a beautiful day. The sun was low behind the glass, it was comfortably warm and it made her drowsy.

The newlywed people in the photo were younger than Brenda herself was now, but Brenda looked on them as her in-laws. Like a dream, she let history play through her mind again. She stroked a finger over the edge of the frame. 'I can still see myself standing in the harbor, arriving in Boston eight years ago, broke, after a journey that seemed like a holiday.' Brenda smiled to herself and kissed the photo. 'We didn't have a dime. With Ted as guarantor, with difficulty we opened a bank account. And six months later, out of the blue, one hundred thousand dollars were credited to it.' Vividly she remembered what a shock it was that they would have been able to buy ten houses with that money. 'I'm still very grateful to you for that, because for David it was a great comfort and enabled him to make a good start,' she said to the couple. 'Your son has used it sensibly.'

Brenda thought back to the journey on the America-Holland Line. Before that time, for the three years they'd lived in Switzerland, David hadn't seemed to show any interest in her. And really, Brenda wasn't ready for a relationship herself. 'At first I didn't want anything with him, but I couldn't let him go either,' she mumbled to the photo. 'Then we went on the boat. There I realized I never wanted to be apart from your son.' Brenda lifted the photo closer to her mouth and whispered, 'you may know now, on the boat I pushed David along a little bit. He couldn't go back anymore. Well, if I had to wait for him, he would still be a virgin right now.' Brenda looked around the small room. 'That's why we have all this now, together.'

After they'd lived in the house with Ted Bates for six months, they bought Ted's business. With the large sum that had been deposited in their account, they could have easily bought a bigger house. At first they didn't know if that money was really theirs or it had been put there by mistake. Later on, when they realized it was really theirs, they didn't have the inclination to move. The house was large enough: the shop was converted into a bedroom, with sets of drawers and a desk where David could work in the evenings. In the bedroom, you could only just fit a double bed. However, the children upstairs had their own rooms. From the very first moment, David and Brenda had felt at home in this house. The children came to enjoy living there too, and so David and Brenda couldn't see the point in moving, just because they had the money. Ted Bates moving out had made a difference in the amount of space that they had. At this point, after being in America for eight years, they could have bought this place ten or twenty times over. Simply put, they were very rich. 'You can be so proud of your son,' she said softly, tracing the edge of the picture again with her finger. 'Since he's been named "Businessman of the Year," he's been invited all over the place to do talks and lectures. Today he's speaking to the students at Harvard.'

Yes, Ted Bates had moved out. 'I'm living in luxury now,' he would laugh. He had paid twenty-two thousand dollars for his 'cottage,' as he called it. The average house price was eight thousand, and that was about three times the average salary. It was a good reward for Ted to have such comfort, recompense for having the original insight about television and radio.

His old little shop, which now served as a bedroom, stored the original television that he'd had in his shop window; the first wooden TV boxes with the small, glass screens. Regularly, Ted would come and rub over the wood with the leather patches sewn to the elbows of his cardigan sleeves. By the time the morning sun had warmed the air a little, Ted would set up a little chair out front and share memories with the local residents and old customers who passed by.

In the corner of Brenda's living room, next to the window through which you saw the apple tree, an RCA television had stood for nearly two years now: the first model with color and, of course, a much larger screen.

'Maybe tonight Sabagh wants to sell us the mansion on the hill,' Brenda thought suddenly. 'No, that's unlikely. Sabagh couldn't have known eight years ago that by now David would have become rich enough to buy it. It's very doubtful that the house is going to be the main topic of conversation. The subject must be something else related to David's youth, or in any case, about Jonathan. It has to be.' With a sense of dread she considered the possibility that perhaps the meeting was something to do with the warning she'd given Sabagh. 'Cha, the warning!' In Switzerland, before coming to America, she hadn't given a single thought to the impact of the contracts that she'd seen. She thought back to the conversation that she'd had with David when she'd seen his parental home, scaring herself remembering what she'd seen in Colijn's paperwork. David hadn't ever really seen why it was necessary for him to warn this man, even if he was about to lose everything as his father had done. They'd attempted to warn him, nevertheless.

Brenda put the photograph back. 'Tonight, perhaps, there will be much more revealed,' she said aloud.

For eight years now, they'd enjoyed making use of the old Ford which David had been given without any cost to himself. In her mind she remembered the day, the day after they'd visited Abdel Amini, when David had been so happy to have the car. She also remembered Abdel's voice that first time they'd met and she'd tried to warn him. 'Don't worry about it, my dear,' he said softly, like a father to a small child. 'Don't be uneasy,' the small man had repeated in the years that followed. And indeed, after eight years now, he did still live as carefree as when they first met in that same large house. Brenda had not expected that it would be so.

In the village of Durgerdam, not far from North Amsterdam, a thin woman and her twenty year old son packed their cases. They were about to embark on a three week-long promotional tour with the most important painting exhibition in France. Paris, Biaritz, Nice…it would be a tiring journey, but also a pleasant vacation. The end of the summer was still lovely weather, and the grape harvest was in full swing. If the weather remained as good as this, they'd be delighted.

Huigje had taken to the countryside in the famine-ridden winter of 1944. She never heard anything more from Sjoerd Colijn. Other people from Amsterdam frequently travelled forty kilometers out of the city to exchange their valuable belongings with the farmers for foodstuffs. With luck, they'd have a bike, although many of these no longer had saddles as everything that was flammable had been used to stoke the fires. Often many of these unlucky inhabitants from Amsterdam would be held up by the Germans on their way back to the city and would have to hand over their hard-earned sack of grain or potatoes.

It was that winter when Huigje and Harm had taken up residence in Hendrik's mill; it had been empty ever since he was picked up by the Germans and had never returned. There she stoked the fire with the wood that Hendrik had carefully hidden. Every day she enjoyed a meal with the two spinsters in their seventies. The two looked after their kitchen garden and kept themselves going all winter on the fruit and vegetables that they'd grown. Once spring arrived, Huigje worked hard to help them with their garden.

She flicked back her long hair and looked over at Harm who was still busy. He still didn't talk much, but there was a strong bond between

Mother and Son. In the beginning, she had been worried that he wouldn't get on very well at school because of his quietness. In fact, the opposite was true. When the war was over, Harm cycled to and fro from Durgerdam to the Amsterdam Lyceum with visible pleasure. With his glasses on, he looked far from tough and athletic, but in his lessons, he ran far ahead of the other children. 'A wunderkind,' some of the teachers had jokingly called him. 'A misfit,' he'd also been called by some classmates. But Harm helped the serious students with their questions and they progressed greatly. He didn't say a lot, but his friends really didn't seem to notice or care.

Harm would go 'on tour' with Huigje tomorrow. It was during the last year of the war that Huigje had begun drawing. Except for the two sisters, she didn't have anything to do with anyone from the village. Across the table from her she would only ever have Harm, with his nose in a book, so she would draw. Sometimes she only had the grey packing paper that Elspeth and Jennifer saved for her. They were always delighted if she drew something for them that was from their garden. Now in the winter of 1954, Huigje had the two spinsters to thank for the opportunity to travel. A year after the occupation had ended, the ladies died and, to Huigje's surprise, they'd left her all their belongings. That proved to be more than she expected. She immediately moved into the spinster's cottage and converted the mill into a studio, dividing her time between her canvases and Harm. Because money was scarce, and she and Harm had to eat, she had begrudgingly sent her paintings to an Amsterdam art gallery.

After being publicized in a Dutch newspaper things had snowballed: the pictures from the newspaper had gone to Italy and France. They were talked about in art journals, and galleries were lining up to display her work. Her technique was detailed and labor-intensive, which meant it was impossible to satisfy the demand for her work. This shortage had an effect on the price. It scared her to find out just how much banks, government institutions and rich individuals were willing to pay for her work. Huigje had never desired wealth but, like it or not, it was coming her way. An Arabian oil sheik had bought one of her pieces and he had invited her to exhibit in New York. 'First we'll do the three week tour of France, and then we'll see,' thought Huigje as she closed the last case.

'Together with Harm.'

Margaret sat behind the wheel of an enormous Chevrolet. The surrounding area was full of people asleep in their beds. Occasionally a light would appear up ahead, signaling an oncoming vehicle. Beside her, Heinrich fiddled with the knobs on the radio. He heard an English-speaking person talk about the race issues in American schools and what was going on in Vietnam. He turned the dial again; he'd had his fill of politics, and eventually settled on a music station playing, as it turned out, Elvis.

Although Heinrich was now past eighty, he ignored all Margaret's objections and traveled, for the first time, to America. Their son David sat on the seat behind them. No longer interested in the barely visible landscape outside, he stared at the ears of his parents in front. He'd been taken out of school for this trip; a trip to America was worth it!

The large car zoomed along the highway. David knew that Americans drove large cars because petrol was so much cheaper for them that it was back home in Germany. However, he hated being cooped up in the car. The country walks with his mother and father around their home in Germany were much more preferable. They did visit some interesting cities by bus sometimes: Paris, Rome, Vienna, Venice. They'd been all over the place and David was proud of that. But to be able to fly over the ocean and then travel further in such a luxurious car, well, that was something special.

David and Brenda had dressed up for the festive occasion. On Brenda's insistence David had put on his blue suit, and it suited him well. The color accentuated his blond hair, and the double-lapels made his shoulders appear even broader. Brenda liked that. She herself looked as glowing and healthy as ever, in her special little suit that hardly ever got taken out of her wardrobe. It fit perfectly around her fantastic body. David too felt a wave of pride as he looked at her.

The two had adapted to American habits; they drove to the mansion although they could easily have walked. As always, Ted watched over their children. The beautiful couple pulled into the gravel drive belonging to the white house, which now was colored red in the setting of the sun.

The mansion seemed quiet with nobody around except for an older man who watched, seated on one of the benches along the driveway. Halfway along the driveway, David pulled in a little to allow a large limousine, with a higher than normal roof, pass by. 'Ping,' went a sound against their door, followed by another. Surprised, Brenda looked around to the car passing them. 'Don't worry, it's nothing important. A couple of pieces of gravel must have flicked up and hit the car. That car must have been specially converted for an invalid,' David continued. 'It must have been someone coming to congratulate Jassar.'

'I wasn't looking at that. I thought I saw…'

David wasn't listening to her and so interrupted her. With one hand on the huge steering wheel, his attention was focused ahead on the large Chevrolet parked in front of the steps. 'Look, there are more people here. They must have gone in already.' Brenda hesitated about whether she ought to say what she was thinking. Then she decided to keep quiet; she was far from certain about what she thought she'd seen. David was far too distracted anyway. 'What old people are here? I'd expected to see more of Jassar's younger friends on his birthday. More family, certainly.'

They parked the Ford behind the large Chevrolet. David and Brenda got out and slammed the doors shut behind them. Brenda pulled David's light blue tie straight. 'You've had your own way, again,' teased David. 'And perhaps this time you were right.'

'I'm always right,' answered Brenda, playfully punching David on the arm as they went up the broad steps to the front door. As evening fell, a damp chill hung in the air. From the steps, the two waved at the old man on the bench.

They didn't have to wait long in the cold air before the door swung open. The servant with the dark complexion, wearing the same white attire with gold buttons that they'd already met encouraged them to come in. The man took Brenda's coat and gave it to a little girl to take away. He proceeded to take them through the hall to the large living room with the huge, open fire and colorful carpets. 'They're waiting for you in there,' whispered the man pleasantly as he opened the double doors.

Inside it looked as if there was a sort of welcoming committee. Tannous, Jassar and Abdel stood stiffly next to each other behind a large table. Beside them was a decrepit man who leaned against his walking stick. Next to him was a woman of about sixty with grey hair. She started expectantly at the couple who stood in the doorway. Jassar stood, strikingly tidy in a ridiculous suit that didn't match his age; he didn't look like a young man at his birthday party. Tannous, as always so supremely elegant that other people faded into the background, was dressed soberly in a grey suit. She held tightly onto Jassar's hand.

At that same moment, Huigje and Harm were on the night train from Brussels to Paris. It was suffocating in the tiny couchette that they had to themselves. The beds were too cramped and too hard. Neither of them could get a moment's sleep, and if they got even close to dropping off, the train would abruptly stop at a station or clatter over a junction and sharply wake them up. 'I don't understand it, Mother. Surely, they must be able to make soundproof trains by now. Everyone knows that metal is a good conductor; therefore it's a good conductor of sound also. Obviously they have to use some sort of material to isolate the metal from the wheels from the carriage.' Harm wasn't usually talkative like this. Huigje usually had to struggle to get anything out of him, and when she did she usually didn't understand a word, as was the case in the middle of this night.

'When we get home, do you think we could buy a television?' It wasn't the Winter Olympic Games in Italy's Cortina d'Ampesso that had put this idea into his head. 'I've heard at school that there's going to be a program about what's been discovered about neutrinos and anti-neutrinos.' Could Harm ever think of anything else?

'What's that now?' Asked Huigje, lying on her back on her bunk.

'They're to do with sub-atomic particles.'

'Oh...well.'

'Subatomic discoveries are going to become really important in the future, Mother. You should take an interest.'

'Why is that?'

'It's like with what we've learned about electrons. Without that knowledge you wouldn't have a radio in your workshop. So who knows what discoveries and inventions await us in the future. In America, they already have television programs in color.'

'Can we see them here in Europe, then?'

'No, of course not. How would they get the pictures to us? They'd need a transatlantic cable of 3620 kilometers. You'll be lucky to be able to have a telephone conversation with America in the near future.'

An idea shot through Huigje's head. 'Would you like to come to America with me in six months' time, Harm?'

'Are you thinking of accepting the invitation to exhibit in New York?' Huigje, shocked, sat bolt upright, banging her head on the bunk bed above her. 'Watch your head, Mother. I've done that too.' While Huigje rubbed her head, Harm utilized the time to think. As Huigje dove back under the much too warm blankets, Harm said, 'yes, if I can rearrange my studies, I would like to come. In America, Ampex are working on video tapes. With them you can record television pictures. I'd like to see how such an apparatus works. And at General Electric, they're making synthetic diamonds. Also very interesting.' Huigje felt sure that diamonds must mean something different to Harm than to her.

Huigje considered the pros and cons of going to America. 'I'm still not sure if I'm going to do it,' she warned. 'I'm not keen on being away from my studio for six months.'

'Then you'll take Betsy with you, surely?'

Huigje was surprised once more. This time she managed to control herself enough to avoid another blow to the head. She wondered how much of her relationship with Betsy Harm understood. He was of an age to understand, but so far she hadn't discovered a single reason for believing he'd any interest in love. If he didn't grasp such matters, then he must have something else in mind. 'Take Betsy with us?'

'Come on, Mother. It was difficult enough with just three weeks in France. Betsy stood crying her eyes out at the station.'

Betsy was a fashion designer. 'You must come and try on some of the swimsuits I've designed,' she had invited when she met Huigje at an art exhibition in The Hague. Huigje had done so, and from that moment had feelings that she'd never experienced before.

'Will it ever be like the relationship between you and David?' Asked Harm from the other bed. The ideas that her son was speaking out loud confused Huigje. It was like he was fishing for information. He had obviously noticed more than she had expected of him. She heard him say carefully, 'I mean…I understand that it wasn't good with Father. After the war you didn't spend a moment trying to find him.' Huigje shuddered at the thought of what Harm might be remembering, meanwhile she heard him say, 'you must know yourself what you're doing, Mother.

I can't see you with another man any time soon.' What did Harm mean with his kind words? Not another man, but with another woman? 'Anyhow, we should go to America. And when we do, I'd really like to visit Disneyland. That's a terrifically large amusement park which opened there about a year ago.' Harm suddenly appeared to have emotions which Huigje had never recognized in him before. 'They use technology there which defies the principles of gravity and other scientific laws. I'd like to see them close up.' Huigje turned onto her side. She was again back in familiar territory, but the talk of science was now just too much for her. At long last, she managed to fall to sleep until morning.

Laura Bradley wasn't a particularly nice or gifted person. A little job at a taxi company seemed about all that she could aspire to. The qualities she did have were mainly negative: she was too direct, foul-mouthed and had no taste whatsoever. If she thought that she was well-dressed, you could guarantee she looked like a car wreck. Her hemlines were too short for her figure; the bright colors she wore, usually red, and her heavy makeup made her appear common. There were many obstacles standing in the way of what Laura wanted: to become rich. Fortunately, with a little luck and enough determination you can get what you want.

By chance, she was given the job of being Sjoerd Colijn's driver. Immediately she saw the possibilities in this opportunity. Perhaps for the first time in her life she did her homework. For a month she studied hard and targeted everyone who could tell her anything about Sjoerd Colijn.

In a tight, scarlet uniform and extra makeup she began her attack. Without hesitation, she focused on her goal and got Sjoerd into bed on the very first night. In the motel where they stayed that night, three years ago now, she had stripped, unasked and unashamed. 'A man in his condition won't initiate anything with a woman,' Laura knew. She knew that sex was the key; if he wasn't willing to go to bed with her, then all she'd ever be was his taxi driver. But, if she could get him to be her lover, then she'd be in control.

Three years after Laura's initial onslaught, she drove the same adapted car along the gravel driveway with Sjoerd Colijn sitting beside her. She passed an old man on a bench and soon after that had to swerve to avoid a collision with and old Ford.

'That was them,' muttered Sjoerd. Laura knew who he meant. He had told her everything, well, nearly everything. For a long time now she'd been his mistress as well as driver. She knew that the smart man in the Ford must have been David Kerzner, the man who had seduced Colijn's wife about ten years earlier. And Sjoerd had also told her about the blond woman who was sitting next to David. She had been after Sjoerd's money and had almost murdered him. 'It's because of her that I'm in this wheelchair and that I've lost my voice,' crackled Sjoerd Colijn angrily from the chair beside the driver.

Today, Laura had heard the whole story afresh. Cautiously she drove back to the port, thinking back to the conversation between Sjoerd and his Palestinian business partner. 'He was a lot smaller than I thought he'd be,' Laura said.

'He is small.'

'I don't know what I'm supposed to think about the Palestinian.'

'So long as he thinks about us the way we want him to, then all will be well.'

'I don't get the feeling that he doesn't trust you.'

Colijn looked at her. 'Then all will turn out well,' Colijn observed, wringing his hands.

The room shimmered. In the large living room, the huge open fire burned, making the room glow red. Tannous also switched on a tall floor lamp, which added more soft yellow light to the ambiance. The room was so spacious that the low coffee table and various pieces of oversized leather furniture seemed to occupy only a small corner of the room.

Brenda and David walked with their hands extended towards the group. Brenda was the first to recognize Margaret under her grey hair. Immediately, she grabbed hold of Margaret and embraced her emotionally. David followed suit. Everyone responded and soon all of them had tears running down their cheeks.

It was a considerable time before they went to sit down on the leather furniture waiting for them. David and Brenda sat on the arms of the sofa that Margaret and Heinrich sat on so that they could stay close to each other. Thus, for an hour or so, they reminisced. Tannous and Jassar listened eagerly, only Abdel Amini remained aloof. So aloof that Brenda tried to bring him in. 'Isn't this wonderful, Mr. Sabagh?'

He couldn't be stirred. Dutifully, Abdel answered, 'Of course, my dear.'

Brenda looked across at David questioningly and nodded towards Abdel. David nodded back. Clearly, Abdel Amini had other things on his mind.

Between Amsterdam and Paris, it was really pitch black. Huigje tried to sleep, but was woken quickly every time she managed to drop off. To try and kill the time, she attempted to look outside. She couldn't see much in the black sky with no moon nor stars. Before long it would be that she'd remained awake the whole night through. In an hour or two the sun would rise. Huigje gazed out the window.

It was not the first time that she'd been to Paris. This time she had no other choice but to take the night train, which she hated. Now and then, the train would stop at various stations such as at Brussels, where the train had stood still for quite some time. This made the journey unnecessarily longer than in the day. She looked forward to arriving at Gare du Nord early in the morning.

The tiring journey was worth it, though. It wasn't the sales or the promotion of her paintings that Huigje looked forward to; she had little interest in such things. Rather, it was the atmosphere in Paris that she was excited about, as well as the museums and the fashion. It seemed that after the war, a period of explosive creativity had come about.

Paris, of course, dictated which way fashion trends would go. Fashion was reflecting the growing independence of women, and that inspired her. More and more women were continuing to work after the war was over and that raised questions as to what they should wear: something that was suitable for the office, but was also easy to commute in. Ladies still preferred to wear high heels, but this wasn't easy if you had to travel by tram or bicycle. They wanted to wear flat shoes to travel in but thought these too inelegant for the office. So many would carry their heeled shoes in a bag to work and then put them on when they got there, coquettishly walking around the workplace until five-thirty.

There seemed to be many different categories of women who the industry had to cater to. On the one hand there were the housewives who tried to hang on to the traditional ideals. They spoke with distaste about the new inventions like washing machines and spin-dryers which were supposed to have been developed to liberate them. They grumbled that they didn't get out all the marks and that they damaged the fibers of the material. Real mothers who weren't lazy washed by hand. On the other hand, you had working mothers who were glad for these machines which saved them from heavy and time-consuming labor.

'Housewife,' seemed like a strange phrase to Huigje, as did 'consumer.' Huigje had discovered that a whole science had arisen around the 'consumer.' Hypermarkets seemed to be the way shopping would develop in the future. The newspapers predicted that the small tradesmen, with their little stores with wooden counters, wouldn't be able to compete with the larger stores. Now you would walk around a supermarket with a little basket, picking up the things you wanted, and you'd settle up at a pay-desk at the front of the shop. Huigje was captivated by such developments.

Huigje painted women in suits who smoked cigarettes; self-important people with sarcasm. Museums sought out so-called modern art. She didn't think much of it. There was a trend towards large canvases and bright colors. Architects used them in their bland, concrete offices with evermore stories. Because of this, many art lovers were looking for a more refined technique. Huigje had read this in an article about her work. Value was determined, not by what the painter presents, but what the fool was willing to pay for it. Huigje's paintings were popular as she really reflected what society was like around her, just as Rembrandt had done in his time. Her work was described as sensitive and attentive to detail. The women dressed in high fashion that she painted seemed as if they were questioning their purpose in life. The naked woman that featured in her paintings had a far-off, ethereal look. Huigje agreed with this kind of appraisal of her work. She painted what concerned and interested her. That wasn't the fashion but she was true to herself.

She never for a moment contemplated what the market dictated or what consumers wanted. She couldn't remember anyone using such terms before the war. Now consumerism had taken firm hold. Companies convinced people they needed every new modern convenience to be happy. In the western world, people queued for these in the same way as they were queuing for food behind the Iron Curtain.

After an hour of memories and tales about their lives in America and Germany, and tales about their children, Abdel Amini stood and noisily cleared his throat. It was obvious that he now had something to add to the discussion and that everyone would listen to it. Abdel walked to stand in front of the fire and looked around at the semi-circle of people. Everyone turned to look in his direction. They all listened attentively as Abdel began: 'Best people, youngsters, my dear friend.' He paused while he took a mouthful of tea and then continued, 'I'm so delighted that you've been able to respond to my invitation.' David thought it all seemed rather solemn for a birthday but didn't say anything. 'Jassar, our Jassar, has this hour become sixteen.' David saw how Abdel looked around the circle and held a finger pointing in the air. 'This hour I said. You heard me correctly,' the little man continued with his feeling for drama. 'Strange that we should call it a birthday, when his birth didn't take the whole day.'

The stout man shook his light brown, balding head to add gravity to his words. He spoke almost solemnly, 'yes, my dear friends present here, I want to call the hour that follows the "Hour of Truth."'

David and Brenda had been expecting something like this, albeit less official and with less solemnity. So far it had been more like a President's speech than a birthday party.

'It's not only that Jassar is sixteen today,' Abdel Amini said to the entire group. 'It has also been sixteen years since Heinrich and I last met.' Abdel Amini turned to face David. 'That was in Geneva…with your father.' David looked across at Heinrich whose large mustached head was nodding in assent. Abdel Amini continued in the shimmering light from the lamp and the fire. 'During this meeting we promised to do some business, which we want to comply with today.'

Again Abdel paused dramatically. He continued, 'today, I have much to reveal to you.' He looked at Jassar. 'Especially to you, my son.' Then looking at Brenda, 'and I have much to ask you, my girl.' Once more he looked around the entire group. 'I have much to tell and much to ask, I need to pour out my heart for the first hour, so I ask that you listen carefully and don't interrupt me. May I begin?'

For a long time, David and Brenda could no longer be astonished by anything. Eight years ago they'd been invited to this occasion. All that time ago Abdel had known what he was going to do this night. Now he asked for an hour to reveal this mystery. Of course, everyone would comply. Again David thought, 'this isn't a party but a meeting.'

Careful to keep hold of their attention, Abdel didn't sit down but continued to stand in front of the hearth. It seemed as if he were at the head of an invisible boardroom table. 'Earlier today, I had a visit from my business partner. You know the man. Mr. Colijn.'

'I knew it…' Brenda couldn't keep her mouth shut. She slapped her hand down on the leather-clad arm of the sofa. 'That was the man in the car.'

'A car which has been altered to allow for a wheelchair,' Abdel continued. 'That good man is an invalid.' David and Brenda forgot Abdel's request not to interrupt him and bombarded him with questions. Heinrich and Margaret remained strangely silent, as if they'd already been made aware of this earlier. But Abdel Amini latched on to one of their questions. 'Why was Sjoerd Colijn here today on a visit? That I will tell you…but first, what this has to do with Jassar's birthday.' This time Abdel spoke directly to his son. 'You, my son, have never heard of the name Colijn. David's father Jonathan and I decided not to tell our sons about our past. That is…' Abdel swallowed and turned to face David also. 'That is what I'm going to tell you now, and, well…it's possible that it will be… how shall I call it? It may be challenging .'

'How so?' Slipped from David's lips.

Abdel Amini walked back to an armchair and, at last, sat down. He looked at Jassar with a fatherly expression on his face. 'David's father and I spoke, with Heinrich as our witness, about giving an honest and unblemished start to our sons.' He paused. 'You must know…before the war, Jonathan and I made our fortune by dealing in arms.'

A light seemed to go on in David's head. His father had never spoken a sensible word to him about his work. His father had escaped every serious conversation about money. Now he understood. He grabbed hold of Brenda's arm who was sitting beside him. 'I thought…I thought it was perhaps diamonds.'

'And I thought it was perhaps from paintings from the old masters and possibly property,' Brenda stammered, crestfallen.

Abdel Amini went on in a louder tone. 'Diamonds, that was his new venture. Amsterdam was the centre for diamond trading, especially for Jews. By the time he was going to start in that market, there wasn't much money left to be made in it.'

'Your father was a very determined man. We did warn him,' David heard the elderly Heinrich say. David could imagine how that went down.

Abdel Amini took up control of the conversation again. As from this moment, he would hardly be interrupted. 'Mr. Colijn did business with your father during the war and after the war; I continued to do business with Colijn. Yes, I see you shaking your head, Brenda. I do continue to do business with him, despite your stern warnings.'

What followed was a brief resume of the war industry during and after World War II. Abdel Amini revealed how he'd decided to swiftly withdraw his interests from that industry. 'I knew I had to spread my personal risk.' Abdel Amini smiled at his own ingeniousness and looked with pride in his eyes at the bewildered Brenda. 'I myself recognized the danger in the contracts that you warned me about. I make it a practice not to skate on thin ice. Of course, I do have some business interests with Sjoerd Colijn. He came to me with a good proposal, for the development of television.' Abdel now looked with curiosity for David's reaction. 'Eight years ago we started Cobagh.' David fell back into his chair. David felt he had done exhaustive research on all his competitors. Cobagh? Abdel looked at him, his eyes twinkling, and guessed what was going on behind David's eyes. He shrugged his shoulders. 'You'd hardly be able to find out about us. It was all a question of the correct legal form. It was all the masterwork of Colijn, I must admit.' Abdel Amini enjoyed watching David squirm. 'You should have figured it out. Listen: Co…Colijn and Bagh…Cobagh.'

David's jaw dropped even further. 'Then…Then you're at the point of…' Brenda kicked him in the shins. David didn't go any further.

'At the point of what?' Abdel was keen to find out.

For the next hour, one surprise followed another. Abdel Amini revealed how, over the last eight years, he had a dilemma. One the one hand his business partner had given him completely plausible explanations about what had gone on. He was a religious man. He had given lodging during the war to a Jewish family. Yes, of course, he'd painted David and Brenda in an unfavorable light. But David and Brenda had done that about him also.

If Abdel Amini were to believe Brenda, then he couldn't be on the same side as Colijn. 'As I heard more from Colijn, I realized that he didn't have a high opinion of you. He told me how his wife had left him. And Brenda, you did warn me about him, but you also hid something substantial from me. You didn't tell me that you tried to kill him.'

'I wish I had shot him dead,' Brenda violently answered back.

'Well, put yourself in my position,' Abdel continued, as if he hadn't heard Brenda. 'Over the eight years, I heard two conflicting accounts of the same story. You were all personally unknown to me. Who should I believe? What else could I do, other than give you both a chance and allow time to reveal all?'

'Give us both a chance?'

'Yes, my dear girl. On the one hand, Mr. Colijn benefits from my investments in our common venture, Cobagh. On the other hand, where did you think your initial capital came from?'

Brenda looked at Abdel with her large eyes. David couldn't keep quiet. 'What I thought about that money wasn't right, was it?'

'That's true, David. Your initial investment, and the periodic lump sums, comes from my Swiss bank account.'

Brenda felt herself become increasingly angry. 'If that's true then David's going to pay you back, first thing tomorrow.' David silently doubted whether that was feasible.

Abdel Amini smiled again. 'Not so fast, dear girl. Not so fast. Just let's wait now and see what the rest of this evening brings.'

The rest of the evening brought tales from Margaret; how David had saved her life by swimming with her across the IJ. Margaret also told all about the escape on the train and what she knew of Brenda's attack. Heinrich added, for the benefit of the others as he'd already told Abdel in his letters, how Jonathan had deliberately sacrificed himself for the sake of his family. Brenda finally told Abdel, for the first time, how she'd tried to get sanctuary for Ricardo during the early days of the war. She revealed how Sjoerd Colijn had refused them lodging. 'How is it possible that you could continue to believe in someone like Sjoerd Colijn,' Brenda gasped angrily through her sobs. Margaret and Tannous comforted her. David thought he knew the answer: money.

Eventually, Abdel Amini decided to try and bring this part of the evening to a close. 'I did warn you. This is the hour of truth.' He shrugged his shoulders. 'Not that it makes much difference to me and Heinrich. We are old people, waiting for death. We realize that there isn't much of an earthly future for us anymore. Our hopes don't rest on weapons, space travel or television. Our hopes rest on God.' The small, tired man couldn't hide the tears in his eyes. Tannous stood and walked up to him. 'My Jassar …our Jassar, is sixteen today. That's an important milestone,' the others heard Abdel gasp. 'Jassar cannot base his earthly future on ignorance.'

Abdel Amini stood up, exhausted and slowly. No one dared say a word. Abdel clapped his hands together twice. The two, large doors on the opposite side of the room from the fire opened. The servant in the white suit and gold buttons came in. He hauled in a large, black object which he could scarcely lift. David and Brenda stared at him and, for this reason, didn't see how Heinrich beamed. Suddenly Brenda pointed towards the man in the doorway. She let out a cry, 'That's the trunk. That's Colijn's trunk.'

She didn't hear what Abdel Amini said. 'Not true, dear girl. That's Jassar's trunk.'

For the next quarter of an hour, Abdel told Heinrich more about Geneva and the secrets of the two trunks. Abdel leaned so far back in his oversized chair that he became almost invisible.

Ted Bates had put David and Brenda's children to bed and there had once again told them tales of Walt Disney's new amusement park. Disneyland was the name of the new park in Anaheim, California; Disney was also the inventor of the world-famous Mickey Mouse and Donald Duck.

Ted still tried to watch as much television as possible. What he'd seen he no longer imparted to David, but to the two children. Of course, Ted had an eye for drama and the children were captivated by his enthusiasm. 'An engineer from the United Kingdom has invented a vehicle which moves on air,' said the oldster.

'Air instead of petrol?'

'No, air instead of wheels.'

'How is that possible, Uncle Ted?'

And Ted explained, 'the machine has a sort of large cushion which the vehicle floats on.'

'An air cushion.'

'That's right, my dears.'

For the last fifteen years, Ted had tried to ignore the more morose subjects: the establishment of the state of Israel, the new threat of war with the surrounding Arab countries, the Suez Canal crisis, Communism and the Cold War. All these things went over Ted's head. He'd much rather watch the films like 'My Fair Lady,' based on the George Bernard Shaw play, 'Pygmalion'.

David believed passionately in a better world. Ted Bates had given up on that dream long ago, and for that reason, he didn't waste a moment thinking about the future. He just did what he could to support David and tried to enjoy life, the same way as the gardener Nabib did, who was by now around eighty but enjoyed life as a child does.

That afternoon he'd been laughing uncontrollably: David's children, Nabib and himself in the beautifully maintained gardens. Nabib had been doing his Donald Duck impression, although it wasn't a million miles apart from what he sounded like naturally. Nabib had chattered about this and that. Ted Bates told him how David and Brenda would be visiting the large house that evening. Nabib knew of the visit, but nothing more.

That evening, when the children were tucked up in bed, Ted Bates sat in David's home reading a book of poetry by Allen Ginsberg: 'Howl and Other Poems.' It was a long poem which rejected materialism and the American Dream. This was another dream which David talked about on every possible occasion.

David and Brenda came home so late that Ted Bates had fallen asleep. 'Let's leave him. He'll wake up by himself naturally enough in the morning,' whispered Brenda.

Ted Bates opened one eye, yawned and sleepily said, 'Hey, I don't think so. Come on, tell all.'

'Ted, you can't be serious. It's almost morning.'

'Come on, now. I'm curious.'

David went to the kitchen and came back with three bottles of beer in his hands. 'Oh, there's not much to tell, Ted,' he pretended. 'One small thing…Sabagh still works with Colijn. Ever heard of Cobagh?'

'Don't be so coy, David.'

David turned around a kitchen chair and straddled it, leaning against the backrest. Laughing, he looked Ted Bates in the face. 'Think about what I just said, Ted. It's simple. Co…lijn and Sa…bagh.'

'Brenda, is David teasing me? It's not true what he's implying, is it?'

'It's true, Ted.'

'Incredible. You know what that means, don't you David? You've been busy thinking of taking that company over.'

'Ted, that's something that only you are aware of. I've been finding it impossible to find out anything about the owners of that company. And now, after a couple of hours, I know why.'

'And what else happened?'

David stood up. He patted Ted on the shoulders. 'Oh, Ted. There's still a lot more to tell you. Margaret and Heinrich were there, and Sjoerd Colijn had been there earlier too. There's too much to tell you in one night so, if you don't think it's too awful, please let us go to bed and we'll tell you everything tomorrow…well, later.'

'Margaret…and her husband. And also Colijn?'

David and Brenda yawned and acted as if they'd not heard Ted's question. Rapidly, they made their way upstairs.

Not more than three hours later they were shaken awake by Ted. 'What is it Ted? It's not even eight o'clock yet. Aren't you taking the kids to school today?' Brenda yawned.

'Get up, Brenda. And you, David. I have to show you something.' Ted Bates spoke nervously and sounded worried. Quickly, David and Brenda threw some clothes over their pajamas. Barefooted, they followed Ted Bates down the stairs. Ted went outside ahead of them. There, at the edge of the pavement, was the Ford Art Deco. Without hesitation, Ted walked over to it. On the driver's side he pointed to two spots on the door. David stooped. They weren't spots: in two perfectly round holes the metal was bent inwards. Ted Bates waited until Brenda had seen them also and then said what the other two were already thinking. 'Bullet holes.'

Laura hadn't had to drive many miles the day before. On her insistence, three years ago Sjoerd Colijn had bought a huge, white yacht. 'You can't live your whole life in a hotel room. I couldn't stand it.' Sjoerd Colijn had taken the hint, and in hindsight, she was right. 'How much time have you spent making your money, and how little time have you had to enjoy it?' Laura asked him, which had got him thinking. Very quickly, he bought the yacht that Laura had her eye on. With that yacht and its crew, they'd traveled to Boston to meet Abdel Amini. The yacht was now docked at the port.

'There you go, Sjoerd. Thanks to this boat, we're home already.'

Laura parked the car on the dock with Sjoerd's door as close to the gang-plank as possible. Thus he could get on board in his wheelchair, with the help of the crew, quite easily. Laura walked on board. Once on deck, the crew left them to themselves.

Colijn pulled on his wheels and twisted to look at the land. 'What is it?' Laura asked, curious.

With a shaky voice Colijn asked, 'did the house please you?'

'The house did, but not the foreigners.'

Colijn pulled on one of the wheels of his chair. This turned him a quarter to face Laura directly. 'It's not going to be much longer before we'll be living in that house.' Laura looked at him questioningly. 'The foreign man doesn't realize it himself yet. His money is almost gone.' A sly laugh played on Colijn's lips. 'And what's worse, he's presently deeply in debt. His company, Cobagh, isn't worth a penny.'

Laura turned from looking at the coast to look at Sjoerd. 'That's awful, Sjoerd. I mean, not for the man, but for you. You own half of Co-bagh.'

Colijn's enjoyment was visible. 'Not for a long time. My share in the company transferred to someone else a long time ago. When we're in-side, I'll tell you all about it.'

Laura pushed the wheelchair along the teak deck to the cabin. The cabin, with its specially broadened doorways, was a good deal larger than their hotel suite. 'A villa,' Laura had said when she first saw it, and so it was. The interior had been lavishly upholstered. A seamless floor-covering ran the length of the interior. The boat builders had worked for six months refitting the boat to accommodate Sjoerd's infirmity and Laura's preferences. They had a large, luxurious bathroom. Their bed-droom was extravagantly decorated, in the middle of which was an os-tentatious, circular bed.

Once inside, Colijn continued his story. 'I'm still married—you know that don't you?'

'You don't have to remind me.'

'Well, perhaps that sometimes seems uncomfortable, but it has its advantages too. My worthless shares are all in my wife's name now. They're untraceable and she knows nothing about it.'

Laura Bradley smoothed down her red skirt and looked doubtfully at Sjoerd Colijn. 'How can you pay for all this then? How do you think you'll be able to take over the house of the foreigner?'

Sjoerd Colijn could hardly contain his pride. 'My kind child, that's actually very simple. Cobagh had become so weak because all the profit goes into my salary and bonuses. And, more importantly, it also goes into buying other companies, profitable companies, which are then put in my name.' It really was staggeringly simple. Laura lit a cigarette.

David and Brenda had got themselves dressed in the shortest amount of time and were now almost at the police station. They parked the Art Deco in the small car park. After they'd told their tale, two inspectors walked with them to their car. One of them crawled into the car, came out after a moment or two and walked over to his colleague holding something small in his hand. 'The bullets,' he said succinctly. Then he invited David and Brenda to come inside again with them.

He directed them to a small consultation room and talked for two long hours about their evening at Sabagh's and eventually also the previous attacks. 'Could it be the Croat?' Brenda asked.

'The Croat that you mean is dead. You know that. We know that one hundred percent for certain.'

'Who then?'

'Sjoerd Colijn?'

'Impossible. We saw him pass us by, with his windows closed.'

'In that case, we're in the dark and we need to warn you.' Brenda and David were aware of the dangers without having to be warned. 'You've already had an arson attack and now another assassination attempt, as well as an abduction which could have resulted in your death. It seems clear that the Croat was probably acting under orders, and the person who gave him the orders has now found another to replace him. It would perhaps be wise to leave the city for a little while. Go somewhere that would only be known by your closest friends.'

'New York?' Suggested Brenda.

'Why New York?' The inspector asked.

David answered. 'We were intending to go there anyway. I've been planning to go there for a long time for business and we already decided to spend Christmas there.'

'Well, okay.' The policeman stood up, extending his hand to shake theirs. 'So long as you let us know how we can reach you if necessary.'

David and Brenda shook his hand and left the somber building.

In the car park the Art Deco was waiting. They swung open the doors and got in. 'You know,' said Brenda, 'I'm starting to get used to this.'

David started the car. 'You've hit the nail on the head. We've been shot at and I'm astonished that I've not been frightened this whole time.

Brenda laughed softly. 'Well, not for myself anyway.' She leaned over to give David a little kiss on the cheek before he drove off. 'We've been here before. It's just the children that I worry about now.'

'Someone's definitely got it in for us.'

'Do you have any idea who?'

'I do,' answered David.

'Me too,' said Brenda.

David looked straight ahead and looked like he was making a decision. 'I think that I'm going to pay Sjoerd Colijn a little visit.'

'Then I'm coming with you,' said Brenda forcefully. 'We need to find out where he lives.'

The engine of the Ford throbbed quietly, but David didn't yet drive out of the police station car park. With both hands on the wheel, he turned to face Brenda. 'Abdel Amini must know where Colijn lives. I think we should go and see him first,' David suggested. 'Perhaps Colijn is staying in a hotel in Boston. If that's the case, then we'd better act quickly.'

Abdel Amini received the two graciously and looked astonished as Brenda, in her usual impetuous manner, asked where Colijn was staying. 'He was visiting here yesterday. We need to speak with him urgently.'

'Can I know why?' Abdel Amini tried to find out.

David gave a resolute answer. 'You can, certainly. But not right now. We want to talk to Colijn ourselves, first of all.'

'Colijn is easy to find. There's only one sixty-foot yacht in the port. That's his. You can't possibly miss it.'

David and Brenda found that to be true when they drove into the harbor that afternoon. On the docks there was also the luxurious, adapted invalid car standing next to a rusty, clapped-out Buick with chrome bumpers. Colijn must have a visitor. David parked next to the two other cars and got out. A thin line of water about a meter wide separated the yacht from the sea-wall. A broad, plain gangplank straddled the gap and David crossed over it with Brenda close behind. They blinked to try and get used to the bright sunlight reflecting from the gleaming white walls. David had expected that Colijn's staff would have stopped him by now, but there was not a soul in sight.

Unhindered, Brenda followed David along the red metal railings to the middle of the boat. Along the beautifully polished teak floors, they passed several doors. 'What now?' Brenda whispered to David. Near one of the doors, one of the port-holes was slightly ajar. 'For fresh air,' Brenda said softly. 'They must be in there.'

David crept closer to the door while putting his finger to his lips. 'Shhh,' he said unnecessarily. He pressed his ear close to the door. Brenda stood behind him, trying to see around him. She too put her ear close to the door. 'I can hear a man talking,' David whispered as he pulled backwards. It was still quiet on deck.

'It must be one of the staff,' Brenda suggested.

David shrugged his shoulders. 'I don't know. It sounds to me as if there's only one person in there. Surely a member of the crew wouldn't be talking to themselves?'

'What's he saying?'

'I can't quite hear. Quiet a minute, the man's not alone. He's talking to someone. I heard someone give an answer back. I can't quite hear them. They're discussing something. By the sound of it they don't agree with one another.'

Brenda moved closer to David so that she could talk softer and listen in herself. 'It must be the visitor who owns the Buick on the dock. There was only one other car there. I don't believe that there are any personnel on board.'

'Come on…let's go inside.' David moved to open the white steel door with the red band. Brenda stopped him. 'What is it?'

'It's much too dangerous.'

'Ah, what? We have nothing to fear. All we want to do is talk. There are only two people in there and one of them is Colijn in his wheelchair.'

'And the bullet holes, then? Someone did shoot at us!' David couldn't deny that. Brenda tugged at David's sleeve. 'I've got a better idea.'

'As usual…go on then, tell me.'

'Let me go in. If I come into any danger, you can go and get help.'

David looked thoughtful. He rubbed his chin and after some time said, 'Okay, good idea. Only, I'll go in, not you.' Before Brenda could protest, he opened the door a little wider and with difficulty edged himself in. Under his feet he felt the deep-piled carpet. He tried to get his eyes to adjust to the dark passageway, only lit by the small porthole. The corridor was empty. The door behind him slowly opened a little wider again and Brenda poked her head through the gap. 'Go away,' David gestured angrily.

David walked carefully along the corridor which went across the ship, keeping one hand against the wall. The voices came from the first cabin on the right hand side. He felt himself breathe more rapidly. After a few steps he reached the cabin. The tension was palpable. Without knocking he held the door handle which gave way with unexpected ease. Without thinking, David stepped into the room. With one step he was in the cabin which had a somber atmosphere. At the back was a small bar. Some of the chairs were piled on empty tables along the wall. Light fell into the room through the portholes along one side of the room. In front of him he saw the hunched shoulders of a man in a wheelchair, and in front of him the long, thin face of an old man. David looked him straight in the face and David seemed to recognize him somehow.

David heard the lock of the door behind him fall into place. The man in the wheelchair also heard the noise but couldn't turn around. 'Who is that?' Crackled his bossy voice. The man who stood opposite him didn't answer. He was transfixed by David. He looked astonished, his mouth open. It was as if he was trying to think how he should react and was finding this difficult. The old, shabbily-dressed man didn't look very clever. You'd get the impression he was kind and friendly, but he was rude and coarse as he finally managed to get out: 'What do you want?'

'I just want to talk with this gentleman here,' said David nodding politely towards the man in the wheelchair and taking a step closer to him.

'Stay there!' The movements of the man in the long disheveled coat didn't seem quite right. You could hear in his voice that something was wrong with him. The man stretched out his trembling hand at David as if repelling him. 'I first,' he said in broken English.

David folded his arms and stood beside Colijn. 'I can wait.'

'Who is that?' Colijn asked again, a hollow crackling sound made by the machine by his throat.

The tall, confused speaker gave no direct answer. 'We're not finished talking yet.' David looked at the man questioningly. He still held out his hand as if directing David to stand still, while with the other hand he groped awkwardly in his coat pocket. David then managed to remember where he had seen the man before. It was the same tired man who was sat on the bench by Abdel's yesterday. The same man who had waved so pleasantly.

The extended arm with the frayed sleeve trembled. The man dropped his arm. He still fumbled in his pocket. It was clearly difficult for him to do several things at once: to follow David's movements, find something in his pocket and keep an eye on Colijn at the same time. David got the urge to assist him and wanted to step forward. 'Stay,' the man ordered. So David stood still and looked on. Everything seemed to be going slowly and David didn't realize what a dangerous situation he had walked into until the man opposite him eventually, triumphantly, pulled out an old-fashioned gun. Two hands as dirty as coal aimed the gun at his face. Instinctively, David raised his hands up. He looked at the man's shaky hands and hoped that he wouldn't pull the trigger accidentally. 'Watch it,' threatened the old man. David was more convinced that the old man wasn't all there. He could kick himself that he hadn't done anything while the man was unarmed. He hoped that Brenda would stay quiet. David dropped his arms and the man raised his pistol more aggressively.

'What do you want?' David asked slowly.

The man seemed to have made a decision and indicated towards a chair in the corner. 'Sit.'

The man had an expression in his tired eyes that David couldn't quite understand. His cheek and jaw bones protruded sharply from his thin face, as if he was being devoured by a terrible illness. His eyes were bulbous. He seemed anxious and almost desperate as if he, and not David, was the one being threatened. He nodded in the direction of the chair again. David obeyed and walked, with his arms still above his head, sideways to the chair under the portholes. He hoped that Brenda wouldn't be as courageous as she always was and storm in. 'If she does, I've had it,' he thought. 'Keep calm. Keep calm,' he encouraged himself.

David sat with his hands raised. That was enough for the man with the pistol to no longer to point his weapon at David's head. David thought about his options. Stand up…five or six paces. The man is old…but was that too dangerous? Was he really the target of this man's anger? No doubt this old and probably poorly-sighted man was the one who had shot at him and Brenda yesterday, perhaps at Colijn's instruction? But why didn't he shoot now?

David tried to understand the body language of these two men. Sjoerd Colijn was clearly not at ease, and the man across from him also had difficulty. It wasn't just the shaking of old age; evidently he was nervous. He seemed to be afraid of Colijn even though he himself was holding the weapon. Who was this man that David seemed to know? He didn't have the confidence and drive that the Croat had had. Here stood a clumsy, anxious person, on the other end of the scale to the Croat, with an old pistol in his hand.

While the old man spoke to Colijn more forcefully, David continued thinking. Yesterday someone had shot at the Art Deco. That surely had to have something to do with Colijn. He must have given the order and it seemed that the old man must have been the shooter. But these two, at this moment, certainly didn't seem to be on the same side.

Brenda had crept into the corridor and listened at the door. Every now and then she heard David's voice which was the only voice that seemed calm, asking polite questions. What he was asking, Brenda couldn't hear. With one hand on the door handle and an ear pressed against the cold steel door, she couldn't make head or tails of the few words that she caught; 'in the past…I know what you're after….it's what you deserve…'

Suddenly Brenda froze. 'Don't do it,' she heard David say. The stream of words from the other man behind the steel door became more intense. 'Don't do it!' David's voice became more urgent. 'Don't. DON'T!' It seemed as if a chair moved.

The voice that was talking now yelled, not from pain but with a crazed energy. 'There's a madman in there,' Brenda thought.

'Don't…Don't do it!' David's voice was raised above the madman. Brenda pushed on the door-handle and put her shoulder against the door. It had locked from the inside and didn't give way. At that moment a shot was fired. The man roared violently and Brenda heard David's voice, 'ooooh, ooooh.' With all her force, Brenda barged against the door but it didn't move a millimeter. Another angry shot was heard.

'David…David, my David.' With both her fists Brenda banged on the door while tears welled in her eyes. She didn't feel the pain in her shoulder and continued to bang on the door with less and less power. Whilst she was crying she heard movements. 'He's coming…the madman…He's coming out.' She was afraid she'd be killed too. She looked around her in a panic. Should she run away? Or find something heavy to hit him with?

The smartly uniformed officer who spoke to David and Brenda a few hours ago had driven up the gravel path to the mansion. The man got out of the black and white car and walked to the step by the front door and looked for the bell. An elderly gardener was leaning on his rake. He said a friendly hello. Before the officer found the bell, it was opened by a large, dark-skinned man in a white uniform with gold epaulettes. The officer asked for the householder, Mr. Sabagh.

Shortly after this he was standing next to Tannous Sabagh in the enormous hallway. She directed him into the sitting room. There Abdel Amini walked over to him with his hand stretched out before him. 'What can I do for you?'

'Are you Mr. Sabagh?' Asked the large officer.

Abdel shook his hand. 'Yes, that's right.'

'You were visited this morning by a young man and his wife?'

'You mean David and Brenda?'

The formality of the officer melted. 'That's them. Are they still with you now?' Abdel Amini said politely how David and Brenda had stopped by and they'd asked about where they could find his business partner, Mr. Colijn. He'd advised them that they'd be able to find Colijn in his yacht in the harbor. The officer decided that he could be more open with Abdel Amini. 'I want to find David and Brenda as soon as possible. Do you think I can find them on that yacht?'

'If they're not at home, I assume that could be possible.' The officer decided to go to the harbor immediately. With a tip of his cap, he turned and left quickly. Abdel Amini walked out of the room with him. 'Do you want me to give them a message if I see them?' Abdel asked.

The officer stood by the large front door, thinking about his reply. 'Just warn them.'

'Warn them?' Abdel said, surprised. 'About what?'

The officer scratched behind his ear. He decided to put his cards on the table. Turning back inside he said, 'Someone shot at the two of them last night. There were bullet-holes in the door of the car. They were extremely lucky. In the last hour we've gotten an idea who the culprit is.' Abdel Amini was shocked. Listening above the balustrades, Tannous' color drained. 'A colleague of mine had a visitor at the police station. It was a foreigner who asked for Mr. Colijn.' The officer shook his head whilst thinking. 'It was an old friend of Colijn's who looked so smart; my colleague imagined it was one of his business partners. My colleague looked at the passenger lists and phoned Amsterdam straight away.' The officer coughed with his fist in front of his mouth. 'It seems as if the man in question was a prisoner there after the war, for six years. Over the last six years in prison he talked only about one thing…' The officer looked around him as if he was going to say something that no one else should hear. '…Revenge. Revenge for the dirty Jewish trick played on him. Do you understand?' He took a deep breath before he continued. 'When I heard that, I thought …the man from your two young guests…he's a …?'

'A Jew, officer? Yes, you're right.' Abdel Amini didn't need any time for contemplation. He wanted the officer to spring into action. Abdel opened the front door wider. 'Your colleague did well in his investigations. I've got an awful suspicion that your instincts are right. Someone has shot at this young couple before.'

'I know.' Sabagh's quick reaction unnerved the officer. He felt he'd been talking for too long, and with quick, lengthy strides walked to his car on the drive.

On board the yacht, Brenda was shivering but she felt strong enough to work out a plan when she heard movement behind the metal door. 'I must get away,' Brenda thought. Squinting, she looked down the corridor to find something with which she could defend herself. Hanging on the walls were turned metal light fittings which weren't alight at this time of day. They were fixed to the wall with large screws. Brenda decided to look outside on the deck for a loose heavy object.

On deck she saw large rolls of cable but nothing she could use to hit anyone with. She ran to the gangplank. Halfway to the gangplank she suddenly stopped next to a pallet full of cartons. She ducked behind them just before the steel door to the deck opened, making sure that she wasn't seen. Bent with her head between her arms, she heard quick footsteps over the wooden deck. Her heart pounded so hard that she imagined the assailant would be able to hear it. The footsteps stopped. The man called out softly but, with her arms over her ears, Brenda couldn't hear him properly. At the moment, her heartbeat and breathing drowned out any other noise.

She could hear the footsteps again. It seemed as if the assailant was walking up and down…searching for her. Brenda crouched down further. The hurried feet on the wooden deck came closer, probably only a few meters away on the other side of the pallet. Any moment now he would discover her. Brenda held still, like a hunted animal. The man called out again and this time she could hear it though the wool of her jumper. She heard her name being called…he knew her name. She shivered. David must have told the man inside that there were two of them and this man was looking for her. About three meters away from Brenda, the man made a decision. He no longer went up and down the deck. He walked quickly with large strides in the direction of the gangplank. Brenda suddenly thought to herself that she would have to take a look at the man, to be able to give a description to the police. 'I'll have to identify him if the police pick him up.' Did she dare to look? She lifted her head out of her arms. She could no longer hear him. Perhaps he'd now gone over the gangplank. Carefully, she looked over the boxes. No one was in sight. She looked all around, still no sign of life anywhere. Timidly she stood up. Was the man still on board? Slightly hunched over, she looked along the deck. It was still and quiet, until Brenda had such a fright. Behind the railings there was a sharp sound of a car horn. Urgent. Again and again. The driver was trying to draw attention to himself, and the noise sounded like the modern hooter that David had installed in the Art Deco.

It just took a few steps for Brenda to get from behind the boxes to the railings. She had to see the man before he disappeared in their car. Without hesitation, throwing caution to the wind, Brenda put both her hands on the red railings and leaned over to look down the docks. There was someone in their Ford. The car started to move. If Brenda wanted to catch a glimpse of the man she would have to be quick. She ran along the railings to the gangplank. The car seemed to be moving with her. She was now on the gangplank and she wanted to run onto the docks. The car stopped. What did that mean? The man was armed—she'd heard shots. She turned quickly. At that moment the door of the car opened.

She started to run back up the gangplank. Behind her she heard a man shout, 'Brenda, Brenda, what are you doing?' What did the man shout? 'Brenda: come on, my girl. Come here!' Brenda stopped at the point where the gangplank reached the yacht. She looked over her shoulder to the seawall. Next to the car, with his arm on the open door, stood a young, handsome man who was waving at her. Brenda started to cry and was angry at the same time. It was her David. Alive and with a smile on his face, David was pleased to see Brenda.

Jassar came home from school, where he studied accounting, and went to his room. He couldn't stop thinking about the things he'd heard last night, as had been the case for the last twelve hours. It had taken him until about three am to translate the handwritten Arabic letter into perfect English and read it out;

Dear Boy,

I hope that you and I have reached the age where you can read these instructions in the presence of your father. The contents of this case are reserved for you with a promise to God, the source of all life for us Muslims as well as Christians and Jews. The God who binds us all, who gives us the future in the form of our children. Often, though, we are ungrateful and disappoint Him with our intolerance, inhuman hatred and our wars, which often abuse His name. Do what you see fit with the contents of this case. Your father doesn't force you to do anything good with it, but he does ask: discern for yourself what you will do, as the God of Abraham encourages. Listen to the prayer of your father, who doesn't oblige you but asks that you use the contents to benefit not only yourself but also your fellow humans. Not just Muslims, but also to the same extent Christians, Jews and other faiths that live under the same sky with us.

Your loving father, with thanks to your mother, Tannous.

When Jassar read it out, he was intrigued by David's response. 'My dream. A copy of my dream,' he mumbled to himself, but for Jassar it was audible. He couldn't get this softly spoken sentence out of his head and he wondered what David meant by it.

At the same moment, not far from the mansion, the officer drove into the harbor. There he met David, alive and well, next to his car, waving to his wife on the gangplank. David walked over to Brenda and talked to her about the two shots that she had heard. He took the officer over to the cabin.

Sjoerd Colijn sat in his wheelchair as if he was still alive. His head was bent slightly forward, with his chin on his chest, as if he was merely asleep. David wondered if he was really dead, as he didn't see any blood. The officer checked Sjoerd Colijn and confirmed that he was dead.

The same was true of the man with the weapon. He was lying on his back with his leg folded underneath him. His face and coat were covered with blood. David knew now who he was. In the last few moments of his life, David had come to know why he recognized the old man; it became clear during the quarrel between the man and Sjoerd. It wasn't strange that David didn't recognize Huigje's father straightaway. Old age and terminal illness makes a person unrecognizable. David felt pity for this cruel man who was wasting away. At least he didn't take life's final journey on his own, but with Sjoerd Colijn.

Brenda had not entered the cabin. Fortunately she was able to leave the yacht as soon as the other police officers came on the scene. David and Brenda decided to go with the older officer to Abdel Amini's.

Abdel Amini understood that something dreadful must have happened as soon as he saw the black and white police car pull on to the drive with the Art Deco behind it. Abdel Amini ran to the door and opened it himself before the servant or Tannous had the chance. His darling wife looked over his shoulder. Abdel didn't send her away. As difficult as life could be sometimes, Allah permitting, he would spend every moment with Tannous. From his bedroom window, Jassar too had seen the police car arrive. Curious, he came downstairs.

Abdel Amini guided the group to the living room: David, Brenda, Tannous, Jassar and the officer. He closed the door behind them as if he expected that things would be said that were not intended for other ears. 'Please sit down,' Tannous invited.

Taking notes, the officer pressed David to disclose all that had happened that day. David told him everything that the culprit had said. 'The dead man in the room with Sjoerd Colijn was indeed Huigje's father, Herbert de Jonge. From his angry story I understand how everything fits together. In Amsterdam, he'd been imprisoned for six years for embezzling church funds; something which Sjoerd Colijn had framed him for. Not long after that, he became terminally ill, TB or cancer. On his last legs he came to Boston. He knew he was going to die, or go on his long journey as he called it. First he sent Colijn on his way, and then he pointed the gun at his own chest before I could do anything.'

'The man wasn't shooting at your car yesterday, then, but at Colijn's,' the officer deduced.

'That's what I think, too.'

'Did he tell you anything about that?' The officer asked.

David thought. 'No, nothing…he did say…'

'Well, tell us.'

David swallowed his words and gulped.

At the end of the evening, after Abdel, Tannous and they had talked for a bit, David and Brenda walked to the car. Brenda couldn't wait any longer. When they got into the car she said, 'Come on, what did the old man say at the end? You can't fool me.'

David started the car and looked at her. 'The man must have recognized me. The man shot himself in the chest and his legs gave way. It was an awful sight. I tried to catch him. When he lay on the ground he looked at me. He took my hand and the last thing he managed to say was: "tell our Dear Lord and Huigje that I'm sorry." He smiled. "You can make Huigje happy," he said, then closed his eyes.'

America–the end of 1956

A murder, large properties, and a sixty-foot yacht mixed in with the collapse of Cobagh: the American newspapers feasted on it. What a story! As fast as they could, the American journalists raced to the door of Abdel Amini Sabagh. None of them succeeded in getting ahold of him.

Abdel Amini, along with his family, went into hiding. David and Brenda were kept out of the picture. As they knew nothing of their whereabouts, they could do nothing more than speculate as the press did. 'Sabagh must have understood that Colijn had dragged him into the collapse of the company,' Brenda had previously said that this would happen and she was right.

'I wish that it was otherwise, but as far as I can see, they're really gone for good.'

For the first few days after the incident, the press camped on David and Brenda's doorstep, but they couldn't help the press any further. 'Maybe they've used the fortune from the case to establish themselves somewhere else,' David suggested when he was alone with Brenda and Ted.

'Well, what's going to happen to the mansion, then?' Brenda wondered immediately.

The beautiful weather-boarding that the old gardener would maintain every year was starting to lose its glory already. The same was true for the steps and the balustrades on the balcony. Through the winter a dirty, green stripe formed under the guttering on the white gables. The shutters were closed. And, as there was no one there to light the lamps, the house seemed to lose its grandeur and soul in the dark, winter nights. With no light shining on the gravel path, you couldn't really see where the grass ended and the driveway began. David began to worry himself about the fate of this house. Sooner or later someone else would live there. If Brenda and he wanted a chance at having it, they needed to make sure they were on the ball. On the other hand, they felt as if their hands were tied somewhat, seeing as the owner was missing. Somehow, it also didn't feel right trying to take ownership of the place in such painful circumstances, as if they were being mercenaries. 'David, love, we're not grave robbers,' Brenda would say if he started talking about the house.

David felt himself get irritated. 'It's not as if we were there on a daily basis. The family only pretended to have a close friendship with us.'

'No, they felt that sincerely,' Brenda retorted, defending the family.

'Tannous maybe. But that man with his "Don't worry yourself, dear girl." You've seen what's happened. You were right.'

'Ach, we'll be hearing from them soon,' reassured Ted, full of faith in the family.

But news of the family was a long time coming. Months went by, months wherein David forgot about the past because his work demanded his attention. And his attention was crucial.

David was looking into buying parts of DuMont, which was seriously in trouble. That's why he wanted to go to New York in December. Also, before too long, parts of the bankrupt Cobagh would be available to be picked up.

In 1938 there was already a DuMont television in Ted Bates' shop window. By this time, the shareholders were causing trouble. The founder of DuMont had been forced to split up the company and sell off parts of it. 'It's all so painful,' David whispered to himself as he read about the company. He appreciated what sacrifices its founder had made and the dedication it had taken to make it the company what it was. In contrast to David's company, DuMont didn't just make televisions. They also transmitted programs; they came out of the DuMont television studios at 205 East 67th Street in New York. It was this studio that David had got his sights on. That's what he wanted to visit when he and Brenda took the children to New York for Christmas.

New York, Christmas 1956

Large amounts of snow had fallen, which complemented the glistening lights in the shop windows. Even some people in the suburbs had decorated their homes flamboyantly. On every street corner you encountered a Santa who called 'Ho, ho, ho' in your face, whether you wanted him to or not. As Jews, David and his family weren't devotees of the Christmas traditions, but they did enjoy spending the holiday season together.

The attempt to buy DuMont's television studios had led to nothing. They simply wanted too much for it. 'Sooner or later the studios would have been profitable for them,' David explained to Brenda. 'But that could perhaps be more than ten years away. But we just didn't have enough money to give them what they wanted.'

'Who does? Who has bought the studios?'

'A foreigner. It'll perhaps be January or February before we know exactly who it is.'

Around Christmastime, all the newspapers featured reviews on the different restaurants, from the surprisingly good small eateries to the grander restaurants. You could also find out about the many musicals and plays that were popular at this time of year. Many people saved up all year to spend Christmas in New York enjoying these things.

David had reserved tables at various restaurants over the few days they were to spend in New York. He and Brenda searched through the newspapers to find suitable shows to entertain both themselves and the children. There was a circus matinee show they were keen on, but this wouldn't fill the two weeks they intended to stay. For himself, David examined the reviews of museums and exhibitions that the journals recommended. An exhibition of Dutch art caught his eye. It wasn't the name of the artist that got his attention; it was the photograph of the painting. In it stood an almost naked woman painted into an Amsterdam scene. There were the typical Amsterdam doorways, with the five or so stone steps leading up to the front door. Along each side of the steps were the dark red, wrought iron railings. The naked woman, painted in minute detail as was the rest of the painting, seemed comfortable in her surroundings, leaning against the railings. A red barge was on the canal in the foreground, and even though David only saw a photograph of the piece, he could see how the artist had carefully paid attention to the smallest of details. It had been painted so realistically, but nevertheless had a surreal quality as, of course, you didn't often see naked women leaning against the banisters. The painting gave David a feeling that he recognized, and it wasn't just the Amsterdam imagery that was conjuring up these feelings. It took a couple of days of looking at the pictures in the newspaper before David realized it was the woman herself that was drawing him in. He realized the feeling was taking him back to 1942-1943. So far it had been smells that brought back the feelings from the past: the smell of wet newspaper, or meals that his mother would have cooked. The painting did make him think of Huigje. Not in a sexual way, but with feelings of freedom and emancipation. 'That's what the painting's all about,' David realized. 'A woman, drawn naturally, as she really is. A woman who can go and stand wherever she pleases, naked and herself.'

David didn't go to exhibitions often, but he took himself to this one while Brenda and the children entertained themselves going to see yet another Santa Claus. On a Tuesday afternoon, David beat the snow of his coat and stepped through the impressive doorway of the museum. He glanced around to try and find the room with the exhibition he'd given himself a couple of hours to look at. As soon as he stepped into the room a strange emotion took over him. He couldn't describe it. It was similar to déjà vu but not exactly, as he didn't recognize anything particular in the room. He felt a little bit like a boy who had come back home; the room's dimensions were very similar to the grand room in the mansion so maybe that contributed to this feeling. Dizzily, he took one or two steps forward. 'Exhilarating,' was the word which played through his mind. And that was how he felt, exhilarated. Crazily, he didn't know why.

'David?' An astonished woman next to him asked. 'Is that you, David?'

'Yes, that's me,' he answered before he turned around. Then David looked directly into the face of Huigje.

The coming days around the Christmas of 1956 were lively and edifying. David, Brenda and Huigje spent every possible moment with each other. Particularly special was the way that the quiet Harm seemed to bubble over with things to say, as if he'd been saving his words up all his life for this Christmas. All the trouble and torment of the war years and the difficult times that followed was all revealed. The families had much to tell each other and there was rarely a silent moment. David explained what had happened over the last few months with regards to Colijn and meeting up with Margaret and Heinrich again. Of course, Huigje was keen to hear about the escape, this being her first opportunity to find out what had actually happened. Then David and Brenda listened as Huigje described the turns her life had taken. It was no wonder that Abdel Amini and his lawyers hadn't been able to find her. She'd been living in New York with Harm for the last three months.

David told Harm about the start of the Ted Bates Company. He spoke concerning the initial investment he'd had from the Muslim, about his friendship with Jassar, and about the events surrounding Jassar's sixteenth birthday. David outlined how Harm would be able to study in America, and before they knew it they were fantasizing about how they could work together to enable transmissions around the world using satellites.

'Us working together? Is that possible? Me, a Christian, with you, a Jew?'

'Yes, it's perfect, beautiful,' answered David. 'Especially together with Jassar, a Muslim.'

Boston 1957

It was January and it was icy-cold in Boston. David and Brenda were at home as Ted Bates had told them they were going to have an important visitor. David suspected that it would likely be the tax inspectors. The doorbell rang; Brenda ran to the door while David tried to see the visitor through the window. In front of the door, by the pavement, stood a large, white Rolls Royce. 'Customs or tax officers in a Rolls Royce?' Thought David. He ran through to the hallway to see Brenda pull open the front door. Outside, four lively people stood laughing loudly. Abdel Amini stood in the middle.

The whole group sat close to each other in the cramped living room: Abdel Amini, Tannous, Jassar and Nabib the gardener. Ted Bates joined them also. There was much to tell.

'We had to escape in a hurry. We had to because of the newspapers,' Abdel began to explain.

'Why didn't you let us know?' Asked David.

'You know the press. We knew that once they'd realized that we'd disappeared, they would be watching you like hawks. Especially if they knew that you'd been present at Colijn's death.'

'Thankfully, the Police have never let that slip to the press.'

'Well, that's a relief. But nevertheless, we didn't want to put you in a difficult position by knowing where we'd gone into hiding.'

'Where have you been hiding?'

'In Europe. In Heinrich's mobile home.'

'What? In his caravan?'

'It's been very cozy,' Tannous reassured him.

'But why, for heaven's sake?' Asked Brenda.

'That I'll tell you, dear girl,' answered Abdel Amini, speaking to Brenda now as if no one else existed in the room. 'All through the war, naturally I had dealings with our mutual acquaintance, Sjoerd Colijn. It was really a little offensive that you didn't have such a high opinion of me because of this,' he teased Brenda. 'From the moment that you came to warn me, though, I knew that I could trust you and not Sjoerd Colijn. Trust was something of value to me, especially considering that we don't share the same religious beliefs. In this world, that's something really special. And so, for this reason I decided to, let's say, sponsor you.'

'Why didn't you tell us all this from the beginning?'

'It seemed wiser to let you to find your own way rather than be in the under the wings of this old Muslim. And for another thing,' Abdel Amini looked at Jassar, 'I wanted my son to be able to draw his own conclusions, as I said to you all previously.'

David whispered, 'I understand that.'

'And what about Colijn and the bankruptcy?' Asked a curious Brenda.

'Yes…how is it with Cobagh?' David was also keen to know.

'Ach,' Abdel Amini leaned back in the chair that was really a little tight for him, with a triumphant look. 'Perhaps you can understand this now that I'm here. In the war I'd already concluded that Colijn, sooner or later, would fall on his own sword.' David's eyebrows rose. 'Yes, first you had the escape affair and then, closely after the Second World War, you had the whole drama about Cobagh. Not badly arranged, if I say so myself.'

David, ever business-minded, instinctively tried to get his head round what had happened. 'You went bankrupt with Cobagh only to see Colijn go under? I just can't believe that.'

'Smart, really smart, my boy.' Abdel Amini was enjoying the moment. 'I felt that Sjoerd Colijn deserved his downfall, just as Brenda had done in the past. For this reason, I can really sympathize with you, dear girl.'

Within a short time everything became clear. 'I'm not going to be coy with you. Since Colijn is dead, all the accounts will eventually come out in the open. Perhaps you are still the owner of the house on the hill and that Rolls Royce outside, but that's far more than I own.' David's jaw dropped open. 'For a long time now I've been penniless, my dear boy.'

'Goodness…'

'Let me finish.' Abdel Amini shrugged his shoulders and shook his little bald head slowly. 'I may well be penniless, but as you know, Jassar isn't. And neither is my friend, Nabib, who's sitting here cozily with us.'

'Yes, I know, he's got his garden.'

'Among other things.'

'What other things?'

'Ach.' Abdel exclaimed, again softly lifting his shoulders. 'Well, not so much…Who do you think is one of the largest shareholders of Lockheed? And other aerospace industries?' It was obvious that Abdel Amini was enjoying the moment enormously. 'Anyone want to guess?'

'Nabib?' Asked David, knowing full-well that he was right.

'Yes, of course. My friend Nabib doesn't know it himself. He owns more than he realizes.' Abdel Amini could hardly hide his glee. 'The trick that Colijn played on your Father and me is one of the oldest tricks in the book. It all depends on how you use the trick–for good or for bad. Since Nabib was young, I've had power of attorney for him; I could sign for him. That's how it could be that Colijn thought that I'd invested all that I had in Cobagh. The papers thought that also. I thought it better to leave it that way. So to escape all the questions here in America, we have spent the last few months in Europe.'

David looked at Abdel thoughtfully. 'I've got the feeling that you've still got more to tell me about that.'

'Yes, you're right. We were with Margaret, looking for Colijn's heirs. I wanted to see if there was some way I could meet up with my new business partners and keep Cobagh intact.'

'Huigje and Harm?'

'Yes, but we were unable to find them. We understand they're in America somewhere.'

'I know,' said David, wanting to tell them about his meeting in New York.

Jassar jumped in. 'Father wants, or rather, I want to make a deal. We've used the time well in Europe to work out a proposition. How would you feel about working together?'

David's mouth fell open again. 'Work together with a competitor?'

'Competitors can become your friends,' Brenda interjected.

'Work together with your father? Is that what you mean? He is Cobagh, what's left of it anyway.'

'Splendid factories that would quadruple your capacity,' persuaded Abdel.

Jassar continued further, 'and that's not all. DuMont's studios have a new young owner who's willing to work with us.'

'How do you know that?' Asked David, astonished.

'Well, the new owner is me.'

It seemed too good to be true: the sales capability of Ted Bates Company joining forces with the production capabilities of Cobagh, via Abdel Amini. In addition to that, Jassar brought DuMont which provided the transmissions which could further encourage television sales. Even better was the thought of the contacts that Abdel must have in the space travel industries.

'You'd be making a formidable team,' Abdel suggested cautiously.

'I can see that. But I need to talk about this. I need to think it through,' David stammered.

'Don't be ridiculous, David,' Brenda interfered. 'This is a fantastic proposal. It's almost like a dream.'

'Your dream,' Jassar continued.

'David's aware of that,' said Abdel Amini softly.

Tannous hardly ever spoke at meetings such as this, especially when it was anything to do with business. This was an exception. She walked over to David and took hold of his hand. 'I think that now, after all these years, it's time to let go of that skeptical attitude, David. By now you should realize that my husband has only ever wanted what's good for you.'

'That's how it is, David,' endorsed Brenda.

That cold evening, grand plans were made around the kitchen table in their small abode in Boston. Abdel Amini openly told how his contacts with the Air Force and the Marines were still in existence. 'Nabib and I are one,' he said. 'The companies which we either own or have shares in are the most important partners of the National Advisory Committee for Aeronautics. They have given the Navy the order to build rockets and are going to send the first unmanned satellites into space this year. You probably read the article last year about AT&T, about the "space mirror" which has given them the capability to handle one thousand intercontinental telephone calls simultaneously. Amazing, when you consider that the first transcontinental cable, which cost fifty million dollars, can only cope with thirty-six at a time.' David nodded. 'So, wasn't it a good job that Nabib was clever enough to invest in AT&T also?' David wasn't surprised about anything anymore.

'War and technology; the two always go together,' sighed Abdel Amini. 'I'll tell you something that not many people know about.' Abdel Amini went back to the end of the war. 'In Germany, at the end of the war, the Americans found two tunnels measuring one and a half kilometers. Therein stood ten thousand V2 rockets. Later they found out that these were made for the Germans by the prisoners in the concentration camps. In 1945 when the war came to an end, the Allies came across a German called Wernher von Braun who had a team of engineers from Bavaria. They were under guard by the SS, who were afraid that they would defect to the Allies. Von Braun, himself one of the SS, wondered to whom he should surrender himself. They were afraid of the Russians, the French would have treated them with contempt, and the British didn't have the money for a rocket program. That left America. In secret, the engineers were transported, together with three hundred wagons full of rocket parts and blueprints. Maybe you've heard of operation "Overcast" or "Paperclip?" The engineers went from Fort Bliss in Texas to Huntsville. A year and half ago, Von Braun became an American Citizen. It's almost impossible to believe, but he's been working for Disney Studios, producing a film to promote public interest in Space Travel. The Navy at that time had the instruction to make sure that they stayed ahead of the Russians in the "Space Race." There are people who doubted their technical know-how. But, I can tell you a secret: Von Braun was working on a better alternative that he was keeping quiet about, not even telling those who commissioned him.' Abdel Amini looked around the table with a serious expression on his face.

'Sooner or later, tens of satellites will be traveling above our heads,' predicted David. Both Jassar and Abdel Amini nodded in agreement.

'It's more than likely that you're right about this, David.'

'Maybe one day people will be walking on the moon,' suggested Jassar.

Abdel Amini stayed completely serious. He looked David straight in the face. 'Maybe I can take away that last bit of doubt in your mind by offering you the chance to use the network that's in Jassar's name and the money that's in Nabib's name. You really don't have to worry anymore about financial support. The only thing that you have to look out for is the technical know-how.' David didn't answer. He stared blankly ahead, deep in thought. 'This is the only way that you'll be able to transmit your own television programs around the world,' Abdel Amini added to add weight to his proposition. David had already come to that conclusion.

'What are you thinking about?' He heard Brenda say.

David picked up her hand which was leaning on the table and sighed. 'I'm thinking about Harm.'

Russia—America 1957-1960

On October 4th, 1957, the Soviet Union successfully launched Sputnik I, the first satellite, about the size of a basketball. A month later, Sputnik II was launched, the dog Laika being onboard. By doing this they proved to be ahead of the Americans. The humiliation was even greater when the Americans launched their rocket and it only lifted off the ground thirty centimeters before it exploded. Only after that, the Navy successfully launched the first satellite, Explorer I. President Dwight D. Eisenhower instituted the National Space Centre. The NACA, set up in 1915, was replaced by NASA.

Three young people, a Jew, a Christian and a Muslim, were working behind the scenes and found the key to the development of such important projects. Satellite television and later on, computers and the Internet, are the realities of dreams that they once had. They dreamed of a world where people could share their lives and their feelings. They hoped that if people got to understand human suffering there would be peace, just as everyone who lived through the war hoped that there would be. With a radio and television in every home, in every corner of the globe, there would never be another war.

Europe—America, Today

At the time of writing this book, David, Jassar and Harm are still alive. Just like David, Jassar also married and had two children. Harm, shy as he was, remained unmarried for a long time. He became the foremost engineer/technician in David's company. He played a key part not only in the birth of satellite television, but also in the development of mobile telephones and GPS navigation.

David and Jassar did their best to help Harm find a wife. Innumerable attractive, intelligent women were hired to become his personal secretary, but none of them clicked with Harm. They tried blonds, brunettes, tall women, short women, curvy women—all to no avail.

One day, Brenda was inspired by an idea. In all the newspapers across Europe she placed an advertisement. Within was a photograph of Harm's half of the friendship token that he'd made, and an address in America. The necklace was recognized by a few different people. Thus, as an adult, Esther was restored to her family. She had survived Belzen and had been living in Europe. In time, Harm and Esther were married, to the great joy of their families. They have one child.

Many people say that David, Jassar and Harm have not been able to achieve their ideal. Indeed, everyone can see their fellow human beings around the globe, but this hasn't brought peace. We know, meanwhile, that the news and information that is seen on TV can be manipulated and used just like a weapon depending on who's using it. David, Jassar and Harm think that this time of peace will still come.

They keep on working. They haven't given up on their dream.